# Acknowledgments

I have to thank everyone who has been involved in giving me the chance to write about Alfie again. He is such a huge part of my life and family now, and the fact I can continue to share his adventures is incredible.

My friends and family have been instrumental in their support and help in getting this book written as always, so thank you to all of you. I love you very much. Thanks also go to my agents, Northbank Talent Management, for your continued support and hard work with Alfie both here and overseas.

To my publishers, Avon, you are fabulous to work with. From editorial to marketing to sales, you are incredible and I feel very lucky to be part of your team. Special mention to Victoria, Katie, Sabah and Elke, and of course sales and everyone else who helps with getting Alfie into the world.

Alfie has been lucky enough to become quite an international cat, so I would love to thank my publishers in Japan, Italy, Spain, France, Holland and Russia for all their hard work and dedication to the Alfie series. I would especially like to send out a huge thank you to my overseas readers for taking Alfie into their hearts. Of course my wonderful readers in the UK deserve a huge mention as well; without you there would be no Alfie, which is unimaginable! I will keep writing the books as long as you want to read them!

I also love to hear from you, so please follow me on Facebook – Rachel Wells, on twitter @acatcalledalfie, and on Instagram @rachelwellsauthor.

*For Becky, Martin, Helen, Megan, Jak and Rory.*

# Chapter One

Chapter
One

I was lying on the sofa, in my favourite spot, the winter sun shining down on me through the window, when my kitten, George, leapt on me. Argh, he wasn't such a little kitten any more; I was winded and a bit squashed.

'George,' I said, trying to squirm out from under his weight. 'You have to stop doing that, you're flattening me.'

'Sorry, Dad,' he replied, with his charming grin and his head tilted to one side. As usual, I melted. My boy was just too adorable, even if he was getting too heavy to jump on me. I couldn't have been prouder of what a fine young tom he was growing into. 'But I have news.' He sat next to me and licked his paws. George did like to draw out any announcements. He was a fairly dramatic kitten. Unlike myself, of course.

'Go on, George, tell me the news,' I coaxed, thinking it would be about a funny-shaped cloud he had seen this morning, or a similar Georgeism.

'There's a big van parked outside so new people are moving in next door.' He looked very pleased with himself, as well he might. I pricked up my ears. New people! On Edgar Road! Well, was there anything better for a doorstep cat like myself? Only a van full of pilchards could beat that.

My name is Alfie, and I'm a doorstep cat. Which basically means I have different families and homes I visit. I do live in one main house, here with my kitten George, in Edgar

3

Road. Our humans are Claire and Jonathan and their children, Toby and Summer. But there is another family on this road we spend time with, Polly and Matt and their children Henry and Martha, and yet another family, who live a few streets away, Franceska, Tomasz and their children Aleksy and Tommy. Phew, it's a lot of families and friends to keep track of. I met them when I moved to Edgar Road after an arduous journey, having been homeless after my old owner, Margaret, died, but that does feel like another lifetime. They say cats have nine lives, well I reckon I've used a few of those up to get to where I am today, although I still have plenty left.

I do credit myself with bringing all my families together and now they love each other the way I love them all. We even have a holiday home together, Seabreeze Cottage, which is in Devon, and we spend time there when we can. But London is our main home, on Edgar Road, where we spend most of our days. There's always something going on here. Never a dull moment. Or if there is, it doesn't last.

Up until now we were experiencing quite a quiet time. Winter was upon us, the nights were drawing in and the air had started biting. I was becoming a bit of a fair-weather cat, preferring not to spend too much time out in the cold and rain. However, my kitten, George, loved being out in all weathers. That's youth for you. Just don't seem to feel the cold. But I did take my constitutional every morning and evening, and I would brave the cold to seek out my friends, the neighbourhood cats and my cat girlfriend Tiger. But now it was cold and darker in the evenings, I preferred to stay in the warm as much as was possible.

But not now. This removal van I had to see. It was still exciting to see new people. Once a doorstep cat, always a doorstep cat, after all. So George and I bounded out to see what we could discover.

We made our way next door. I knew the house well – not too long ago my first girlfriend, the one before Tiger, Snowball, lived there. She was my first love and it wasn't the easiest of starts but after many attempts to woo her she came round to my way of thinking eventually. Don't get the wrong idea, I'm not exactly a cat lothario, I've only been in love twice, once with Snowball and now with Tiger, who is a mum to George. And George is adopted; he's not my natural kitten but he, Tiger and I are a family.

Because I've learnt through the years that family comes in all shapes and sizes and no one is the same. But as long as you have love then you have family.

'Look, Dad,' George said, his eyes as wide as saucers. We stopped on the pavement and looked at the large van. The back door to the van was open and men were unloading boxes. I gestured for George to follow me and we snuck into the back garden where I knew we would find big patio doors to look through. My first thought whenever I saw new people was, were they in the market for a part-time cat? My second was that I sincerely hoped they didn't have a dog.

We peered through the glass door, making sure not to be too visible in case we upset anyone (or dog). I could see activity. In the kitchen a woman, perhaps a similar age to Claire who, I believe, was in her forties but didn't like to talk about it, was unpacking. Near her was a younger girl; she was tall and slim, perhaps a teenager? She was attached

5

to a device, a phone. Aleksy had one and didn't tear his eyes away from it for a minute if he could help it. His mum despaired. Tommy, who was younger than Aleksy, had one too but he was more interested in sports, so he was a whole different kettle of fish. Yum.

Suddenly, my excitement increased as I spotted what looked like a cat bed.

'Oh George, I think a cat lives here,' I said. Which of course meant the owners probably wouldn't want another two cats but this cat could maybe be our new friend, which was even better. You could never have too many friends. We craned our necks a bit further and I spotted a tail. Quite an interestingly patterned tail. As the cat turned to face us, we both gasped. This cat's fur had white, black and light brown markings, a pretty tail, pointed black and brown ears and exotic features. It was fairly small and sleek and I had never seen a cat quite like it, definitely unusual. I guessed she was female as she looked far too pretty to be a male, and she was a good few years younger than me but perhaps a similar age to George.

'Wow, she looks lovely,' George said. I raised my whiskers. I didn't want him getting a crush on her just yet, not until we knew her character. George had developed quite a thing for a cat when we'd spent our first summer in Devon. Chanel was the meanest cat I'd ever met, but George had been smitten and he'd pined for her all summer. His crush had also led to the near drowning of her, him and Jonathan, but thankfully they'd all survived. I wasn't sure I was ready to cope with that again, just yet.

'Perhaps we'll wait until we meet her, eh George,' I said.

'You can't keep falling in love with just looks you know, personality matters.'

'Oh don't worry, Dad, I'm not planning on falling in love with her. After Chanel I'm pretty much off girls for good.'

If only I could believe that.

We watched for a while longer, but there wasn't much to see. Boxes being unpacked. The girl putting her phone down and petting the cat. They seemed serious and perhaps a bit sad too; being quite an intuitive cat I picked that up. We weren't spotted and, after a while, George got bored and begged me to take him to the park. I reluctantly tore myself away, I was curious and I wanted to know more. They say curiosity killed the cat but not this one, no, curiosity is my middle name. Although not literally.

George went to play with Summer and Toby upstairs after the children had their tea. It was like having three children in the family. Toby and George had a special bond; Toby was adopted, like George in a way, and they both slept in the same bad every night, and had done since Toby came to live with us when George was tiny. Summer was younger, bossier and a 'madam', according to Claire, but she could pretty much do no wrong in my eyes. I loved all the children and part of my job was taking care of them.

I padded into the kitchen to see if there was any sign of dinner. Claire was cooking, and Jonathan had just got home from work. He was sitting at the kitchen table with a beer. My food bowl was still empty.

'Oh Jon, can you feed the cats?' Claire asked. 'I think Alfie's after some food.'

'Meow.' I was.

'Sure, I'll give them some left-over roast chicken,' he replied as I licked my lips.

'You really do spoil them,' Claire said, almost chastising him but not quite. Thank goodness he did, otherwise we had to settle for food that came out of pouches. There was nothing wrong with it, but it wasn't quite the same. For a cat I did have a pretty sophisticated palate and a love of fine dining.

I started eating, knowing George would be down later, but I was hungry. As I lapped my food, I listened to the easy conversation between Claire and Jonathan.

'I was talking to Frankie and Polly about Christmas earlier,' she started.

'Already?' Jonathan pretended to be not the biggest fan of Christmas, but deep down he loved it, especially with the children. We all loved it, and I pricked my ears as it sounded like news.

'Jon, it's less than two months away and you know how quickly it'll come round. Anyway, we were saying that perhaps this year we can spend the day together, here.'

'We were saying?' Jonathan raised an eyebrow.

'OK, I was. I was thinking about Devon, but then Matt has to work between Christmas and New Year, so they literally only have two days off and Frankie said it would be very nice to have Christmas in London.'

When Tomasz and Franceska had first arrived from Poland they had very little, but they worked hard, especially Tomasz and now he owns four restaurants. Not on his own – he has partners and Franceska works with him now the children are older. They are doing very well and I am incredibly proud of them. They also introduced me to sardines which remain, to this day, my second favourite fish.

'I haven't even spoken to work about time off yet, but I'm happy for Christmas in London.'

'And Frankie said they would do all the side dishes, I'll do the turkey and Polly will make the pudding.'

'You mean she'll buy it,' Jonathan replied.

'Well yes, we know Polly's not much of a cook, but at least it'll be from Waitrose.'

I licked my lips. Christmas dinner was one of my favourite meals. I even liked some vegetables, which Claire said was very unusual for a cat. I think cats, in my experience, like a far wider variety of food than anyone gives them credit for.

'And it'll be nice to be together,' Claire said wistfully. Her parents went to Spain every year for Christmas now, where her brother lived, and Jonathan wasn't close to his family, so our friends were our family. It wasn't a bad family at all.

'The excitement levels of Summer and Toby will be cranked up this year.'

'Oh, Summer is already talking about what she wants. Although I ought to warn you, she wants a baby.'

'A doll?'

'No, for us to have another baby.'

Jonathan choked on his beer, his face turning a funny colour. 'What did you say?'

'I said that we had a lovely family already and, as Santa knew that, he'd probably not be able to send us a baby, and she then said perhaps a talking doll would do instead.'

'Thank God for that.' Jonathan started to return to a

normal-ish colour. 'It's not just beyond Santa's remit, it's way beyond mine,' he said.

'Don't worry darling, our family is perfect and I don't want to change a thing,' Claire said, going over to kiss him. Warmth flooded me as I let the feeling of happiness wash over me. Then I went to tell George it was time to wash his paws in time for dinner.

A parent's work was never done.

Later that night, when George was tucked up with Toby and Summer was fast asleep, I set out to see my girlfriend Tiger. She lives just down the road and we usually met up most evenings, weather permitting – she's even more of a fair-weather cat than I am – to watch the moon and chat about our day. We would also bring up any worries we had about George. We were parents first, which is what had prompted our friendship to develop into something more.

I sat on her back doorstep and meowed, which normally means she comes out. But she didn't. I pushed the cat flap with my nose then waited but nothing. I couldn't go in, her humans weren't too keen on other cats in their house, although they tolerated George but not me. I guessed she had probably fallen asleep. Tiger wasn't always the most active of cats.

I was about to give up and head home but I couldn't resist going for one last look at our neighbours. As before, I found myself peering through the back doors, the house was fairly dark. But sitting at the table in the kitchen was the woman, in front of her was a glass of wine, and on her lap was the cat. The cat had her back to me, so no one noticed as I watched. The woman picked the glass up slowly and took a drink, before carefully placing it back on the table, and pushing her hair out of her eyes. I saw her head fall as she stroked the cat, and I saw what I thought were tears glistening in the darkness. Even from outside it was as if I could feel her sadness, her pain. I went home wondering what her story was, their story, and why she was upset. But I knew that somehow and at some point I would get to the bottom of it.

That was the kind of cat I was.

# Chapter Two

'I fell asleep,' Tiger said the next morning when George and I called on her. I hadn't even opened my mouth.

'I thought so.'

'It was quite cold and I snuggled up with my human on the sofa, and the warmth from the fire, you know.'

'Tiger, it's OK, you don't need to explain.' Normally she didn't offer explanations, but I didn't say that.

'Mum, Dad, can we go for a walk to the park?' George asked. He had boundless energy this morning. I wished I did, but I was feeling the cold. I had an old injury which I had suffered when I first moved to Edgar Road. It was a long story involving saving Claire from a horrible relationship, and eventually bringing all of my families together, but it did leave me with a slightly bad leg which seemed to get worse and stiffen up in the cold or the rain. I mainly got on with things, I was pretty used to it by now. However, at the start of every winter I would be reminded of it.

'Of course we can, George,' Tiger said, nuzzling him. 'It's not raining, and hopefully it'll stay dry.'

We set off and, as George hopped in front of us, I told Tiger about the new people.

'So this cat is very pretty, is she?' Tiger narrowed her eyes.

'She's unusual-looking but nearer George's age than mine,' I replied. Tiger did have a jealous streak, so I needed to tread carefully when talking about other cats.

'What does George think?' She immediately switched from sounding jealous to maternal.

'He told me that after Chanel he's sworn off girls for life.' I grinned.

'Good, because no one is good enough for my boy.' I couldn't have agreed more.

The park was pleasantly empty. We trailed around after George who bounded from one activity to the next. He stared for ages at his reflection in the small lake – I urged caution because when I was younger I'd done the same and nearly drowned. Then we made piles of leaves which were browning and a little soggy, but still quite fun to play with nonetheless. There were no butterflies to chase at this time of the year but George did manage to climb one of the smaller trees. By the time we headed back for lunch I was hungry, Tiger said she was tired – I swear she was getting lazier by the second – and George was still full of energy. He would only come home when I promised he would be allowed out later to the other end of Edgar Road, on his own.

It had been a hard decision to let George out alone, and I know that human parents had the same dilemma as Franceska had been through it with Aleksy and Tommy. Aleksy was a teenager now and wanted more freedom, a bit like George, but at the same time we, as parents, knew there were dangers out there. Letting go was possibly one of the hardest parenting lessons we had to face.

When George first went out alone, although he promised he wouldn't go far, I was a bag of nerves until he came home. When he did come home I almost smothered the poor lad but I had never felt relief like it. Well, apart from the time he was catnapped and I found him, or the time he ran off after Chanel and we found him . . . But this was different, it was the first time he had gone out with permission.

Now he went out alone a fair bit, but never at night and never for too long. I tried to make him tell me where he was going as well, although to be fair he didn't always seem to know. Sometimes he said he was going to the park, sometimes to see if any of the other cats were around. So far I had resisted the urge to follow him, but only just. Instead I would pace up and down or watch out of an upstairs window for his return. And thankfully he always came home and never stayed out too long. Otherwise the worry would probably have turned my fur even greyer than it already was.

So, this afternoon I thought I would catch up on some of my personal cat business. I enjoyed time alone to have a thorough grooming session – after all, when you're a parent you always seem to be having to rush your ablutions, and then I would enjoy some thinking time. It's hard to think when you've got youngsters always wanting your attention. So, as much as I worried about George, now he was more independent I was beginning to enjoy some 'me time' as well. I settled on Claire and Jonathan's bed – Jonathan didn't like me being on there, Claire didn't mind – because it was incredibly comfortable and one of my favourite places to muse.

The front door opened, and the rush of voices and children interrupted my thinking time. I stretched, yawned and then headed downstairs where to my joy I found my families all together in the kitchen. George was hopping among them.

'Oh hi, Alfie,' Tommy said, coming over to pet me. I saw a number of fat pumpkins on the kitchen table. Ah, of course, it was the weird thing that humans celebrated called Halloween.

'I want to carve my pumpkin all on my own,' Summer said. Claire looked terrified and I agreed. The idea of Summer with a knife was not good.

'Sum, let me help you and Martha,' Tommy suggested kindly. 'It'll be better than letting the adults take over.' She considered his offer and agreed.

'And Aleksy, maybe you can help Toby and Henry?' Franceska suggested.

'Do I have to?' Aleksy answered, sounding surly which wasn't like him, although it was lately. 'I'm too old for all this.'

'Yes you do,' Franceska snapped and she, Polly and Claire exchanged glances.

'We'd be very grateful if you would,' Polly said, trying to calm the situation.

'Fine.' Aleksy made it sound as if it was anything but.

Claire made drinks for the grown-ups as the children sat at the table in the kitchen and began carving their pumpkins.

'Hey,' Henry said. 'Let's have a competition to see which one is the scariest.' They all seemed to like this idea, although I knew from experience the only one who would end up liking it was the child who won.

'What costumes are everyone wearing this year?' Franceska asked. 'I miss my boys dressing up.'

'We're too old to dress up,' both Tommy and Aleksy said at the same time.

18

'Summer wants to be a witch, and Toby is insisting on being a superhero,' Claire said.

'And I'm going to be a superhero too,' Henry said. Toby and Henry were quite close and often copied each other.

'I'm going to be a cat,' Martha announced.

This news surprised me; after all, there were two cats here.

'Oh, you can be Summer's cat,' Franceska said.

'And George,' Summer piped up.

'Sum wants me to dye George black,' Claire explained.

My whiskers twitched and George looked terrified. Imagine, my lovely kitten being dyed black!

'Don't worry George, it won't happen. But I had to promise to make you a little witch's hat to compensate.'

'So, Summer, Martha and George will all share a broomstick,' Henry explained. I wasn't sure about George and a broomstick but we'd have to see.

'Where are we getting a broomstick from?' Claire asked, worriedly. 'I've only got a kitchen broom.'

'We need a proper broomstick,' Summer shouted.

'Don't worry, I've ordered one from the internet,' Polly said. Halloween was a lot of work, it seemed.

George was on the kitchen table and I could barely watch as he dodged the knives, seemingly unaware of the danger he faced. I heard him make a funny sound, which worried me.

'Ahh,' Toby cried. 'George spat pumpkin over me.' We all looked and Toby had a splat of pumpkin on his face. George glanced over to me as if to say, 'I didn't know it wouldn't taste good.' I raised my whiskers again. My curious son would never learn, it seemed, as he tried to lick Toby's face.

The rest of the carving passed without incident. As the four children proudly presented their finished pumpkins, it was up to the adults to choose a winner. As Aleksy and Tommy had done most of the work it didn't seem fair but then the older boys didn't seem to mind as Aleksy wandered off to do something on his phone and Tommy went to the fridge to find a snack.

'It's a draw,' Polly announced diplomatically.

'Absolutely,' Claire agreed, 'they are all far too good.'

Thankfully the children all seemed to accept this. Summer and Toby's pumpkins were placed on the front doorstep, with a lit candle in each – I warned George to stay away – so that Jonathan would be able to admire them when he got home.

As everyone said their goodbyes, Henry and Martha proudly clutching their pumpkins to their chests, they arranged to go 'trick or treating' the following day after school.

'I can't wait to go trick or treating,' George said to me when we were alone.

'Well, you know Claire said you had to wear a hat,' I pointed out.

'Yeah, I'm not pleased about that but at least they're not going to dye me black,' he replied. And I had to agree.

'Oh, and George, no more eating the pumpkin.'

'No Dad, it tasted really weird.'

# Chapter Three

Chapter
Three

Even I had to admit to being excited. George had been unbearable today; he was so keen to go trick or treating, that from the morning he was badgering me about the time. It was a very long day until I bundled him off to find Tiger, telling him how much she would love to hear about the pumpkin carving and the evening ahead. It did buy me a little bit of peace and quiet and I would apologise to Tiger later.

What I was most excited about was the fact that when trick or treating we would definitely go to the new next-door neighbour's house and hopefully meet them. Despite not having a costume or being given a specific role I would join them, as the other parents did.

While the children got ready upstairs, I groomed myself in the living room. I was sad that Aleksy, Tommy and Franceska wouldn't be joining us, but the boys refused point blank to go on the basis that they were too old. Growing up was hard, but it was definitely difficult for parents, I knew that with George. They became more independent, needed you less, wanted you less even, which could be hurtful. It was something that I was having to learn to accept and Franceska and I were in a similar situation on this one.

The children emerged giddy with excitement. Toby was in a Spiderman costume and Summer was dressed in a black cape with a tall pointed black hat and a false nose. She looked a bit scary in a very cute way. George, being carried by

Summer, had a little black hat on and he looked adorable. I was sure he would earn the kids extra sweets this year. Claire picked up the broomstick, and we all headed out to meet Polly, Martha and Henry.

All assembled, they decided to start at the end of the street. I was slightly disappointed by this. Edgar Road is a long road and it meant I would have quite a wait before we reached next door.

We approached the first house. Summer, Martha and George were all at the door, trying to balance on the broomstick, when it tipped and George fell off.

'Yowl.' He landed on his tail.

'Martha, that was your fault!' Summer stormed.

'No, it was yours,' Martha bit back, and Martha never got cross. Polly picked George up and petted him, Claire picked the broomstick up and as the girls glared at each other with their arms crossed, a kindly woman answered the door, and thrust sweets at them. They soon forgot to argue and were happy to get back on the broomstick. However, Toby took George from Polly and offered to carry him, which seemed the safest bet.

We crossed the street to a house opposite which was a real mess. The garden was overgrown, the house had peeling paint, and it looked sad, if it was possible for a house to look so. I saw Polly and Claire exchange a glance.

'Maybe we should give this one a miss?' Claire suggested, but the kids were already half way up the path. We all followed, reluctantly. There was a light on in the front room and Toby knocked on the door, George still in his arms. The children all stood expectantly on the front doorstep, discussing what sweets they might expect. A man came to the window. He was old, moving slowly. He looked out at us, then, to our surprise, he raised his fist at us, shouted, 'Get lost', and pulled the curtains closed.

'Why doesn't he want to see us?' Martha asked, her eyes full of confusion.

'Maybe he forgot to buy sweets. Come on, we've got lots of houses to visit,' Claire chivvied them up. As we made our way back down the path I glanced back at the house. I didn't understand why he didn't want to see us either.

Finally, with weary legs – me – and full bags of sweets and chocolate – the children – we reached the house next door to us. I could barely contain my excitement as I waited with everyone on the doorstep. The woman who opened the door didn't look sad, not like the crying woman I'd seen last night. She had short-ish blonde hair which fell over her face, and was tall and slim. She looked composed, smiling, her head tilted to one side questioningly as she stood in front of us.

'Trick or treat,' the children chanted.

'Oh my goodness, Connie, come here,' the woman shouted and the teenager I'd seen joined her at the front door.

'Hi, I'm Claire and this is Polly.' Claire beamed as the children held their bags out hopefully. 'I live next door, Polly is down the road. We would have come round properly to introduce ourselves, but with it being Halloween . . .'

'Hi.' Polly held out her hand and the woman took it.

'I'm Sylvie, and this is Connie. Lovely to meet you.' The woman paused for a moment, then she said, 'I'm sure I've got some chocolate inside, why don't you come in for a

25

moment?' The children didn't need to be asked twice, but Polly swiped George out of Toby's arms and put him next to me on the doorstep.

'Oh, who are these two?' Sylvie asked.

'Our cats,' Polly and Claire said in unison. They both laughed. 'You guys wait here,' they said as they followed the children inside and the door was closed on us.

'Oh well, Dad, I guess when they come out we'll hear all about it.'

'Yes.' But I was impatient. I wanted to know about the new family, and the cat. And was there a man? Because we'd only seen Sylvie and the teenager. So many questions.

We waited patiently by the front gate and it wasn't long before Polly and Claire and the children emerged. They were laughing and Sylvie was smiling.

'Oh how sweet, your cats waited for you.'

'They enjoy trick or treating,' Polly said.

'It's funny, so different for us. My Hana is a house cat, she's never been outside – but that was normal in Japan.'

'Hana is such a pretty cat,' Claire said, and I agreed from what I had seen.

'She's a Mikeneko, which is Japanese of course. Cat with a coat of three colours. The English name would be a tortoise-shell.'

'But Hannah is an English name?' Polly asked.

'It's actually H-a-n-a, it's Japanese for flower.'

'That's lovely, a sweet name for a sweet cat,' Claire said.

Bingo, I already had more information at my paw tips than I thought I would. A house cat, and what was Japan? A coat of three colours. Oh, this was most interesting.

26

'Right, well we'll see you soon. I'll text and we'll have that dinner,' Polly said as she gave a wave. I was delighted, it seemed the women were already the best of friends. But how we were going to befriend a house cat?

Later, when the children were upstairs having managed to sneak a number of their sweets up there, despite being told not to, and Polly and Claire were sitting on the sofa with a glass of wine, I learnt more about Sylvie.

They both seemed to like her so far. She was English, but she and her daughter had moved back from Japan which was a place quite far away, by the sound of it. They had lived there with her husband, who had left her for another woman and they were now getting divorced and she was very upset about it. Already things were beginning to make sense. Claire had been divorced when I first moved in with her, before she met Jonathan of course, so they had that in common. Anyway, it was difficult because not only had Sylvie split up with her husband but she'd also had to move away from the country that had been her home for many years. Her daughter, Connie, who turned out to be the same age as Aleksy – fourteen – was also upset about leaving her school, her friends and her dad. I guess that explained the late-night wine drinking in the kitchen and crying. Claire had done that a lot too.

As I listened to them talk about how they would make Sylvie feel really welcome and how they would also introduce Connie to Aleksy who would be at the same school in the same year, I began to feel excited. New friends. Now I just had to figure out how to get their cat, Hana, to come out so we could meet her. Either that or we'd have to find a way to go in. It was just a minor hiccup; after all, I'm a pretty resourceful cat, if I do say so myself.

I heard a clatter of footsteps on the stairs and Toby burst in with Henry at his heels.

'George has been sick on my bed!' he cried.

'He ate lots of our chocolate, by accident,' Henry explained.

'Great, right, well I better go up and clear up. And you guys, I already told you no more sweets,' Claire shouted.

'I feel a bit sick too, Mummy,' Toby said. We all did what I call a parenting eye roll, and rushed upstairs to sort it out. I would be having stern words with my kitten later.

'So, I missed the trick or treating,' Jonathan said, not exactly sounding disappointed.

'Yes, funny how you had to work late tonight,' Claire bit back.

'I did, honestly. Anyway, the kids had a good time?'

'Yes, I took photos.' Claire handed him her phone. 'But there was one house which was a bit of a nightmare, at the end of the street, overgrown, peeling paint. There was a light on but when we rang the bell, an old man glared at us then drew the curtains. Who would do that to a bunch of kids?'

'Oh, I know. That's the guy who Vic and Heather Goodwin were moaning to me about. Apparently they have been trying to talk to him about tidying the place up, even offered to do the garden for him, but he told them to go away. Although I'm not sure he was that polite. They said he's a bit of an ogre and they think he might be dangerous. All bulging eyes and shifty behaviour, according to them.'

28

'Great, so I took our kids to a nutter's house?'

'Oh I wouldn't worry, you know how the Goodwins exaggerate. He's probably just a grumpy old man who doesn't like people. I understand, after all I'll probably be one one day.'

He was right, he definitely would.

# Chapter
# Four

After breakfast, as the children all went to school, George and I headed out to see the other neighbourhood cats. Sometimes I felt as if I was far too busy, so many people – and cats – to see that it was hard to fit it all in. I was hoping to see Tiger as well, as I made my way to near the end of the road, where we often convened on a patch of grass we called our recreation space. It was quite isolated from the main road, and there were hedges to play in – George still loved a bit of hide and seek – and even a couple of trees. Best of all, our friends knew to go there.

I had made many cat friends since being on Edgar Road. We had new ones coming in, and had lost one or two of our members, but the core group remained the same: Elvis, who was pretty much an old man now, Rocky and Nellie, but there was no sign of Tiger.

'Alright, Alfie, George,' Rocky said.

'What's going on?' I asked.

'Nothing much, you?'

'We've got a new cat next door,' I said, too excited to keep the news to myself. 'But she doesn't go out, or she didn't in her old home, so we haven't been able to meet her yet.'

'Claire and Polly said they lived in another country,' George said. 'What's that then?'

Nellie, Rocky, Elvis and I all looked at each other. We were cats, after all, and not experts in geography.

'It's very far away,' Elvis said, finally as if he knew. 'We live in London, and other people live in other places which are countries.' None of us, including him, knew if that was true.

'Like Devon?' George asked.

'Exactly,' I said quickly. After all, it didn't really matter, did it?

'So Japan, which is where they come from, is another country,' George said. 'And there, cats don't go out, apparently,' he added. I was surprised and pleased that he'd paid so much attention. He went off to hide under a hedge.

'You can pretend to look for him today, Nellie,' I said. She was like an aunt to George and also had more patience than I did. After all, George always hid in the same place and it did get a bit tiresome pretending that we didn't know where he was.

'OK.' She grinned.

'Has anyone seen Tiger today?' I asked.

'Nope. She's been a bit elusive lately if you ask me,' Rocky said.

'I said the same to her but she said she just didn't like the cold any more. Though I thought she might be here this morning.'

'Nah, not so far. Although it's still early.'

We settled down to our activities, gossiping, watching George play and watching the world go by, and before long Tiger appeared. I was relieved to see her, and I'm not sure why I was worrying. It was just something I always did. I am a worrier by nature. And when, like now, life was coasting along very well, I tended to worry more.

'Hey,' I said, greeting her excitedly.

'Calm down Alfie, you're acting like you haven't seen me for ages.'

'Well, you weren't out last night.'

'No, sorry, I fell asleep after dinner again, and when I woke up, I thought it was probably too late. Honestly, I am not a fan of winter,' she declared, examining her paw.

'I love winter, I hope it snows,' George said excitedly. He'd had his first experience of snow the previous year and he was a big fan. I was not; it was cold, wet and you sank into it, a bit like sand actually, which I also wasn't too fond of.

'Yes, well, George, you might not say the same when you get older,' Tiger said, but indulgently. 'Right, come on and we can go and climb a tree if you're good.'

They set off together to the nearest tree. All was normal as I watched George jump about with Tiger, then Nellie went to join them and they started a game of tag. Rocky, Elvis and I watched and caught up on more local gossip.

'Salmon tried to tell us about your neighbours as well,' Rocky said.

'Of course, his owners will have gone around already, won't they?' I replied. Salmon was a pain and used to be my arch nemesis, but we were civil now. He lived across the street from me with the Goodwins who were the self-appointed neighbourhood watch coordinators on Edgar Road. Translation: they were incredibly nosy busybodies who annoyed most of us. But Jonathan had to admit that, with them around, Edgar Road was a low crime street. No one got away with anything. 'What did he say?'

'Oh, he was doing his usual, acting as if he knew more than he did, being cagey, but we're used to it now. He didn't even mention the fact they'd lived in another country, so my guess is that your humans found out more than his.'

'Well that makes me happy,' I said. I was still curious though. Our chat was interrupted by a commotion and we rushed to see George perched precariously on a high branch. My heart sped up.

'Oh my goodness, George,' I said.

'Get down at once,' Tiger was shouting.

'He's ever so high,' Rocky exclaimed.

'And that branch don't look too secure,' Elvis yowled.

'Oh no, poor boy, what's going to happen?' Nellie asked. We all started panicking, running around in circles and yelping. As we came to a halt I noticed that George had started his descent. My heart was in my paws as I watched him climb down. I had discovered my fear of heights a long time ago, whilst being stuck up a tree. Not only that, but I'd had to endure the humiliation of being rescued by the fire brigade. It was all for love, but that was another story. Trees had not been one of my favourite things ever since.

'What were you all shouting about?' George asked innocently as he reached the ground.

'Oh thank goodness,' Nellie said, sitting down and looking exhausted.

'George, you were so high, too high,' Tiger chastised.

'No I wasn't. Look, I got down, didn't I? Sometimes you adults panic about the most ridiculous things.'

Unfortunately no one could argue with that.

Tiger and I decided we'd had enough excitement for one day so we took George home. He was reluctant, having had so much fun. But while we were on our way I saw the next-door neighbour, Sylvie, and her daughter, Connie, in the street. I couldn't resist making myself known to her.

'Oh Connie, here are the next-door cats again.'

'They're cute,' Connie said, bending down and petting us.

'We'll meet them properly later as we're going over.' Sylvie smiled in the way that people did when they weren't really very happy. A fake smile, or putting on a brave face as I thought of it. We all did it, us adults.

'Great,' Connie said but I noticed how her shoulders sagged and she dragged her feet. Her voice definitely lacked enthusiasm.

'Come on, if we get your school uniform sorted quickly then I'll buy you some more exciting clothes.' Sylvie was trying hard.

'Fine,' Connie said as they walked off.

'I think those two need a lot of cheering up,' I said. Tiger nodded her agreement.

'Well, they've come to the right street,' George finished.

They really had.

My slumber was disturbed by one of my favourite noises: my families. From my place on Claire and Jonathan's bed, I heard the loud cheery greetings. I stretched and rushed downstairs where George was, as usual, centre of attention. I meowed loudly to make myself heard and Aleksy and Tommy came over and took turns fussing me. I nestled into them enjoying the warmth.

Our house, which wasn't quiet at the best of times, became louder, more crowded, and heaps of fun. Claire and Jonathan's was the biggest house which was why we all convened at ours, but Tomasz and Franceska came in loaded with food from the restaurant, Polly and Matt always had wine and beer with them, and the adults – which included me – would all go to the kitchen to prepare food and drinks while the children, with George in tow, went into the living room. The older children would set up games for the younger ones. I had noticed that lately Aleksy hovered a bit before joining the kids; he thought himself too grown-up and I had been warned what that meant. He was a new creature now, something called a teenager.

I had heard about teenagers, notably from Tiger whose humans didn't have one but knew one who visited, and I'd had first-hand experience of one when I was in love with Snowball and she lived with a teenage boy who spoke mono-syllabically and never smiled. Well, my Aleksy, who I had known for years, since I first moved to Edgar Road and before he even started school, was now one. He had had his thirteenth birthday last year, and everyone had made a big deal about him becoming a teenager, but I didn't know why because as far as I could see there was nothing to celebrate. It seemed that turning fourteen hadn't improved things at all.

It was about losing my sweet best friend – although he was always still lovely to me, I didn't know if the real him would ever come back. Teenagers were not an exact science though, apparently, but this one, hovering in the hallway, looking at the phone clasped in his hand, ignoring everyone around him, had definitely become one of them.

Eventually he went into the living room.

38

'Aleksy, help me make a den,' Tommy said.

'I'm busy,' Aleksy mumbled and sat on the sofa doing something with his phone. Toby looked disappointed.

'But Aleksy, you make the best dens,' Henry complained.

'Please,' Summer asked, looking at him with her big blue eyes.

'OK, but just for a minute,' he sighed, as he started gathering the sofa cushions.

I went to the kitchen where Polly had just finished telling Franceska about Sylvie.

'She'll be here in a minute, but remember, guys, it's been hard for her,' Polly reminded them.

'Hey, I lived in Singapore, remember,' Jonathan said. 'And I wasn't exactly thrilled when I moved back here, so I'll be able to properly sympathise.'

'God, he's right,' Claire said. 'I hadn't thought of it before, but at least you and her can talk about expat life if needed.'

'And also how, if you hadn't left that sunny, fun-filled life, you'd never have met Claire, or had the kids,' Matt joshed.

'Hey, he is so lucky he got fired from his job in Singapore,' Claire said.

'Meow,' I shouted.

'Of course, you'd never have met Alfie either,' Tomasz said and thankfully everyone seemed to agree what a terrible thing that would have been.

Throughout dinner, Sylvie and Connie were quiet. The younger children had been fed earlier, Tommy insisting on eating with them, and they were in the living room watching a DVD while the adults, Aleksy and Connie ate. Claire, Polly and Franceska talked about the local area, schools, and the men were polite, but no one wanted to ask too many questions. Aleksy and Connie sat next to each other but they weren't exactly chatting either. It was fine but it did feel a bit awkward, rather than the usual conversation and bickering and teasing. I paced around the table, wondering what I could do to bring this evening to life, and then I had an idea. I knew I'd be in trouble, but I jumped on the table.

'Alfie, get down!' Claire screeched. Aleksy burst out laughing and then Connie looked at him and did the same.

'Bloomin' cat,' Jonathan huffed, lifting me off the table and trying not to laugh.

'He is such a naughty cat sometimes,' Claire huffed.

'But so cute.' Tomasz grinned.

'You two will be going to the same school when Connie starts on Monday,' Claire said, the ice having been broken.

'Really? What year?' Aleksy asked.

'Year Nine,' Connie mumbled, but then she looked up. 'I haven't been to school in England before,' she said. 'So I don't know much about it.'

'I'm in the same year. Hey, listen, I can meet you and walk there with you if you want, I mean on your first day.'

'Would you?' She looked relieved, as did her mum.

'Sure, I mean I know nearly everyone in our year and school's OK, so I can help you meet people.' Aleksy blushed; this was the most I had heard him say in ages.

'That's great, thank you Aleksy,' Sylvie said. The teenagers looked as if they had said too much and glanced back at their plates.

40

Things got easier after that. Sylvie seemed to relax as she and Jonathan chatted about Asia; they both had been to lots of the same countries although Jonathan admitted never having been to Japan. At one point Polly went to check on the children, then Aleksy asked to be excused and Connie and he left, both grabbing their phones from the kitchen counter on their way out. I spent a while listening to the adults, satisfied that although it wasn't quite there yet, Sylvie would make a nice addition to the group. I could still feel her sadness and she was guarded but when she smiled, or laughed, I could see that she was lovely.

I followed Aleksy to where he and Connie sat on the stairs.

'I'm actually really nervous about school,' Connie admitted. I looked at her properly for the first time. She had shoulder-length dark hair, big eyes and pale skin. She was almost as tall as Aleksy and slim, although she wore baggy trousers and a hooded sweatshirt, which was pretty much what Aleksy wore too. They both had trainers on their feet as well. It was, I believed, the teenage uniform.

'I guess it might be different to your school in Japan. Do you speak Japanese?' Aleksy asked. Connie said some words which neither of us understood.

'Yes, I do.' She smiled. She was pretty when she smiled. 'But now that we're here I'm not sure how useful it will be. I didn't want to come home,' she admitted.

'You know, I lived in Poland when I was born,' he said.

'Do you remember it?'

'No, but we do visit. And I speak a bit of Polish.' He said some words again which I didn't quite understand, although

I recognised it a bit as I'd heard Franceska and Tomasz speaking Polish over the years. 'But I think of here as home now.'

'I still think of Japan as home. I miss it,' she said, sounding sad.

I was surprised at how open she was; it seemed that perhaps teenagers only knew how to speak to each other.

'It'll be alright. Hey, is that the iPhone 7?' he asked, looking at her phone.

'Yes, it's the same as yours,' she replied and they both grinned.

Family evening came to an end soon after that. Tired children were either taken home or upstairs to bed, George was tucked in with Toby, Aleksy and Tommy bounded off, still full of energy, with their parents, and Connie and Sylvie went next door. Once everyone was settled I went to see if Tiger was out, but it was raining so I was pretty sure that she wouldn't be. I was right: there was no sign of her. As the raindrops dampened my fur, I thought about going home, snuggling into my warm bed but, before I did, I couldn't resist sneaking next door.

I saw Sylvie sitting at the kitchen table, this time with lights on, Hana the cat on her lap again, and in front of her was a computer. She was talking to someone and I knew from experience that she was probably talking to a friend through the screen – I was quite technologically savvy for a cat. I was pleased to see she was smiling and I hoped that being with us had cheered her up a bit. The rain started coming down much heavier and, in danger of turning into a drowned rat, I went back next door to the warm, dry home that was always there to welcome me.

# Chapter Five

I was thinking about how to get to meet Hana now the weekend was over. Connie had started school and Sylvie told Claire she had some job interviews, and now I had spent a bit of time with both Connie and Sylvie I really, really wanted to meet this exotic cat. Not only was I keen to let her know that she had friends around if she wanted them, but I also was interested to get her opinion on how her family was coping.

Connie had told Aleksy that they'd had Hana since she was a kitten and she had never been outside, she'd always been a house cat which was customary in the Tokyo suburb where they lived. I could understand that in some places cats didn't go outside and I also knew it suited some of them, but I couldn't imagine being a house cat. Although, after some of the trouble we had got into in the past, it probably wasn't a bad idea. And in George's case it would make life much easier for me . . . No, being a house cat, on reflection, sounded terrible and I needed to rescue Hana from this life of incarceration now she was in England.

These were my thoughts as I hung around outside Tiger's house – George had gone off for a stroll with Nellie – when I saw her owners come out with her in a cat carrier. I narrowed my eyes and wondered where she was going. Her owners were older than any of mine and didn't go out very often. But they got into a car, a taxi, and drove off. Tiger hadn't been looking so she didn't see me. I forgot all about

Hana and fretted about Tiger, where was she going? What was she doing? Was everything OK? I calmed myself down as I went to find the others. Her owners didn't have luggage with them so they couldn't be going away. Perhaps they were taking her to visit a friend. I found Elvis and Rocky at the recreation ground, grateful that I could take comfort in their routine.

'The lad and Nellie have gone to the other end of the street,' Rocky said.

'Yeah, and Nellie never says no to him,' Elvis added.

'No one says no to George,' I pointed out. 'But I wanted to ask you, I just saw Tiger going out, does anyone know where she's gone?' I asked. I doubted they did but, before they could answer, Salmon loomed over us. He had a habit of doing that, almost appearing from thin air.

'Are you wondering about Tiger?' he asked. He sounded his usual smug self. But I wanted information, so I needed to play along.

'I was, I saw her go out with her owners, I had no idea what she was up to,' I said, trying to sound nonchalant.

'Well, my owners went to see hers this morning, important neighbourhood watch business. Apparently they are taking her to the vet.'

'The VET??!' I immediately panicked.

'Calm down Alfie,' Salmon said, almost sounding kind. 'It's just a check-up. Tiger probably didn't even know she was going but they said they'd locked the cat flap so she couldn't go out this morning.'

'Thank you Salmon, it's really kind of you to let me know.' I wasn't used to him being so helpful.

'That's alright.' He tried to sound cool again. 'No fur off my nose.'

'Hey, I was just thinking about Hana, the cat who's moved in next door to me,' I said, thinking I owed him.

'Oh yes, have you met her?' he asked. He couldn't hide his interest now.

'No, but her owners came to our house last night. She doesn't go out, ever. She's a house cat. Something common in her country of Japan apparently.'

'Well I never,' Rocky said. 'A house cat?'

'Yes, she's never been out, ever,' I said, enjoying having the authority on something.

'That's a shame,' Elvis said. 'It means we'll never meet her.'

'Oh we will,' I said.

'What do you mean?' Salmon narrowed his eyes at me.

'I don't exactly know, but I will figure something out.'

'I can't stand around here all day chatting, things to do, people to see.' Salmon grinned before stalking off.

'Gosh, he's almost going soft in his old age,' Rocky said as we watched him swinging his tail behind him.

I didn't tell George about Tiger. Salmon had said it was just a check-up but I wanted to talk to Tiger and get some reassurance before involving George. He was surprised as I actively encouraged him to go out on his own after lunch, but he was quick to take advantage as he rushed off with my blessing.

I sat by Tiger's back step and it wasn't long before she appeared.

'Thank goodness,' I said, nuzzling her. 'I was worried about you.'

'I know I'm sorry, they sprang the vet on me. This morning I went to go out and I bashed my head against the cat flap, which hurt.' She paused to rub her head with her paw. 'They closed it without telling me, and they shoved me, well not shoved, but put me in the carrier and off we went.'

'You poor thing.' No cat I knew was a fan of the vet, they had a habit of poking around where it wasn't their business. Well, actually it was their business but it was still very personal and intrusive. 'What did the vet say?' I took a long, hard look at Tiger; she seemed fine to me.

'Oh nothing really, it was just a check-up. They poked and prodded and ran some tests but I'm right as rain. You know how my humans fuss. I heard them say that at my age we needed to check more often. I mean the indignity!'

'God, I hope it doesn't occur to my family. I'll have to make sure I always appear in the best of health in front of them.'

'Good plan, Alfie. Although the vet was nice, she was very kind, but still. Where's George?'

'Off playing somewhere. To be honest, I wanted him to go off so I could talk to you. You know, in case anything was wrong. Hopefully he'll be back soon.'

'Oh Alfie, what will we do with you? Come on, I'll come with you, let's go find our boy.'

We set off, the wind in our fur, the cold air whipping around our legs as we set off. We walked in companionable silence and I couldn't help but think how lucky I was to have so many cats around me that I'd known for years, and that I cared so deeply about, and that cared about me. It made me return my thoughts to Hana, I really had to figure out a way to see her and make sure that she wasn't too lonely. Loneliness was the worst thing and although it had been so long since I had experienced it, I had never forgotten.

George and I walked Tiger home and then went back to our place, where we bumped into Aleksy who was with Connie.

'Hey guys,' Aleksy said, petting us.

'Meow?' Aleksy didn't normally come to our house on his own.

'I just walked Connie home, but I better go, Mum will worry if I don't get back soon. Not to mention that we have a mountain of homework, right Con?' he grinned. I was startled, Aleksy hadn't been this chatty for quite a while, or looked so animated. He wasn't even staring at a screen. Was being a teenager over now? I certainly hoped so. I wanted my sweet Aleksy back.

'Yes, and it's only my first day,' Connie giggled. I stared at them both, raising my whiskers. It looked as if they had become friends already which made me very happy. So, as I took George home for tea, all seemed right once again.

# Chapter Six

'So, I got a job,' Sylvie said as she arrived at our house a few nights later, a bottle in her hands. 'I know you might be busy, but I wondered if you fancied a drink to celebrate with me?' She shrugged. She looked so attractive, with her eyes, which were a bit like Connie's, sparkling.

'What, already? The job, I mean.' Claire said.

'It's nothing fancy but I got it through a friend of my sister's, so total nepotism. But, you know, I haven't worked for years, I've been an expat wife, so I was lucky to get anything, I think.'

'Congratulations, come in, of course we can celebrate. The kids are in bed, Jon's at the gym, so you've picked the perfect time.' Claire ushered her in and I followed. Claire led her to the kitchen, pulling some glasses out of the cupboard and opening the bottle which was fizzy.

'I really hope you don't mind.' Sylvie chewed her lip nervously. 'I don't normally go anywhere without arranging it . . .'

'Don't be silly. Honestly, I would rather you felt like you could pop round whenever you want, if we're busy I'll say, and you won't take offence. That's how it is with us, you know Polly and Frankie,' Claire said.

'That's so kind, I can't believe how lucky I was moving in next door to you!' Sylvie said.

'I moved to London years ago without knowing anyone so I understand how daunting it is. And, Sylvie, I moved here after my first marriage broke down in a horrible way. I made a friend from work, Tasha, she basically saved me from loneliness,' Claire explained.

'I've been away so long that I've pretty much lost touch with my friends from the UK. My sister lives in Bristol with her husband, but I gave my life up for my ex-husband, basically. Moving back here, well, it made me realise how much my life was tied up with his and that's so sad. Thank goodness I got Connie out of it.'

'What happened, exactly?' Claire asked, putting two full glasses in front of them.

'Total cliché . . . Um, that's nice,' Sylvie replied, taking a sip of her drink. 'My husband met a younger woman through work, and I now know they were having an affair, but then he declared himself in love with her and asked for a divorce.'

'Wow, that's awful. Is she Japanese?'

'No, actually American, beautiful of course and young. Only in her twenties.'

'Oh God, that's so horrible. I am so sorry Sylvie.' Claire's eyes glistened with concern.

'I'm sorry.' Sylvie wiped a tear away. 'I'm not good at celebrating yet. I felt as if my life was over, does that make sense? I'd devoted it to him. I gave up my career to follow his, I brought up his daughter for him, I didn't really have anything but my family. Looking back that was very stupid of me but . . .'

'Hey, no one knows what's going to happen. He's, well, I won't say what he is, but I am so sorry.'

'Then he gave me the option of staying to watch him

with his new woman, so he could see Connie, and I just couldn't. I was too humiliated, so I moved Connie back here, but I know she misses her dad and I feel so guilty about pulling her away. But Japan was about my marriage, I couldn't stay there without it. There was nothing there for me but humiliation and I had to get away.'

'You did what you had to do, honey,' Claire said. 'Look, don't for one minute ever think it's easy. I moved here after splitting from my ex-husband, as I said, but I only moved within this country, not from a million miles away. You must miss your friends.'

'I do, and I Skype them, but it's not the same. Anyway, sorry I'm being so maudlin – but I have to admit worrying about Connie settling in here is giving me sleepless nights.' She lifted her glass.

'And that's understandable. But, cheers to your job – oh, what is it?' Claire laughed. 'I almost forgot to ask.'

'It's in a clothes shop, a gorgeous boutique in Clapham. Lovely clothes actually, quite expensive, but I did work in fashion in my old life, and I have a bit of a passion for it. I know I'm just a shop girl but it's not too far away and it'll just give us a bit of income.'

'Well, I think it's great. I'll come and have a look but of course don't tell Jonathan if it's really expensive.'

'Promise I won't. Anyway, my sister's friend, Jessica, she said if it works out, she'll let me help with buying and display down the line, and so it will be quite fun. It'll get me out of the house while Connie's at school and it's a good, positive move, I think.'

'It'll just do you good to have routine.'

'Yes, I need to feel that I have a purpose. For so long now I've just been a wife and a mother.'

'You're never just a mother. But I do understand. I used to work long hours but I've been part-time since Summer and Toby, but to be honest I don't miss it as much as I thought I would.'

'I can't pretend I don't miss my old life although I wasn't exactly a modern woman. I organised the house, my husband's social life, took care of Connie and spent a lot of time with friends. But now being home . . . well, it's different and the older Connie gets the less she'll need me. I think it was the whole expat thing. I didn't work, most of us wives didn't. I made sure that Philip, my ex, that his life ran like clockwork. If he was home I cooked for him, made sure his laundry was done, packed for his business trips, arranged holidays, basically ensured his life was relaxing, and I kept most of the stress away from him. I dealt with any problems with Connie, he got the fun bits, but he had a pressured job so I thought it was important and in return I got to lunch with my friends, travel, buy pretty much what I wanted, and for so long I thought it was enough for me, I thought it was enough for us.'

'But it wasn't?'

'Not for him. And of course I worry about Connie. He's still her father and she loves him.'

'Oh God.' Claire and I both shuddered. 'I couldn't cope with that, poor Connie.'

'Anyway, time to rebuild. I might have been married for sixteen years but it's time for me to look to the future. And to ensure that my little girl, who isn't so little, isn't too badly damaged by all this.' She spoke with purpose.

'Did Connie get on OK at school?'

'She seemed happy enough. It's very difficult because she's used to her very nice international school. I think it's a bit different from a comprehensive in London. I did think about trying to make my ex pay for private school but the fees are eye-watering, even for him, so I decided to try this first. If she's unhappy, though, I would find the money somehow, or I would make him pay. I should make him pay.'

'Hey, we're not going to talk about him, remember. Positive. Aleksy will make sure Connie's OK at school, you have a job, your ex is a . . . a word I shouldn't use and, one day soon, you'll see there's a future.'

'Gosh, Claire, I'll say it again: we were so lucky to move next door to you.'

'Meow!' I said.

'And Alfie of course.' Claire winked.

'Oh for goodness sake, Claire, give it a rest,' Jonathan said later as they were in bed.

'What?' she asked. 'I just asked if you knew anyone.'

One of my skills is matchmaking. I bring people together, both romantically and in friendship, and Claire has learnt from me. She is an enthusiastic student.

'The last time I set one of your friends up with mine she ended up moving to Dubai.' He was talking about Claire's best friend Tasha, who was also a very good friend of mine. We both still miss her.

'OK, yes, but I just thought it might help Sylvie get settled if she had a bit of a social life.'

'I agree, but she's probably not ready for a man yet, she's

been through a huge upheaval, Claire, and I think the best thing is for us to offer friendship. Honestly, not every woman needs a man.' Jonathan shook his head. 'I can't believe I actually said that. I almost sound like a feminist.'

I grinned, Jonathan wasn't exactly a 'new man'. He said he tried it but he liked being lazy and looked after. I had to agree with him. I respected women, as did Jonathan, but I didn't mind if they liked taking care of me. Although I took care of everyone, so I might have been a 'new cat' after all.

'Hell will freeze over before you're a feminist. But, OK. For now,' Claire said. I did agree with Jonathan, Sylvie didn't seem ready for a new relationship at all. But friendship was good.

I fell asleep thinking about that. How Sylvie went from happy to sad in an instant, the way Claire had when she first moved here. I understood, I really did, she wanted to move on with her life, but it was never that easy. I had been there myself. I had lost people I loved, lots of them, and I'd been through my fair share of heartache, so when I saw Sylvie, I understood how she was feeling as if I could see right into her heart.

# Chapter Seven

It seemed like ages before I actually got a chance to see Hana properly. I cased the house, looking for a way to break in, because it was clear that Hana wasn't going to be coming out. When my old girlfriend, Snowball, lived in the house they didn't have a cat flap, but if the family were all out, they would leave a window open in the kitchen for her to come and go as she pleased. Otherwise she would wait at the glass doors to be let out and in. It worked well for her, although I preferred the freedom of a cat flap and I also found that having to climb on windowsills could be a bit tiresome. As Hana was a house cat, there was not only no cat flap but also, as it was cold, no windows appeared to be open. It was frustrating me, and the more I found I couldn't get in, the more I wanted to.

This morning, George had refused to go out as it was raining hard, and he suddenly decided to develop an aversion, so I decided I would take the opportunity of knowing he was safe at home and go and see if I could find a way in. The rain seemed to cling to my fur as I made my way round the back of the house, but there I struck gold, or maybe silver, as one of the kitchen windows was slightly open. Unfortunately it was a small, narrow, high-up one, but I was determined. I jumped onto the windowsill – so far so good – and then I made an attempt to jump for the window. My first one failed; it was higher than it looked. I rebalanced myself and tried again. This time I managed to hook my paws over the open window and, with great effort, pulled myself up. It was only open a bit and I soon found the gap was narrower than it looked. I began to squeeze my way through it and soon realised that perhaps I had misjudged. I was about half way through, but my bottom was a bit stuck as I wiggled and squirmed and regretted eating quite so much breakfast.

'Yowl,' I cried out in frustration as my body moved only a tiny bit at a time; at this rate I'd be here all day.

'What are you doing?' a voice said. I looked down and saw Hana on the floor, looking quizzically at me.

'Oh hi, I'm Alfie, your next-door neighbour, and I've been wanting to come and welcome you to Edgar Road. But it hasn't been easy as you don't go out by all accounts, and so I thought I would have to come in. And that's what I am trying to do.' It wasn't the introduction I had envisaged.

Hana hopped onto the kitchen counter. She was even prettier close up, with sweet light green eyes. I had never seen a cat quite like her and I also really would have liked her and George to become friends. She would make a great companion for him; he didn't have anyone his own age in Edgar Road.

'That's nice, I haven't met another cat before,' she said, looking at me with interest.

'What, really? Never?' I couldn't believe it as I gave my bottom another wiggle.

'No, well I must have done when I was born, not that I remember, but then I came to live with my family, in Japan, and I didn't get to go out, and no cat ever came to visit me like you're trying to do.' She was sweet and warm, if a little bit confused. 'I always had lots of humans to play with though, so that was nice,' she added.

'We have many friends on this street. Honestly, if you did go out you might like it,' I said. Huffing a bit as I tried to squeeze myself to a smaller size.

'I don't know if I'd even be allowed. Anyway, it's very nice to meet you.'

'How did you get here?' I asked. I felt myself easing forward a bit, I was making progress, thankfully.

'I was in a carrier and we went on an aeroplane. Connie, my human, she said it was like a giant bird that flew in the sky. I had to go into a special place but slept mostly and then suddenly – well, it wasn't sudden, it was a very long time – we were here and then I had to have a check-up with a vet before I was reunited with my family.'

'It sounds exhausting.' I wondered if I would ever get to go on the giant bird, but it was doubtful. When we went on holiday it was always to our house in Devon and we went in the car.

'It was a very long time and I did feel a bit strange for a few days, but then that might be because we moved so far. The man of my family, he didn't want them to bring me but Connie refused to leave Japan without me, which I am thankful for, as I love her very much. I miss my home, but I think I would miss Connie more.'

I was going to reply when, with a final squeeze, I found myself almost sliding through the window. In my surprise I ended up falling, landing on my tail, in the kitchen sink.

'Ow,' I said, trying to regain my composure and thankful

that the sink was empty. 'Oh well, at least I'm in.' Always look on the bright side, that's my motto.

'Um, yes but I'm not sure how you're going to get out again.' I turned my head to where Hana was looking and saw that not only had I managed to get through the window but I'd somehow knocked it closed. Not that I would have had the energy to get back out that way again in any case, but still it did leave me with something of a problem.

I would like to say that this hadn't happened to me before but that wouldn't be true. I had been known to get trapped in places on occasion – especially cupboards. But I couldn't worry about that right now, I was here, in front of Hana, and I wanted to make a new friend.

'Why don't you give me a tour of the house?' I asked, thinking I would come up with a plan to get out later. After all, I was a cat who was known for being very good at plans.

By lunchtime, I was beginning to panic. Although spending time with Hana had been pleasant and we had managed to cover quite a lot of ground. Not only had I toured her entire house, but I'd explained all about Edgar Road. I told her about George, who I thought would make an excellent playmate for her, and she told me all about Japan, specifically her house in Japan, and the strange language they spoke, the raw fish she ate, and how happy her family had been. Since coming to London they had all been very sad – which I knew of course. But Connie was trying hard to get used to it, as she didn't want her mum to worry, and vice versa. Hana was the confidante of both her humans the way I was with all of mine. She listened to Connie before she went to sleep and then had late-night chats with Sylvie. It kept her very busy.

'What about the husband/father?'

'Oh yes, you see I thought he was lovely,' Hana said as we stood in Connie's bedroom. It was painted a bright yellow, and she had put big pictures of pop stars on the wall. There were lots of photos of her and other girls on a pin-board – they were her friends in Japan, Hana said, which was one of the reasons she was upset; she missed them. I understood all about that. 'But then one day he said to Sylvie that he was in love with someone else, and that he wanted a divorce. Sylvie was so devastated, she still is, and I don't think she's coping as well as it seems.'

'It's very sad,' I said. Then I turned my attention back to the problem at hand. 'But you know, if I don't go soon, George might start worrying about me.'

'I feel terrible, you came around to make me feel welcome and now you're stuck.'

'Oh no, I'm still glad I met you, I just wish you could come out, and then you could meet the others, our cat friends.' That would be my next plan. As soon as I came up with one to get myself out of her house, I would come up with a way of getting Hana out of the house too.

We both looked around for any sign of being able to leave, but it was hopeless. There were no windows open, or anything that I could use to get outside. As I was beginning to despair we heard a sound, like a key in the door.

'That's the front door,' Hana said and we both bounded towards it. The door opened and I saw my chance. Without hesitation I ran as fast as I could through Connie's legs and outside. It was only when I was on the front path that I stopped, turned around and saw that Connie and Aleksy were both looking at me with bemusement.

'How did Alfie get in here?' Connie asked. 'Hana, are you OK?' I took offence at that, what did she mean? What did she think I had done to her?

Hana mewed, softly. I hadn't even stopped to say goodbye to her but I raised my whiskers and she raised hers back.

'I'm sure he was just being friendly and, after all, Alfie is one clever cat, he would have found a way,' Aleksy replied, and I bounded off to get home to George, as they closed the front door. Not feeling that clever – after all, it had taken hours to get out.

When I told George all about my adventures next door, he went into a sulk because I hadn't taken him with me. When I reminded him of his refusal to go out because of the rain, he still took umbrage. I promised him the next time I would take him with me but of course I wasn't sure how there would be a next time. After the hazard of getting in and out, it just might not happen. I wasn't ready to cope with that again.

It was only much later, when I was alone, about to take a short nap, that I thought about it all again and realised I hadn't stopped to wonder what on earth Aleksy and Connie were doing at her house in the middle of the day. Weren't they both supposed to be at school?

# Chapter
# Eight

Chapter
Eight

Word about my visit to Hana got around quickly. I was surprised. I had thought that if Connie told her mum she would have had to explain not being at school, but that only goes to show how wrong I was. It turned out Connie had gone home at lunchtime because she'd forgotten one of her text books. She obviously hadn't mentioned Aleksy, because when Claire was telling Jonathan, in front of me, his name didn't crop up.

'Did Sylvie mind about our mad cat being in her house?' Jonathan asked. I waved my tail, I wasn't mad.

'She was a bit surprised at first but when I explained that Alfie always liked to make friends with other cats she didn't seem too upset. She said she always worried about Hana being bored, she wasn't alone very often in Japan.'

'Maybe we can persuade her to put a cat flap in so Alfie can visit more often,' Jonathan laughed.

'Yelp!' I jumped onto his lap; that was a very good idea.

'Alfie, I think Jon was joking,' Claire giggled. 'Anyway, I invited her to lunch on Sunday at the restaurant. I checked with Frankie and she didn't mind.'

'Great. Hopefully she'll start to settle in a bit more.'

I was excited at the news. Not that Sylvie and Connie were joining us, although that was nice, but mainly about the fact that we were having lunch at the restaurant. It would give George and I a chance to catch up with Dustbin, the restaurant cat who was a very, very good friend. He lived outside and was a bit feral, but he liked it that way, and he might have been rough around the edges but he had a heart of gold. I hadn't seen him for a bit, probably because life in Edgar Road was keeping me busy, so we were due a visit.

In the meantime I had to find Tiger. She was still being a bit elusive of late, and I did want to see her. I missed her. George had seen more of her than I had, but that was because he went into her house. I wouldn't go because if I got caught by her owners they threw me out. They didn't mind George quite as much, but nor were they laying out the red carpet to welcome him either. He assured me she was fine but I still wanted to see for myself.

I went to Tiger's house and nudged the cat flap. As I waited on the doorstep I was anxious, but Tiger appeared after a short time.

'Hi stranger,' I said.

'Don't start,' she replied, giving me a quick nuzzle. 'I've had my family all keeping me in, it was to do with the vet. I thought I was fine but it turned out I had some kind of infection, and I had to take some medicine, which is why I haven't been out. It's all gone now and I'm allowed out again.'

'But George said you were staying in because of the weather.'

'I didn't want him to worry, or you. I was only allowed dry biscuits to eat for days, can you imagine?'

'No, frankly I can't. But you say you're all better?'

'Yes. The tablets, which my family thought they were being very clever in hiding in small bits of chicken – which I ate because it was the only respite from the biscuits – have all gone, and that means I am back to normal.' She grinned.

'Oh thank goodness.'

'You know, Alfie, you worry too much. Tell me, what's been going on in the world while I've been stuck in.'

'Walk with me and I will do.' I grinned. It hit me how much I'd missed her. I was a softy after all.

As we took a stroll, I told her about Hana and being stuck in the house.

'It's a shame, you know, she'd make a perfect companion for George,' I said, not for the first time.

'Stop trying to matchmake, Alfie,' she replied. 'George will make his own friends.'

'I know, I was just saying, they aren't that far apart in age and she's lived a very sheltered life.'

'That sounds like an understatement,' Tiger pointed out. One of the many things I loved about her was the fact that she paid such good attention to everything I told her.

'Yes, right, so I thought her sweetness would be great for George. Anyway, I don't see it happening, she doesn't go out and there isn't an easy way for us to get in . . .'

'Don't tell me you're going to give up that easily.' We both stopped and I looked at her. She knew me so well.

'Of course not,' I replied, with a grin.

When I got home, feeling lighter than I had for a while, probably because of seeing with my own eyes that Tiger was fine, Claire was at the kitchen table with Polly and Sylvie. After establishing that George was outside, playing in the small back garden, I joined them, sitting myself on Polly's lap and enjoying the sensation as she ran her fingers lightly through my fur.

'So, the job is good?' Polly asked. She had a big bag with her, which meant she had been working herself. She was an interior designer and although she tried to work part-time she could sometimes find herself very busy. Luckily, Claire was always able to help out with the kids if necessary, that was how we all did things on Edgar Road.

'Yes, it's strange though. I haven't had a "job" since we moved overseas.'

'That's a long time to be out of the workplace,' Polly said.

'It is. And, you know, getting out of the house is good, the hours aren't too long so I can be there for Connie . . . Not that she seems to want me to be.' Her brow wrinkled.

'Is everything OK?' Polly asked.

'If you ask Connie, it is. She says she likes school, she's getting good grades already, she even has a sleepover with a couple of friends on Friday, so it seems she's settled in pretty well. But, well, she's very quiet and when I try to talk to her she gives me one-word answers, then makes any excuse she can to be in her bedroom with her phone or iPad.'

'I think, from what Frankie says about Aleksy, that that is being a teenager,' Claire laughed.

'I hope so. I know it sounds strange but it's like she's gone from being this chatty little girl who loved to tell me about her day, who seemed to love me, to someone who acts as if I am torturing her by asking her if she's alright and can barely stand the sight of me. I'm worried that she's just putting a brave face on everything.'

'Does she speak to your ex?' Polly asked, gently.

'Yes, he Skypes, or FaceTimes her a couple of times a

week, and she's pretty surly with him, but of course he doesn't have to deal with her moods on a daily basis.'

'Listen, I honestly think it's just the big upheaval, but hey, you said she's doing well at school?' Claire said. Sylvie nodded. 'She's not got an eating disorder or a drug problem?'

'Oh God, I hope not. No, she still seems to eat like a horse and she isn't losing weight. I'm pretty sure she's not on drugs,' Sylvie replied with a slight grin.

'Right, as far as I can tell that means you're winning parenting her. I said the same to Frankie about Aleksy. He's the sweetest kid, always has been, sensitive, caring, but he has started acting as if he's a bit too cool for all of us, especially his parents.'

'Meow!' I shouted.

'OK, apart from Alfie then.' The three of them laughed.

'Actually, even Alfie at times,' Polly whispered but I heard and narrowed my eyes at her.

'I need to stop worrying so much,' Sylvie said.

'Yes. My dad, he was a social worker and pretty good with children and teens, he told me that he got through me and my brother's teenage hormonal phase by not pushing us too much. He said he gave us space and one day we started being pleasant again,' Claire explained.

'Oh God, I was a nightmare,' Polly said. 'I drank, smoked and was boy crazy, but then I started modelling when I was fifteen so I guess that explained it a bit.'

'Was modelling a bit wild?' Sylvie asked.

'Yes, it was, but after a while I rebelled against the bad behaviour.'

'Oh God, you know also, we didn't have all the pressure

of social media when we were growing up,' Claire pointed out.

'I know, I didn't want Connie to have any, but she said that she didn't want to be the only girl at school without Snapachat or whatever, so I had to give in. I can't make her feel different, that's the worst when you're a teenager.'

'Trust her – as much as you can anyway. She seems pretty good to me,' Polly said, giving Sylvie's hand a pat.

'Meow,' I said again. Polly was pretty good as well, all my women were.

'I will do my best to give her space, but I can't help worrying.' Sylvie's brow was furrowed.

'None of us can, really,' Polly agreed.

'Meow,' I thirded. That was what us parents did best: worry.

# Chapter
# Nine

'The cats are coming?' Sylvie asked as we all set out to lunch on Sunday.

'Yowl,' I replied. Of course we were.

'You'll soon learn that our cats go pretty much everywhere with us,' Claire explained, as if it was perfectly normal. Over time, I have learnt that it's not. Dogs, they go to many places with humans, cats not so much. But for George and I things were different. And we liked it that way.

'It makes me feel sorry for Hana,' Connie said. She wasn't being surly at all today, she had a big smile on her face. She really was very pretty, a bit like her cat; they matched. 'You know, at home on her own so much of the time.'

'Meow,' I said. Good, it seemed the seed had been planted.

'Yes, but darling, Hana doesn't go out, I'm not sure she'd cope very well.' Sylvie sounded worried.

'I know, but seeing the freedom Alfie and George have, well it got me thinking. I really am worried that she's lonely here.'

'Ah, well maybe we'll get her a treat later, some fish maybe, just in case.' Sylvie gave Connie's shoulder a squeeze. That wasn't what I had in mind.

George and I kept up with the humans, although at one point Toby picked George up and carried him for a while. No one thought to offer me a lift. But Franceska and Tomasz didn't live far away, so it wasn't so bad. I was used to the journey, it was one of my regular routes.

The family used to live in the flat above the restaurant,

which was nice but small, so when Tomasz became more successful and the boys got bigger they bought the house next door. They still had the flat, but a couple of the members of staff lived there. Thankfully they'd knocked down the back wall so the yard to the restaurant and the house was adjoining, which meant when George and I stayed with them - which we did if Claire and Jonathan and the children went away without us – I could see Dustbin whenever I wanted.

'Hello, welcome,' Tomasz said, standing at the door, and scooping me up as he ushered everyone in. They had a rule that the place was always closed on Sundays, to make sure everyone could have a day off, so when we had family day here we had the place to ourselves. As hugs and kisses were exchanged, Toby and Henry went to find the boys, Martha and Summer took their dolls over to the table which had been set for the children, whilst the adults all chatted and sorted out drinks. Connie stood, looking slightly awkward, but as soon as Aleksy spotted her he bounded over. I was offended that he didn't even say hello to me.

'Let's go and find Dustbin,' I said to George, affronted, and we made our way through the kitchen – where we normally weren't allowed – to the backyard.

'I heard you were coming,' Dustbin said as he greeted us affectionately.

'Hi, how are you?' I asked, pleased to see my very good friend.

'Yeah, not bad. Got a few mice yesterday, the blighters keep coming back for more, it's like they never learn.' He gave his head a small shake.

I shuddered, I hated all talk of hunting. In fact for a cat

I was a pretty poor hunter. I had done it out of necessity, when I was homeless, in order to survive, but I didn't like it and since becoming so pampered I had lost my knack. George showed an interest in it, disappointingly, but more for the thrill of the chase than anything. I tried to discourage it but it was his instinct, so I had to accept that.

'Dustbin, can we go and find some mice?' George asked, looking hopeful.

'Maybe later, lad. They've all scarpered for now.' He gave me a 'look' and I thanked him silently.

'Anyway, they'll be bringing us some lunch soon,' I said. When we visited it was the only time we ever ate outside because Dustbin didn't like to come inside. Which reminded me to tell him about Hana.

'Well, I never heard such a thing. A cat who doesn't go out? I wouldn't like that.'

'But if you didn't know any different you might,' George said, sagely. He was a chip off the old block.

'True, George, true. And what suits some cats doesn't suit others, eh Alfie?' I nodded my agreement. 'Anyway, Alfie, you might want to know this: Franceska was on the phone out here last night, talking to one of your ladies no doubt, and she said she was worried about Aleksy.'

'Oh no, what about?' My fur stood on end. I couldn't bear it if anything was wrong with my Aleksy.

'He's acting all secretive apparently, home late from school, spending all his time in his bedroom on his phone, only coming out for meals – and you know how close he and Tommy were. Well, apparently he basically ignores his little brother, these days.'

'Oh,' I said, a bit relieved. 'I know what this is, the women were talking about it the other day: hormones. All teenagers get it, it's like an illness I think, you know, makes you not a very nice person for a while, but they all said it passes eventually.'

'That's good to know. Poor Franceska's very upset, she misses how close she and Aleksy used to be.' It was the same conversation that Polly and Claire had with Sylvie.

'Thanks Dustbin, and I will keep an eye on things, but our new next-door neighbour, Connie, is suffering from it too. Thank goodness us cats don't get it,' I said, raising my whiskers at George.

'Oh no, we are just lovely and fun and sweet all the time,' George said as he pounced on a mouse which seemed to appear from thin air.

'Good catch,' Dustbin said, proudly. I shook my tail. I bet the mouse didn't think George was sweet.

We dined on sardines and as always it was delicious. We had a very pleasant time with Dustbin before we left him to go back to our families. In truth I was cold, chilled to my bones actually, and George was tired. Dustbin didn't seem to get either cold or tired, he was a super-cat. As we said a reluctant goodbye to him, I said I'd see him soon. I would put visiting more often on my to-do list.

Back inside, I began to warm up as I let the human chatter wash over my fur. A good meal had been eaten, dishes were piled up, but Franceska and Tomasz refused to let anyone clear up, saying they would do it when everyone had gone home. The children were playing in one part of the restaurant; Tommy had set up an elaborate obstacle course and the younger children were enjoying it, along with George who quickly joined in, easily shedding his tiredness, it seemed. Aleksy and Connie were watching them, but set apart from the others. Both had phones in their hands. They were talking though, laughing, and they seemed happy. The adults were enjoying drinks, and talk turned to Christmas.

'I have so much to do,' Franceska was saying. 'Not only for the boys but for work too.'

'I know, but I love Christmas.' Claire sounded dreamy.

'It costs a fortune,' Jonathan huffed.

'Bah humbug,' Matt teased.

'It's going to be nice this year, all together,' Tomasz said, then the table fell silent.

'Are you staying in London for Christmas?' Claire asked Sylvie.

'Yes, I think so. My sister has invited us to go away with them, but well, Connie and I aren't used to being here yet, so I think staying might be best. I just don't . . .' Her voice cracked and I went to rub her legs. 'I haven't really thought about it,' she said. Then she tried to smile.

'You must come to us,' Claire suggested.

'Only if you want to, of course,' Jonathan quickly added.

'We're all having lunch together, it'll be loads of fun,' Polly said.

'Well, I hate to impose.' Sylvie sounded uncertain.

'Why would you be imposing? The more the merrier I say,' Matt said.

'And you can bring something,' Franceska added. 'Claire

and Jonathan will do the turkey, we will bring potatoes and vegetables, Polly brings pudding.'

'That doesn't really leave much,' Claire pointed out.

'I'll bring champagne,' Sylvie said. 'How about that?'

'Well we never say no to champagne,' Polly laughed. She was right, they didn't. They didn't say no to wine either, to be frank.

'Great, that's settled,' Tomasz said. 'We'll have a proper traditional Christmas.'

'An Edgar Road family Christmas,' Jonathan added.

'Let's drink to that,' Claire said and I licked my lips. I was thinking already about turkey and all the lovely left-overs that George and I would be treated to. I really did love Christmas, it's my favourite time of the year.

# Chapter Ten

# Chapter Ten

Never one to give up, I had found a way of introducing George to Hana. We both stood at her patio door and we had a conversation through the glass. We had to shout and sometimes words got a bit lost, but it was better than nothing. And Hana said she looked forward to our visits – well, I think that's what she said, we couldn't be sure. We'd started going round to see her most days. Remembering how Connie was worried she was lonely and bored, we took it upon ourselves to make sure she wasn't.

'Why don't you try to come out?' George asked.

'I don't know how, or if I'll like it,' Hana said. 'And after watching Alfie get stuck in the window . . .'

The only window in the house that was ever open – and not always – was the one I had squeezed through. I wasn't sure Hana, having never gone out, would be up to it. After all, it had nearly defeated me, a far more experienced cat.

'Maybe one day I can come in and see you?' George said but Hana obviously didn't hear. Instead, she squinted at him.

'What does "comtinbeya" mean?'

I sat back a bit and let them continue the conversation. I was right, George and Hana seemed to have hit it off, even in this unorthodox way. As I listened I marvelled at Hana's nature. She was always sunny it seemed, she never complained, although to my thinking she had a lot to complain about. Her family were unhappy still. Although Sylvie put a brave face on when she visited my humans, she was still crying most nights and not coping as well as she was pretending to. Sylvie would let her tears drop onto Hana's fur and Hana would try to comfort her, but she didn't know what to do. And Connie was still being quiet and solitary. She barely spent time with her mum, despite Sylvie trying very hard. She spent most of her time in her room, on her phone, and Hana didn't know what was going on there either. George told her Aleksy was the same and we all hoped it was just this illness known as 'teenage hormones', and that it would soon pass.

But although it seemed that Hana had a lot on her plate, she never complained, not even that she was stuck in the house alone for most of the day, and I thought we could all take a lesson from her.

'It is nice that you come and see me,' she said, or shouted, as we got ready to go home for lunch. 'It does brighten up the day.'

'One day you will come out with me,' George said, confidently.

'I don't know about that.' Her eyes widened. 'But maybe one day you can come in. If they ever leave the bigger window open . . .' We all glanced at the closed windows.

We bid her farewell, she put her paw up on the door, and George and I matched it on our side, before we set off back next door.

'You know, if I was ever going to fall for a girl again I would probably fall for Hana,' George said, sweetly.

'And if you hadn't sworn off them forever then I would probably give you my blessing,' I replied with a grin.

I did have one resolution though. I'd heard it said that no one should be alone on Christmas Day, it was something I'd learnt throughout life and I didn't want that for Hana either. If her family was spending the day with us, then she would too. I just had to figure out how.

After lunch I put my thoughts of Hana aside as I had to go and find Tiger. I had ignored it for the past few days, but I had growing niggling doubts about her. I had barely seen her since she'd told me she was fully recovered from her illness. Even George was complaining that he hadn't been able to find her. The other Edgar Road cats had also noticed that she was acting out of character. Not only was she barely around, but when she was she was quiet and not her normal feisty self. She hadn't even bothered to be rude to Salmon the other day. I had a bad feeling, and was pretty sure something wasn't quite right. I could feel it in my fur.

So, without drawing George's attention to it, I needed to go and sort it out once and for all. I was quite a perceptive cat and my intuition said that all was not well, and for once I refused to be fobbed off. If Tiger wasn't wanting to spend time with me any more then she had to tell me. But she couldn't do that to George; he thought she was his mum and that was a relationship that you didn't get to walk away from. Or you shouldn't get to walk away from anyway. I went from worried to angry and back to worried again. I really did need to get to the bottom of this.

George had gone out, saying he had things to do. He really didn't but I went along with it. However, I was grateful, as I wanted to confront Tiger on her own. I wasn't going to let her wriggle her way out of this one.

I bashed on the cat flap and waited. It seemed to take a

long time, so I bashed again. Eventually she appeared and as she came through the small door my first reaction was shock. She looked thinner than the last time I saw her.

Tiger had been a bit chunky when we first met; she liked her food and she was lazy but I had introduced her to the joy of exercise and she'd slimmed down, but even so the cat in front of me looked as if she was mainly skin and bones. I wondered how long it had been since I last saw her, maybe a week. How did she get to be like this in a week?

'Tiger,' I said simply. I found my voice choking. I missed her, my boy missed her. We were a family.

'I'm sorry I've been avoiding you, Alfie,' she said. 'But you know, I'm not exactly looking my best,' she tried to joke, but it fell flat between us.

'What's going on? I need to know, not just for me but for George too. He misses you and he's only young. And you look terrible.'

'Thank you.'

'You know what I mean,' I corrected.

'I don't know how to tell you.' Her voice became sad. 'I've been avoiding you, both of you.'

'What, have you met someone else?' I asked. It would explain the weight loss. Claire said she always lost weight when she first fell in love. Tiger narrowed her eyes at me.

'God, you are ridiculous sometimes, Alfie. No, I haven't met anyone else,' she snapped.

'Then what?' My heart was beating right out of my body and my legs had turned to jelly. I sat down.

'I lied to you. When I went to the vet I wasn't just having a check-up, I wasn't feeling too good. I've been feeling tired

88

for ages, and I've been struggling to eat, and they ran loads of tests. I did have some tablets, like I told you, and I did feel a bit better for a while, but there's bad news, Alfie.'

'No,' I said, but then I reasoned that she could get more tablets. It might just take longer than she first thought. Poor Tiger, all that dried food though.

'I, I thought if I carried on as normal it might just resolve itself but it isn't going to. I'm tired all the time, I can barely get to the end of the garden let alone the street. Alfie, my family were talking and I don't have long left.'

'What do you mean?' I felt a chill in my fur. My heart sunk into my paws.

'I'm dying, Alfie. I'm so, so, sorry but I'm not going to be here much longer.'

'No, that's not possible.' I couldn't even comprehend what she was saying.

'Alfie, it's true, I'm not going to get better and I don't have long left.' I blinked. She sounded so matter of fact about it.

'I can't, I can't . . .' Words failed me.

'Oh Alfie, I've been trying to come to terms with it, you know, but it's so hard. I don't want to leave you, I certainly don't want to leave George. I love life but it's quickly slipping out of me and there's nothing we can do. I have to accept it and unfortunately that means you do too.'

'Surely there must be something someone can do. The vet, another vet? I could make a plan—'

'We've exhausted everything. My family are sad which is heart-breaking. They are old and they've had me since I was a kitten, they say they're going to be lost without me.'

'I'm going to be lost without you,' I said, selfishly.

89

'I know. But you know, you have great families, you have great friends, and you have George.'

I shuddered as the thought hit me square between the eyes.

'How are we going to tell George?'

'I don't know.' I saw Tiger falter then. She had been so strong when she spoke, composed, but not any more.

'We'll tell him together,' I said. 'But not today, not yet, I need to let it sink in too. It doesn't feel real.'

'No, I understand, it's taken me a while and I still wake up and forget.' We both looked up at the grey sky. A lone bird flew overhead, the wind whistled, the clouds threatened to unleash some rain. And next to me was Tiger, my love, my best friend, the cat who, next to George, meant most to me in the world and I was losing her. I knew as I looked at her, trying to remember every stripe in her fur, every speck of colour in her eyes, that I would have to say goodbye, and I felt as if part of me was dying too.

I have had more than my fair share of goodbyes in my life. When I was younger and lived with Margaret I had to say goodbye to Agnes, my sister cat, who was much older than me and died. That was hard, but then Margaret died, which was even worse as it rendered me homeless. I had to say goodbye to Snowball, although she didn't die, but I knew I would never see her again. I had to say goodbye to Tasha and her son Elijah when they moved to Dubai, although I did expect to see them again sometime. I have said goodbye, in my words and heart, many, many times and, you know what, as I looked at Tiger and committed every inch of her to my memory, I realised that it didn't get any easier. Saying goodbye never got any easier.

# Chapter Eleven

It was hard to tear myself away from Tiger, but she needed to rest. While I was with her, she was still my Tiger, she was still here. I knew the minute I was alone, thinking about losing her, I would fall apart. And we still had the problem of George to contend with. My poor boy. My heart was breaking for me but, more than that, it was breaking for him. His first taste of loss was going to be one of the worst, and I wished with all that I was that I could protect him from it. But I couldn't. I couldn't protect either of us from this one.

I'd discovered a lot since becoming a parent but this was another level. I knew that not only could I not protect him from Tiger dying, I couldn't stop the devastation he was going to feel. There was a terrible feeling of hopelessness, there was literally not a thing I could do. For a cat who believed there was a solution to all problems, knowing that there was nothing any of us could do to stop this was horrific. It was the worst feeling ever.

I wanted to wallow, of course I did. I wanted to lie in my bed and cry, and yelp and brood and feel sorry for myself but I couldn't. Until we told George, which we hoped to do the following day, I had to put a brave face on. I licked my whiskers, and prepared to act as if everything was alright, when in fact at the moment it was exactly the opposite.

George came home just after me.

'Where were you?' I asked, hoping my voice sounded normal.

'I went to see Rocky and he and I chased around a bit then I went to see Hana, who was very pleased to see me in fact,' he said proudly.

'I bet she was. Did you have a nice time?'

'Yes. Dad, your voice sounds funny.'

'I might have a bit of a furball,' I said, hoping he would believe me. He nodded and seemed to accept it.

'Anyway, I want to tell you that there is trouble next door,' George said.

My ears pricked up. Trouble? Not more, not today. All my energy was going into trying to stay calm, to not fall apart, I had nothing left for trouble.

'Hana said that Sylvie and Connie had a big row last night. It seems that Connie has been seeing a boy, whatever that means, and Sylvie said she was too young and it had to stop.'

'Do you mean she's got a boyfriend?' I asked. I had learnt a lot about the complexities of human relationships in my time. We cats had relationships but we were far more sensible about it. Though not always, I admitted, thinking of George's first crush. There was nothing sensible about that.

'I think so. Hana said that Sylvie was so angry and Connie said she hated her mum, before storming off. Apparently Sylvie took her phone away from her.'

'Gosh,' I said, thinking of Aleksy. 'To a teenager that's like chopping off one of their limbs.'

'Well, she couldn't see what was on the phone as it was locked and Connie refused to unlock it for her. She even threatened to call her dad.'

'Who, Sylvie or Connie?'

94

'Sylvie. Then Connie shouted that her dad didn't care about her, so to go ahead and she stormed upstairs and slammed her bedroom door, so even Hana couldn't go and see if she was alright.'

'Well I'm sure they'll sort it out, parents often row with their teenagers,' I said, thoughts of Tiger weighing heavily on me. 'But if they need help we're here,' I added, as brightly as I could.

'That's exactly what I said, Dad.'

I tried not to think about Tiger, and how much losing her was going to affect us all, but as I looked at my lovely boy, it was, in fact, all I could think about.

George was playing with Summer and Toby when Franceska called round. She was on her own and Claire let her in, giving her a warm hug. I rubbed her legs, Franceska was one of my favourite people. She was so calm and loving normally but today she didn't look it.

'You don't mind me dropping in?' she asked, chewing her lip anxiously.

'Don't be ridiculous, Frankie, you're family. Anyway, what's up? You look worried.'

'I am stressed. Tomasz is off early today so he's with the boys, and I had to get out. My Aleksy, my lovely, sweet, sensitive boy, has turned into a monster and I don't know what to do with him.'

'OK, first wine, then tell me everything.' Claire poured out two very large glasses and they sat at the kitchen table. I was just wondering if there was something in the air – just as everything seemed tranquil in my life a bulldozer came and disturbed it, all of it. I was trying to focus on what Frankie was saying and I was worried, of course I was, but my head was so full of thoughts of Tiger, I was struggling to follow.

'He just doesn't talk to me any more. I've said it so many times but now we've had a big row. I asked him about school, he didn't look at me and said, "Fine", and I got angry, shouted at him that I was his mum not a stranger and he needed to talk to me. I said I cook and clean and buy his clothes and he shows me no respect. Even Tomasz intervened and told me to calm down which is why I am here. I think he threw me out!' She started laughing and then she started crying. Claire leant over to give her a hug.

'Frankie, you never get angry,' she said, which was for the most part true.

'I know, but you know he's so infuriating. I know everyone says it's just a phase and he'll grow out of it, but I miss my boy.'

'I know, I'm dreading it when mine grow up, I can see how hard it is. Aleksy is changing and it's confusing. He probably has temporarily forgotten how to speak to adults. He's discovering girls and trying to find his place, being a teenager, trying to fit in, can be really hard too.'

'I know and I am pushing it, which is wrong. Tommy is still so much fun, I guess that just makes me miss Aleksy more. And also then I worry Tommy is going to be like him soon and I can't have two of them ignoring me in my own home.'

'You have to try to give him space, and Sylvie is going through the same.'

'Yes, but with Connie I understand it more. She's had to leave her home country, her friends and her dad and start again, right at the wrong age, but Aleksy, well nothing has changed for him, or nothing major.'

'I know, I feel so bad for Connie but then I also feel bad for Sylvie because she's struggling too.'

'Oh goodness, I am such a foolish.' Franceska's English was perfect but sometimes, when she got stressed, she got her words a bit muddled. 'I have Tomasz, who is amazing, I have the restaurants, which are all great, and I have Tommy. And one day I will get my Aleksy back. I should be counting my blessings, not moaning.'

'That's not what I meant but when you put it like that,' Claire laughed. 'You know Aleksy is so handsome and clever, and he's kind, he'll find his way back to you.'

'Oh Claire, how do you always know to say the right thing?'

'Meow.' I had taught her well.

Franceska helped Claire get the children ready for bed and was about to leave when Jonathan came home.

'Hey ladies,' he said kissing Claire and giving Franceska a hug. 'How are we?'

'Good, and about to leave,' Franceska replied. 'You know, before Tomasz sends out a search party. Thank you again, Claire,' she said, as she kissed her cheek, then she petted me before going.

'What was she thanking you for?' Jonathan asked.

'Oh, she's worried about Aleksy. You know, the terrible teenager.'

'Yeah, Tomasz mentioned it. If you ask me he's discovered girls.'

'I did think that. Do you think he's got a girlfriend? He's only fourteen after all.'

'Fourteen, going on twenty. They start young these days.'

'You won't be saying that about Summer,' Claire pointed out.

'No, I'm locking her in the house until she's thirty,' Jonathan said, and I wasn't sure if he was actually joking or not.

But, later, when I was in bed, I got to thinking. Yes, I was consumed with thoughts of my beloved Tiger and how on earth I would cope with losing her, but I couldn't help thoughts about Aleksy and then Connie popping into my head. And I knew that as soon as I'd visited Tiger in the morning I needed to make a trip. I would go and see Dustbin. Because, if anyone knew what was going on, it would be him and if he didn't he would help me find out. And perhaps it would distract me from what was happening with Tiger, although at the moment it didn't feel as if anything would.

# Chapter
# Twelve

'Tiger, we have to tell him,' I said, as I sat on her door-step.

'OK, but not today. I have been feeling sick, and I really do need to sleep. Can you make an excuse for me, and I promise I'll tell him tomorrow.'

She looked so sad and I didn't know whose pain was whose any more, I could feel mine and hers, mixed up together. I know I was feeling sorry for myself, and devastated at the idea of losing her, but suddenly I stopped being selfish and focused on how awful it was going to be for her. She was the one that was ill. I hadn't even thought about how much she was hurting, but now it was all I could think about. I needed to be kinder, less selfish. It wasn't easy.

'Of course, you need to rest, Tiger, and you will not tell George tomorrow. *We* will tell him tomorrow. I'll meet you here after breakfast. And I love you.'

'I love you too, Alfie, and I'm sorry . . .'

'You have nothing to be sorry for. You just think of yourself for now and I will worry about everything else. After all, it's what I'm good at.'

We both managed a small smile before we parted. So, I just needed a plan to keep George away and, of course, taking him with me to see Dustbin would be perfect. It was not too far, as I have already said, but it was far enough away to keep him from Edgar Road for a few hours. Hopefully by the time we got back the children would be home from school and things would be too hectic for him to think of going out again. It was the only plan I had right now.

I found George in the back garden, about to go into the house.

'Have you been to see Hana?' I asked.

'Yes, but Sylvie is home today so we couldn't chat. I was going to see Tiger mum.'

My heart felt as if it was being stabbed.

'Good idea, but I have to go and see Dustbin. Do you fancy coming with me first?' I asked, trying to act nonchalant.

'Oh yes, I'd love to see Dustbin. After all, I can see Tiger mum any time I want.'

Oh God, just as I thought my heart couldn't break any more.

George chatted away as we walked and I think he failed to notice how quiet I was. It felt as if I spoke I wouldn't be able to hide the truth and it was important, for George I believed, that Tiger and I both told him together. That was parenting after all. So I tried to mew in the right places and I tried to concentrate on his cheerful chatter. I couldn't help but think of Edgar Road without Tiger and that didn't seem right. Not right at all.

'Dad, we're here, you were miles away,' George said, as we weaved through the back way to the restaurant yard.

'Sorry, son,' I said. I really did need to pull myself together, not only for the next few hours but after . . . No, I wasn't ready to think about after.

Dustbin was giving himself a wash when we found him.

'Oh, this is a nice surprise,' he said. As usual he seemed genuinely happy to see us.

George went straight for the bins to see if he could sniff out any mice and, instead of telling him off, I let him, so I could talk to Dustbin.

'I thought I'd ask you if you knew what was happening with Aleksy?' I asked. 'Franceska was at ours yesterday and she was upset.'

'Oh, interesting. You know, I heard her and Tomasz talking last night as they checked the restaurant last thing. He told her that she was being silly, that Aleksy might be a bit secretive and glued to his phone but he wasn't drinking, smoking or taking drugs.'

'God forbid,' I said. 'He isn't, is he?' None of that had occurred to me.

'Nah, Alfie, you see, Aleksy sneaks down here when he thinks his parents don't notice. From what I can gather, he seems to have got himself a girlfriend.'

'Oh, is that all?' I felt relieved. A girlfriend, that was a nice thing, not something to worry about.

'Yeah and he was saying he wanted to tell his mum and dad but his girlfriend doesn't want him to. It seems I've become a bit of an eavesdropper since meeting you.' He laughed, as did I. Dustbin used to keep himself to himself until he met me. He did try to keep me at paw's length when we first met but I wasn't having that and now we were the best of friends and he knew everything that went on.

'Sorry, well actually I'm not sorry. The more we learn about our humans the easier it is to solve their problems,' I pointed out.

'Right you are. Anyway, from what I could hear of his conversation, his girlfriend obviously told him not to tell his parents and he said he was finding it hard to lie to them, but the girl must have said something else because then he said, OK, he would leave it a bit longer until she was ready.'

'Let me get this straight. The reason he's being secretive is that his girlfriend can't tell her parents so she's asked him to keep quiet?' It seemed to make sense.

'Yes, and I gather that her mum thinks she is too young for a boyfriend.'

'You really did listen, didn't you?' I raised my whiskers, impressed.

'Oh yes, and I know who the girl is, by the way.' He grinned. I hadn't thought to ask that question, where was my mind? My eyes nearly popped out of my head. Who was she?

'So do I,' George piped up. I hadn't noticed him but he was behind us, having heard it all.

'Who?' I asked. And how did George know?

'Connie,' they both said at the same time.

It seemed George, clever George, had worked it out by listening to me and also to Hana. Hana had said she knew the boy went to school with Connie and also he'd been to the house, which must have been Aleksy. Dustbin had heard Aleksy call her by her name. Perhaps all the trauma with Tiger had taken me slightly off my game, but it hadn't even occurred to me. I guess no one could blame me though. I suddenly felt like crying. Aleksy and Connie were beginning their relationship and mine was ending. Oh dear, I was back to being selfish.

'Well, I think it's great,' I managed. 'Aleksy is a good boy, Sylvie should be pleased that her daughter has met a lad like him and not one of those horrible ones that hang around the park sometimes with their trousers half way down their bums.'

'Oh Dad, you do sound old sometimes,' George teased. 'It's just fashion.'

'I do not,' I replied. 'And fashion isn't always right.'

'Actually, you do a bit,' Dustbin agreed. 'Reading between the lines, it seems that Sylvie is a bit overprotective of Connie, not only with everything that has been going on but also because her life in Japan was very sheltered.' Dustbin was a pretty perceptive cat.

'It was,' George added. 'Her school only had girls in it, and she didn't really have any friends that were boys, let alone boyfriends. Hana told me that.'

'Is Hana the cat who never goes out?' Dustbin asked.

'Yes, and she's my new friend,' George replied. 'And we talk through the glass door. It's a bit strange but we're making it work.' He sounded so grown-up, I was proud.

'Anyway, so her mum doesn't know about Aleksy?' I checked.

'No, and Connie wants to keep it that way for a while, because she is worried that she'll go mad and stop her from seeing him,' Dustbin continued. 'But that's all I know.'

'It's a lot,' I said. 'And I wish he'd tell Franceska and Tomasz. They won't be angry with him, in fact they would probably be able to help.'

'But you can't make him tell them,' Dustbin pointed out.

'Well, actually I probably can,' I said, and we all laughed.

Although my feelings about Tiger weighed heavily on me, I was relieved to find out the only thing wrong with my boy

Aleksy was that he had his first ever girlfriend. I found it quite moving; he was growing up. They all were, and that included George. As much as you wanted to protect them all, you couldn't protect them from everything – I was learning that the hard way. The problem was my children were too.

'So, what are you going to do, Alfie?' Dustbin asked.

'I'll think of something,' I said. 'But in the meantime, do you think someone might be out soon with left-overs?' I felt a bit hungry after all this emotional activity.

'I'll stand at the door and they'll think I am too cute to resist,' George said, and he did just that. It didn't take long before one of the staff came out with a bowl of food for each of us; it never failed to work.

I was aware that some people would wonder how I could think of my stomach at a time like this but I knew that I needed to keep my strength up. Whatever happened the next few days, weeks, or however long I had my precious Tiger, I would need it all, and with the humans adding in their issues to my already complex emotional mix, I knew I needed to make sure that I was in peak physical condition. Even if my feelings were broken and they would never ever recover, I would have to get through this. Too many people relied on me: George, my human kids, the adults, and now we had Sylvie, Connie and Hana to take care of.

As I ate I realised I was needed by many, and most of all, Tiger needed me. I would somehow have to reassure her that it was going to be alright, that she shouldn't be scared, that she mustn't fret about leaving us behind because George and I would somehow cope. I knew that she needed to be at peace and the only way for her to do that was for me to ensure she didn't worry. I had no idea how to do that, but I knew it was right at the top of my priority list. I still didn't know how I was going to be able to say goodbye to her but I needed her to think that I would be fine, and most importantly that George would too.

'Are you alright?' Dustbin asked. 'You don't quite seem yourself.' I looked at him, his kind eyes, his scruffy fur, and I wanted to tell him everything, but then I looked at George sitting beside him, gazing hopefully up at me, and I knew I would keep it to myself for now.

'I'm fine, just thinking about all the work we have to do to fix our humans,' I lied.

'Oh well, you know I'll help you with anything you need. I'll keep my ears open with Aleksy anyway and if there's anything urgent I'll come to you,' Dustbin said, reassuringly.

'And you don't have to worry about me, Dad,' George said.

'No, son, I know,' I lied, for the second time that day.

# Chapter
# Thirteen

'Summer, you are in big trouble,' Claire said as we got home to find Toby, Summer, Jonathan and Claire all in the living room. We had hung out with Dustbin until it began to get dark and then I said we better go straight home so that they didn't worry. George accepted it all with his usual good grace and I felt guilty, but at least he had one last night before he knew the horrible truth. George and I both watched from the doorway of the living room.

'Why?' Summer asked, crossing her arms defiantly. Claire sounded cross, Jonathan was scratching his head and Toby seemed a bit nervous, but then he didn't like conflict and I can't say I blamed him. Claire had tried to protect him from it when he first came to live with us but she and Jonathan then realised that he needed to understand some arguing was normal and it would be best for him to learn to cope with it. It was a work in progress.

'Sum,' Jonathan said. 'You cannot go around trying to kiss boys against their will.' Ah, that was what she'd done.

'I didn't. I only did it with one boy. Zack.'

'That doesn't make it better,' Claire said. 'You know he shut himself in the toilet and refused to come out, even for lunch. It took your teacher ages to calm him down and he's still terrified of you.'

I glanced at George. We knew Summer well; when she wanted something she didn't let anything stand in her way.

'He's a big baby,' Summer continued. She wasn't going to back down.

'He is a bit,' Toby supported her. 'I mean, he just had to tell Summer to get off him and be stern with her, and I'm sure she would have stopped.'

'Yes I would.' No, she wouldn't.

'The point is that you shouldn't have done it in the first place. You have been told to leave Zack alone before, Summer, and your teacher is really cross. And I have to phone up Zack's mum and apologise to her, which is just embarrassing.' Claire was pacing up and down, she was agitated. Jonathan seemed more amused, actually.

'He must really not like you,' Jonathan said finally.

'Not helpful, Jon, a bit of support please.' Claire said that a lot. Jonathan sighed.

'OK. Firstly, Summer, you will apologise to Zack tomorrow in front of your teacher. Then you will apologise to your teacher for disrupting her lesson by her having to get this kid out of the toilet. And you will not go around trying to make boys kiss you. In fact, you shouldn't be kissing boys at your age anyway, what has got into you?' Jonathan used his best parental voice. Summer was six, but she was going on sixteen, Claire often said.

'Hormones,' she said. 'I just can't help it.'

'Where the he— I mean, where on earth did you get that from?' Jonathan asked, totally aghast.

'Mum and Polly say it about Aleksy.'

'Aleksy is a teenager and you're not,' Claire pointed out. 'So really that doesn't wash with us, young lady. You'll do as

Daddy said, and then you will stop trying to kiss Zack once and for all.'

'Well, I was going to stop anyway,' she said.

'Why?' Toby asked.

'I need a man not a boy,' Summer said.

'Right, go to your room now,' Claire shouted, and Summer stamped her foot but scurried off. As soon as she did both Claire and Jonathan burst out laughing.

'Oh my goodness, hormones? I mean, really, I have to watch what I say in front of her from now on.'

'She's needs a man not a boy. Hey, Toby, you better warn Henry. Or even Tommy!' Jonathan had tears running down his cheeks he was laughing so much.

'So it's OK?' Poor Toby's voice was full of confusion.

'Yes, I mean, no she is still in trouble, but I'm sorry Tobe, your sister is quite bonkers.' Claire hugged him.

'She's funny though, everyone at school thinks she is.' Toby looked thoughtful. 'Apart from Zack, that is.'

'Yes, and thank goodness she's got an older brother like you to help keep her out of trouble.' Claire gave him another hug.

'Should I go and check she's alright?' he asked, sounding very serious.

'Good idea, but don't tell her we were laughing, it'll only make her worse,' Jonathan said.

'Right, got it, come on George,' he said and George and Toby trotted upstairs.

It took ages before Claire and Jonathan stopped laughing and I was cheered up too. Laughter was a tonic, they all said that, and I really did believe it. For a few minutes anyway it helped.

Claire calmed down enough to give Summer a bit of a chat as she was tucking her into bed.

'Darling, I know your intentions were innocent but you really shouldn't kiss boys, Daddy was right.'

'I'll stop, but you know it is just so funny when they scream and run away.'

'One day, which will come far too soon for me and Daddy, they won't scream and run away, and then you'll be stuck with them.'

'Is that what happened with you and Daddy?' Summer asked.

'Something like that,' Claire replied and kissed her daughter.

I nose-kissed George goodnight as he settled in with Toby. I checked on Summer who was sleeping, her breathing so sweet, and I remembered when she was a baby, which didn't seem so long ago, and I would watch her sleep a lot. It was sort of hypnotic watching her, and I also felt that I was protecting her somehow.

I padded back downstairs where Claire and Jonathan were snuggled up together on the sofa, watching something on TV, and giggling together. They were happy. I then went out, quietly, to Polly and Matt's house. I let myself in through the cat flap, which they'd had put in years ago just for me. I didn't spend as much time there as I used to any more, because of George, but I did go and see them when I could. I made my way upstairs, and checked on Martha who was

114

sleeping, and sounded a bit like Summer, then Henry who had kicked the covers off but was also fast asleep, clutching a toy spaceman.

'Hello, Alfie,' Polly said as she emerged from the bathroom, wrapped in a towel. She had come out of the bath, I guessed – each to their own. I hated water but humans seemed to like it. Matt shouted up asking if she wanted a cup of tea and when she put her pyjamas on I followed her downstairs to where he was waiting with tea and biscuits laid out on a tray.

'Fancy watching *Game of Thrones*?' he asked, giving me a fuss. 'Nice to see you, Alfie.'

'Perfect,' she said and gave him a kiss. They went into the living room, and sat together on the sofa. I spent a bit of time on Polly's lap, enjoying her affection. Just as I was beginning to feel sleepy, I decided to leave.

'Meow,' I said, quietly, and bid them goodnight.

I had an urgent need to check on everyone I loved, but it wasn't possible to go back to Franceska's house. It was too late now to go so far from home, but knowing Dustbin was keeping an eye on things was reassuring. I was glad my Edgar Road families were all happy, and peaceful. How I wished I could be.

I went to see if there was any movement from Tiger's house before I returned home. There wasn't. The house was shrouded in darkness and I knew her family normally went to bed early, so I wasn't surprised. I quickly popped to the back of Sylvie's house and saw that Connie was at the kitchen table, with her computer in front of her, and it looked as if Sylvie was helping her with her homework while Hana sat next to the computer. They looked more harmonious and I wondered how Sylvie would react when she found out about Aleksy. But that was a worry for another day.

I went home and curled into my bed and thought about Tiger. I replayed certain scenes with her in my head. How she was protective of me since we first met on Edgar Road. How she was always the more aggressive of the two of us and had got me out of trouble a few times. She was unafraid, she seemed so fearless. How she teased me about my vanity and conceit but still liked me for it. How she'd been jealous of me and Snowball, and I'd felt our friendship was really under threat, but she had been so mature about it and we had worked through. How she was the one who helped me when I was broken-hearted after Snowball left and how quickly she took to helping me parent George and never complained. She didn't complain about much. And when I told her I loved her, which was a long time coming, she was so happy, but she also would never have pushed me into it. She was the best friend a cat could ever have, and as I finally let myself fall apart, when no one could see me, I realised I had no idea how I was going to cope with her loss. For an ideas cat, I literally had no idea how I would carry on without her.

# Chapter
# Fourteen

Chapter
Fourteen

George's head moved from me to Tiger, and back again. He blinked and then he looked at us both again.

'I don't understand,' he said. The poor kitten really didn't.

'I'm not well, George,' Tiger said. 'I can't get better. It happens sometimes and soon, but I don't know how soon, I won't be here any more.'

'But where are you going? On holiday?' It was George's first experience of loss, and goodness, what I wouldn't have given to protect him from it.

'No, although it might seem a bit like that. I'm going far away so you can't physically see me but I will always be watching you.'

'Well that makes no sense at all,' George said. 'If you're so far away how can you watch me?'

'Well I'm kind of going to be in the sky, so I will be able to see you but you won't be able to see me.' I'm not sure Tiger was actually doing a good job of this. She was confusing the poor lad even more. Not that I was sure I could do any better, but I thought I'd have a go.

'What Tiger means, George, is that sometimes people, or cats in this case, have to leave this earth, but they will be in your hearts forever, so they never properly leave you.'

He blinked at us both again.

'So you won't be here, in this house, on this road?'

'No.'

'And I will never see you again?'

119

'No.'

'But we don't know exactly when I will never see you again?' George asked. He seemed composed but I was still unsure what he was comprehending, after all it was huge.

'No, we don't know for sure,' I said. 'But we have been led to believe that it's not going to be long.'

'Before Christmas?' George asked. I hadn't thought about that, I hadn't thought about this being close to Christmas. Would this be Tiger's last ever Christmas, would she even make it to Christmas? It was unbearable.

'I honestly don't know, George, but I won't be able to come out much, so you'll have to come and see me. I'm pretty sure my family will be alright with that but come even if they aren't, because I want to see you.'

'I want to see you too, Tiger mum, and I promise that I'll come in, whether they shout or not. But please, try to be here for Christmas. I don't want to have Christmas without you.'

'And nor do I, love,' Tiger said and I could see she was about to cry, in a cat way of course.

George seemed to accept this and I was relieved. He was behaving with a maturity I didn't always credit him with.

'Do you mind if I go now? I need to think,' he said.

'Of course, but come and see me later?' Tiger asked, giving him a nuzzle.

'I will, Tiger mum.'

As George went off, we decided that I ought to go and fill the other neighbourhood cats in on the situation. Tiger didn't think that she would be able to make it. Not only was she feeling weak but she was also distraught about George.

'I'm not sure he understood,' she said, clearly worried, on top of the fact she was also exhausted. Whatever this illness was, it had changed her almost beyond all recognition already, she was a shrunken version of herself and she was struggling. I knew she was in pain too, but she refused to complain about that.

'No, but we'll help him, and you know he needs time to let the news sink in.' I knew I had needed time and I wasn't sure it had still fully sunk in with me.

'You promise you'll take care of him, when I'm gone.'

'You know I will,' I said. 'But let's not speak of that.'

I didn't know why but I was suddenly filled with optimism that this would all sort itself out. She said that the vet told her family she wouldn't get better but that didn't mean she wouldn't. Vets weren't always right. I had heard Claire say the same about doctors. What if they'd got it wrong, what if Tiger was just bad now but would recover? She wasn't that old, not even in cat terms, and by rights she should have years left in her. And I knew that due to her laziness she hadn't even used up half of her nine lives. No, I narrowed my eyes, there was no way that Tiger could die.

'But you have to promise me something,' I said, suddenly energised.

'What?'

'That you'll try to fight this illness. For me, and for our boy.'

'I will, Alfie.' But I could hear the hopelessness in her voice. She didn't think she could, but luckily I had enough belief for all of us.

\* \* \*

121

I left her to rest as I went to see the other cats. Rocky, Elvis and Nellie were joined by Tinkerbell, a cat who was a boy, but had a girl's name. He didn't often hang out with us, he was normally too busy looking for food, but he did at times, and was a very pleasant cat, one I was happy to call a friend.

'Have you seen George?' I asked.

'Yes, he ran past here a while back, going at some speed I should say,' Nellie said.

'When I asked him where he was going, he shouted back that he had to be somewhere important. Well, I don't know about you, but I don't see anywhere important at that end of the street.' Rocky sounded confused.

'And it's not like the boy not to stop and pass the time of day,' Elvis said.

'Maybe he heard about somewhere to get food.' Tinkerbell narrowed his eyes, as if he was thinking about following him, but then he sat down. 'Not to worry, I've just had two lunches.'

I filled them in on Tiger's situation. Nellie immediately started yowling. Elvis and Rocky seemed very quiet.

'I knew there was something amiss. I mean, we've barely seen her and normally she's always with you or the lad,' Rocky said, eventually, his voice full of emotion.

'I don't know, the place won't be the same without her,' Elvis said.

'She's not gone yet. She might recover,' I said.

'In my experience, when the vet says your days are numbered, they are generally right,' Tinkerbell said. 'And, Alfie, I'm not trying to be mean but, you know, sometimes it's better to try to accept it, especially as you've got George to think about.'

'I know but I just don't want to lose her,' I said, lying down on the soft grass, feeling like I never wanted to get up again.

'Hey, we'll be here for you, and the lad, and Tiger of course. How about tomorrow morning we go to her garden, show her our support?' Rocky said.

'That's a good idea,' Nellie agreed. She had come over to nuzzle me, we were all united in grief.

'As long as I've had my breakfast of course,' Tinkerbell said, and I managed a grin. Sometimes when the world seemed to be changing, falling apart, breaking hearts, having someone act as if everything was normal was a comfort.

'Do you think I should go and look for George?' I asked. Now I had stopped feeling sorry for myself I was worried about him again.

'I'd leave him for a bit, give him some space. We'll all keep an eye out for him.'

'I am so lucky to have such great friends,' I said, before going home so I could crawl into my bed and wallow.

George returned just in time for tea. I could tell he wasn't feeling very good, his eyes were downcast and he didn't have his usual bounce about him. He ate a bit, but not as much as normal, and I knew I would have to get him alone so I could have a chat with him. I took my chance as Claire took the children upstairs to get them bathed and ready for bed.

'Come outside with me for a moment,' I said, and George followed me through the cat flap.

'Will she really die, Dad?' he asked.

'You know, son, I keep saying to myself that it's all a big

mistake but that is what the vet said, and she's not feeling well at all. So, as much as we don't want to, I think we have to face facts. You must have noticed how thin she is.'

'I did today, but she's my Tiger mum, and I don't know what I'd do without her. What happens when she's not here?'

'I don't know, son.' I felt my eyes glistening with tears and cats don't cry. 'I know we will miss her, our hearts will hurt and we won't feel good at all, but together we'll get through it. I know you are young and you shouldn't have to say goodbye to someone you love, not at your age, but I can't stop it, I can't protect you from it.'

'I'm scared, Dad.' He looked at me with his big, innocent eyes.

'So am I,' I admitted and I moved in as close to him as I could while we both yowled about what we were about to lose.

# Chapter
# Fifteen

I could tell that Christmas was creeping closer, because there was an excitement in the air that wasn't there before. It was only a few weeks into November but Claire always started making lists early. Polly also started talking about ordering things from the internet to get ahead of the game. Jonathan, of course, moaned about money and Matt, who loved Christmas, talked about how he was going to decorate the house, for the kids, and how Jonathan should do the same. Jonathan didn't share his enthusiasm and wasn't keen, saying the houses looked tacky when they were all done up. He could be so miserable but I knew, deep down, he loved Christmas.

Tomasz and Frankie were gearing up for the restaurants' pre-Christmas rush. For most of December they spread themselves very thinly, as Christmas menus started to be served, office parties booked, and with a few restaurants to run, they were kept busy.

But the most important event, according to the adults, more important than the letters to Santa and the arguments about when to decorate the house, was the nativity play. This play was only taking place in the younger children's school, but it was a big deal. Claire and Polly were chatting excitedly about it when they got a letter saying that the school was holding auditions and the children were all enthusiastic about their potential parts.

'Right, kids, what are you going to do for your audition?'

Claire asked as she, Jonathan, Toby and Summer were in the living room after tea. George and I were also in attendance.

'I'm going to sing,' Summer announced before launching into a rendition of 'Jingle Bells'. It wasn't great, more shouting than singing, but Jonathan and Claire clapped enthusiastically as she finished. Parents were a little biased. I knew this as I could be too, but not when it came to that sort of noise.

'Great, Summer. And Toby?' Jonathan asked.

Toby cleared his throat, then got down on all fours. 'Hee-haw,' he said.

'Right, is that it?' Jonathan had his hands ready to applaud but then he scratched his head.

'I want to be the donkey,' Toby explained.

'Oh, in that case, it was excellent,' Claire announced and they all clapped loudly, before getting the kids to do it over again. I raised my whiskers; in my opinion, once was more than enough.

'You are going to kill these auditions,' Jonathan said, enthusiastically.

'Jon, it's the school nativity not the West End,' Claire pointed out but she looked pretty excited about it too.

Despite being heart-broken about Tiger, I decided to focus on the Aleksy situation. I needed Franceska, who was worried about him, to know the truth, because I knew she would be relieved. Aleksy wasn't ill, he wasn't miserable, there was nothing wrong with him, apart from first love. And I knew that if Franceska saw that she would be reassured. And, anyway, it was not good for them to sneak around together. I had learnt that the best way to deal with things was to be open about them.

I had a foolproof plan. I went to see Dustbin, and chatted it through with him. We knew that Aleksy usually walked Connie home from school – I'd seen him – and I also knew from Franceska that she was letting him have a bit more freedom as long as he was home for his tea. So, all I needed to do was to get Franceska to our street so she could see them together. Simple. Although, from past experience, I knew that getting humans to do as I told them wasn't always easy. It could be quite exhausting, in fact.

I waited until Franceska and Tomasz came out of the restaurant and were about to head inside the house. Then I started behaving oddly. I yowled, meowed, yelped, hopped around in circles and almost cried myself hoarse. I scratched at Franceska's trousers, careful not to hurt her, and just as I almost felt as I was going to pass out, they seemed to get it. I tried not to catch Dustbin's eyes, he was rolling around with laughter behind a dumpster.

'I think he wants us to do something,' Tomasz said, scratching his head.

'MEOW!' Yes.

'I go with him, you stay home because the boys will be back any minute,' Franceska said, glancing at her watch.

Tomasz nodded. 'But call me, to let me know everything is OK.'

'MEOW,' I shouted again. Finally. Although I was exhausted, I set off round the side of the yard to the main road. I managed to get Franceska to follow me, although she seemed very confused as she did so.

'Is something wrong?' she asked. I tried to tell her it wasn't but I don't think she understood. I managed to dodge a chubby dog who tried to leap at me, luckily his owner pulled his lead back. He snarled at me as I grinned back at him. Dogs were no match for me, even when I was tired and emotional. We made it to our street without further incident, but of course I am a cat and I wasn't sure about the timing. Had they come home? Were they on their way? I had no idea. I led Franceska to Connie's front door, hoping that somehow this was going to work.

'Is something wrong with Sylvie?' Franceska asked, looking at me with concern. 'But why didn't you get Claire or Polly?'

'Yowl.' Honestly, did she understand nothing? She shrugged at me and then she rang the doorbell. There was no answer. I wondered how I would come up with a plan B, because let's face it, this one had really taken it out of me. We stood on the doorstep, poor Franceska looking totally bemused, and me so tired I thought I might pass out. Instead I sat down.

'Alfie, what on earth is going on?' she asked. I put my head in my paws. She turned to leave, and then she stopped. 'Oh my,' she said. I looked up. Bingo. Walking towards us, holding hands, were Aleksy and Connie.

'Aleksy and Connie?' she asked.

'You're welcome,' I thought as I lay down and tried to get my breath back, relief flooding my poor, tired body.

They both stopped short as soon as they spotted Franceska, and they untangled their hands, as if we hadn't already noticed. I wondered whether those suffering from 'teenagerness' temporarily lost a few brain cells as I'd always thought of Aleksy as being quite clever.

'Hi Mum,' Aleksy said, trying to sound casual. 'I was just walking Connie home from school because . . .'

'He's borrowing a book from me for English,' Connie quickly added, sounding as if butter wouldn't melt but looking embarrassed, and a little awkward.

'Is that what they call it these days?' Franceska arched an eyebrow.

'What?' Aleksy asked.

'It's fine, I was hoping to see your mum, but she's not here.'

'No, she'll be home in about an hour,' Connie said, still red-faced.

'No problem. Right, Aleksy, go and get your book and then you can walk home with me,' Franceska said.

'Sure, Mum,' Aleksy said.

When they went inside, Franceska bent down and gave me a tickle. Then she lifted me up for a cuddle.

'Is that what you wanted me to know?' she asked.

'Meow,' I said, quietly.

'Oh Alfie, you are such a good, clever cat. I can't believe my Aleksy has a girlfriend. Oh, I am so not ready for him to grow up, but at least it's nothing bad, thank you.' She kissed my fur and put me back down.

# Chapter
# Sixteen

Claire was having one of her 'girls' nights', although why they called it that I had no idea, they were hardly girls after all. Polly and Franceska were coming round and Sylvie would be joining them; they were so determined to make her feel welcome that they included her now. I was so proud of my women, their friendship had been built over a number of years but they never excluded people and I believed that I might have had a paw in that.

Polly and Franceska arrived first, both brimming with excitement.

'Quick, tell Claire what you told me,' Polly said, shoving Franceska into the kitchen.

'What?' Claire looked bemused.

'My Aleksy, he told me. OK, he didn't exactly volunteer the information, but when I caught him, he came clean. I mean, Alfie led me there, so because of Alfie I know everything now.'

'You're making no sense,' Claire said. 'Take a deep breath.'

'I found him at Connie's house and reluctantly he told me he liked her.'

'Oh wow, you mean Aleksy has a crush?' Claire grinned. 'Now this calls for wine.' I didn't like to say anything but really these women would use any excuse for wine. If I was like that with catnip, I would never get anything done.

'No, it's not a crush, it seems that she likes him too. He has a girlfriend.'

'Aleksy's first love,' Polly sighed. 'Gosh, I remember my

first boyfriend, Peter Spencer. I was twelve, he was in the year above and we held hands every lunchtime until he dumped me for an older girl. I was devastated.'

'Oh God, I was much older than that, at least fifteen,' Claire said. 'Unfortunately I ended up marrying him.'

I raised my whiskers, this was news to me.

'Really, he was your first husband?'

'Yes, but we broke up for about two years, got back together at nineteen, and well, the rest is part of my pitiful history.'

'Not sure these stories are helping,' Franceska pointed out. 'But I was a late starter. I didn't have a boyfriend until I was seventeen. And no, it wasn't Tomasz.'

'That is so sweet,' Claire said.

'Ah, young love.' Polly looked dreamy. Probably because we were all way past that.

'And is Sylvie alright with all of this?' Claire asked.

Franceska shrugged.

'I don't know, Connie hasn't told her yet. Because apparently she's so overprotective, that Connie is scared to tell her – which explains all the secretive behaviour – but of course I told Aleksy that she needed to tell her mum, as it was wrong to keep things from her, especially now I know.'

'Did he know you were seeing Sylvie tonight?' Polly asked.

'Yes, and I said I wouldn't lie to her, so he is going to speak to Connie about it.' Franceska now looked worried. 'It's not fair that she doesn't know and we all do. Aleksy wasn't happy when I said that but us mums need to stick together. And then I made Tomasz give him "the talk".'

'You mean he hasn't already?' Claire asked.

'Yes, we did do that, or Tomasz did, years ago, but he was

so awkward that he kept swearing in Polish, and after he blustered through it Aleksy said they already did it in school. But this time I made Tomasz give him a talk about respecting women and not rushing into anything.' I was slightly disappointed I hadn't been there for that one.

Claire's phone beeped with a text.

'Sylvie's on her way.'

'That's good, isn't it?' Franceska said.

'Hopefully.' Claire didn't sound so sure.

Our nice relaxed girls' night had taken a bit of a stressful turn, however I had to have faith. Sylvie was a lovely woman, sensible, and she fitted right in on Edgar Road, so what could go wrong?

I cowered under the kitchen table next to Polly's legs. I felt as if she might like to dive under it with me. Franceska looked as if she was ready to cry and Claire's eyes were as big as saucers. Basically, Sylvie hadn't taken the news well. And that might be one of my biggest understatements.

I had gone with Claire to open the front door when Sylvie pushed past us both with barely a glance. I had to practically run after her, and when she got to the kitchen, she really lost it.

'My daughter has just informed me that she's got a boyfriend. And it's your son.' She glared at Franceska, who looked surprised and then a little afraid.

'Well yes, we just found out—' Polly started.

'And you are all sitting here as if the most normal thing in the world is that my fourteen year old, who has never really been around boys much in her whole life, now after only a short time in London thinks it's OK to have a boyfriend.' Her eyes were on stalks. She was clearly distressed, and slightly unhinged.

'Hey, it kind of is normal,' Polly pointed out, then flinched because Sylvie's eyes were blazing with anger.

'Not for my daughter. She's a good girl. She works hard, she gets straight As, she doesn't care about boys and make-up and clothes. Well, she didn't until your son corrupted her.'

'God, Aleksy couldn't corrupt Donald Trump,' Polly tried to point out. I had to admire her insistence on not backing down; both Claire and Franceska seemed to have become mute.

'Not the point,' Sylvie shouted. But I thought it was the point.

'Meow,' I said, trying to convey that Aleksy was a lovely boy and any parent should be pleased it was him spending time with Connie.

But she ignored me; she was angry and started pacing up and down the kitchen. 'We've had a huge upheaval and I knew it was a mistake letting her go to the local school. She begged me, said it would be a way for her to make friends who lived nearby, but somehow I am going to have to get the money for her to go to an all-girls' school. Maybe if I tell her dad what she's been up to he'll cough up.' She was muttering now as if she was talking to herself. She was definitely unhinged.

'Sylvie, Connie seems like a sensible girl and Aleksy is one of the sweetest, most sensitive boys I've ever met,' Claire said, her voice gentle. She tried to offer her a glass of wine, but Sylvie ignored it. 'You know, it's very innocent between them, just a bit of hand-holding, and if Summer had to have a boyfriend, which I know is a terrible thing for us mums to get our heads round, I would like it to be someone like Aleksy.'

Franceska looked at her gratefully.

'I brought him up properly, to respect women, he won't do anything bad, he doesn't do anything bad. Oh, and by the way, Aleksy is a straight-A student too.' It was the first time since Sylvie had lost her temper that Franceska had spoken.

'That is not the point. The point is, Connie is too young for a boyfriend, no matter what. If her father was here, he would go mad.' I could feel Sylvie's frustration vibrating in her voice. 'I forbid them to see each other.' Her voice was angry, but also I could hear sadness in it. Because she was suddenly having to parent her daughter alone and she clearly didn't know how to do so.

'Sylvie, I say this out of friendship,' Polly started. 'Doing that will just make them want to see each other more, and they go to the same school.'

'I do not need any of you telling me how to raise my daughter,' she almost spat the words. 'I'll tell Connie that she has to come straight home from school, and if she sees Aleksy in school I can't control that but I can forbid her to see him otherwise. And I'll take her phone, so she can't contact him. Yes, Polly, she might be mad at me initially but in the long run she'll thank me. She is too young and too naive to be exposed to boys like Aleksy.'

'How dare you!' Franceska now stood up. I jumped onto Polly's lap. 'Boys like Aleksy? My son is a good boy. They are both fourteen, it's normal, there is nothing wrong with it. I will not tell you how to bring up your daughter but I will not have you speaking bad about my son.' I could feel Franceska's anger.

139

'I'll say what I want, and you women, well you can keep your friendship, you obviously don't care about me or my daughter. And I wish I'd never met you or moved to Edgar Road.'

Leaving all three women gaping, Sylvie stormed out of the house.

'Well, that went well,' Polly said, but no one laughed.

'I really didn't see that coming.' Claire finished the rest of her wine quickly.

'Oh no, poor Aleksy,' Franceska said as she burst into tears. Claire and Polly tried to reassure her that it would be fine, and I tried to think but I had no idea what to do next. They all seemed to think that Sylvie would calm down and they would be able to sort things out. I felt they were being a little optimistic, but of course I couldn't say that.

Then I had an idea. I left my women, reluctantly as I didn't like to leave when they were still upset, and I headed next door. I wondered if I would be able to see how it was playing out. At least if I knew what was going on, I might begin to get an idea of how to fix things. Because I knew Aleksy was good, as was Connie, but I also could see how scared Sylvie was, probably because of what she'd been through. I could see both sides, although of course Sylvie was wrong. Connie was lucky to have someone like Aleksy in her life, but I couldn't tell Sylvie that, and even if I could have she wasn't going to listen.

I made my way to the back garden and when I peered through the darkness into the lit kitchen my worst fears were confirmed.

I couldn't hear what was being said, but the muffled sound of raised voices came through the door. Sylvie was running her hands through her hair, Connie was shouting; her face was red and I could see tears beginning to fall from her eyes. Hana was cowering, and my heart went out to her. Us cats always got caught up in the crossfire but, because of Hana's sheltered life, she probably had no idea what to do. I watched, slightly mesmerised as Connie, crying properly now, handed her phone over to her mum who was pointing at her. Connie turned on her heels and stormed out of the room. Sylvie sat down at the kitchen table, put her head in her hands and sobbed.

So much unhappiness, I thought, when it could have been a happy time. Aleksy would have been good for Connie, he would have helped her adjust to life here. I knew that, because I knew him. But Sylvie didn't and I had no idea how I would fix this one.

# Chapter
# Seventeen

Chapter
Seventeen

I woke up feeling weary, as if I hadn't slept. The last few days had been trying and it was taking its toll. Claire, Polly and Franceska were all still very upset about Sylvie, and although Jonathan said that it would all blow over – that seemed to be his solution to most things – I wasn't so sure. They were lucky I wasn't like him.

Although Claire and Polly had discussed it yesterday and tried to come up with a plan, they both felt that, although Sylvie was clearly having a difficult time, they had to be loyal to Franceska. They agreed that they could try to broker peace, but they needed Franceska to know they were her friends first and foremost, and also, she was right and Sylvie, according to Polly, was insane.

I felt exactly the same. They discussed trying to reason with Sylvie and, while I wasn't sure that would work, I was pleased they were trying. However, they argued about who would go and see her and in the end they rolled a dice from one of the kids' board games. Polly lost. Claire, from her position of not having to go near Sylvie, was happy to offer advice, but Polly wasn't thrilled.

Of course I was worried about Tiger as well, and seeing her was becoming increasingly difficult. With a lot of effort we were still managing, and every time I saw her face I was filled with happiness that she was still with us. I was also concerned about George. I tried to have numerous conversations with him about Tiger but he kept changing the subject or saying he was fine. He was brushing me off, which of course made me fret about him more, but I didn't know what to do. I couldn't make him talk to me.

Instead, I told George about the situation with Sylvie before he went to visit Hana. I schooled him on the importance of information gathering so we could help them. And George, bless him, was a very good student. When he came back he reported that Hana was very upset. Connie wasn't talking to her mum, but when she spent time with her in her bedroom, she confided in Hana. She cried a lot and talked about how unhappy she was, how she missed her dad and her home and how Aleksy had made it more bearable. She did say, however, that luckily Aleksy was being supportive and they were spending time together at school, which they accepted for now. They were sensible kids, I was right. It was a friendship first and foremost, I could see that, but if only Sylvie could see it too. If only there was a way to make her see it.

Sylvie wasn't coping and Hana said that she had no one to turn to. Having cut herself off from the women, she wasn't even talking to her friends via the computer any more. Hana told George that no one really comprehended how much Sylvie's life had been turned upside down and that trying to hold things together for Connie, as she had been so far, was making her ill. Sylvie had even done as she'd threatened and spoken to her ex-husband, who had suggested Connie come and live with him in Japan, which had sent Sylvie almost mad. Now she felt she couldn't talk to him about it, in case she lost her daughter. Because I knew this, but my women didn't, I felt for Sylvie and thought it would be down to me to fix things for her.

As winter settled, cold whipping at our fur and nights and mornings dark and gloomy, my tranquil life was over. However, Tiger had to be my priority. I didn't know how long I had left with her and I wasn't going to miss a moment if I could help it. I knew I had other problems to solve, other fish to fry, and I had my paws full, yet everything would have to work around time with Tiger. That was something I would never get back again and I refused to miss it.

She was waiting on the back step for me. 'Hi Alfie,' she said. When I saw her these days, I had to gulp back my feelings, try not to show the shock in my eyes, which I knew, for a split second, was there. She was getting thinner, her fur had lost its gleam and she was permanently exhausted. But she always kept her spirits up, which I thought was for my sake and George's.

'Tiger, looking good,' I said and gave her my best grin.

'I know that's a lie. Anyway, I'm glad you're here, tell me about the drama with your humans.' She shivered.

'Are you cold?' I asked.

'Yes, it's harder and harder to keep warm, but I'll be alright.'

I snuggled into her. 'You don't want to hear about my humans, all that drama,' I said.

'Alfie, don't treat me as if I'm ill. Normally you would tell me all about the problems and I would listen to you, I need that. I need normality.'

147

'OK, but before I do, how do you think George is coping?' I asked. She nestled her head into my neck.

'I don't know, he's putting a brave face on with me, and he visits me, which is sweet – my family don't even mind at all any more. But when I try to talk to him he changes the subject.'

'Same with me,' I said. 'He seems fine, but I know how much he loves you. And he seems to be avoiding me. Or maybe he just needs to be alone to process things. I know he sees Hana every day, and you, but he seems to be out for an awful long time and when I ask him he's evasive.'

'Alfie, he'll be fine, he's got you, and he's probably just trying to get his little head around everything. Now tell me about this row between the women.' Tiger had always been a bit like my voice of reason, and I fleetingly wondered who would be that when I lost her.

I told her all about how the relationship was fractured between them now, and how Claire and Polly were trying to resolve it.

'But if Sylvie was so rude about Aleksy why do they want to be friends with her?' Tiger asked. One thing I loved about Tiger was how she sometimes saw everything in black and white.

'Well, firstly they want to resolve it for Aleksy and Connie's sake, but also they know how badly Sylvie has been hurt. They know she's not really horrible, but she's scared, terrified even.'

'I see. And do you have a plan?'

'Not yet. I am going to see what happens when Polly tries to reason with her and also tomorrow, when I've left you,

148

I'm going to go and see Dustbin, see if he has any news, about Aleksy mainly. But you know you're my priority before I worry about anything else.'

Tiger sighed. 'Look, Alfie, I know that you are going to put me first, but I also want whatever time I have left to be as normal as possible. And that means I expect you to do what you always do and come up with your mad plans, which inevitably involve some kind of disaster before working out.'

'They are not mad, they are very good plans.' I bristled.

'What about when you nearly died?'

'It all worked out in the end, but yes, maybe not that one,' I conceded. I had tried to protect Claire from a boyfriend I knew was no good and I ended up being injured by him, but it did bring all my families together, so you know, it was kind of worth it.

'And when you got stuck up the tree and had to be rescued by the firemen?' I could tell she was grinning now.

'Well yes, that might not have been my finest hour.' I had been trying to woo Snowball, my first girlfriend, but I discovered a fear of heights and couldn't get back down the tree. It was most humiliating.

'Or when George got catnapped?'

'But at least we managed to rescue loads of cats in the end.' That had been a terribly worrying time though, not knowing where my little George was. We called them the 'Lamppost Cats', because cats were disappearing on and around Edgar Road; pictures of them were being hung on lampposts. At the same time, my families were all unhappy so I tried to get George to hide with Tiger for a while, the idea being that it would bring them all together again. And

149

it did in the end but only after it went a bit awry as George got taken by the kidnapper – catnapper. It was the worst time of my life before we managed to rescue him and all the other cats.

'Or when you nearly got set on fire?'

'OK, Tiger, enough now.' But I was smiling. I was glad to talk about old times with her, it was some comfort actually, even if she was teasing me. And I didn't nearly get set on fire, I actually foiled a fire that was going to be set in our holiday house in Devon, so there.

'So, promise me you won't ever stop with your plans, Alfie,' she said and I felt her eyes close and she fell asleep right on the doorstep, snuggled up with me in the cold. I wanted to tell her that I wasn't sure I could give up my plans even if I wanted to, how when she was gone I would need to keep busy more than ever. There was so much I wanted to say to her.

I stayed still, and breathed in the scent of her. I was trying to commit it all to memory – how she looked, how she felt, how she smelt, how her fur tickled mine – because it was painfully clear that despite my optimism, despite the fact that I was the cat who fixed everything, there was no way I could fix this. One day soon, I would have to say goodbye to someone else I loved. And all I would be left with was my memories of her, so I wanted to make sure that I had lots of them.

# Chapter
# Eighteen

Chapter
Eighteen

Matt and the children were with Jonathan in the living room and Claire was clearing up the kitchen when we heard the doorbell. Wiping her hands on her jeans, Claire went to open it with me at her heels. Polly, face like thunder, stood on the doorstep.

'Oh dear,' Claire said. Polly pursed her lips and walked in. The adults all made their way to the kitchen, leaving the children playing.

'I'm actually really worried about that woman,' Polly started.

'So, she didn't take kindly to your reasonable chat?' Matt raised an eyebrow. 'I did tell you to leave well alone.'

'I told Claire as well,' Jonathan said. The two men high-fived, looking pleased with themselves. Honestly, if we left it to them nothing would ever get resolved. I swished my tail against Jonathan, angrily.

'Oh, for goodness sake, grow up. Anyway, I will tell you what happened. Sylvie now blames us – that's me and you, Claire – for this whole thing. Apparently if we had left her alone, hadn't tried to make her our friend, then Connie wouldn't have met Aleksy and none of this would have happened.'

Even I had to admit that was terrible logic. Connie was in the same year as Aleksy in the same school.

'I said,' Polly continued, 'very calmly, I might add, that they're in school together so they would probably have met at some point. And do you know what she said?' They all

153

shook their heads. Polly can be a bit scary when riled. 'She said that she was still going to figure out a way to pull Connie out of school and send her to an all-girls' one. The thing is that she is behaving madly, and I think she needs help but she won't let us anywhere near her.'

'Oh dear,' Jonathan, the master of understatement, said.

'I asked if she would sit down with Franceska and Aleksy to talk, and she basically threw me out of her house.'

'She must have been so badly affected by the divorce.' Claire shook her head.

'Yes, and I'm out of ideas. I do want to help her, not just the kids, but she really isn't behaving rationally.'

'I feel sorry for her, but I have no idea what to do.'

'Maybe you can try next time,' Polly said. Then she smiled. 'Though if you value your life I wouldn't recommend it. She's feistier than she looks.'

'If only there was a way though, to get her to see sense.' Claire chewed her lip, thoughtfully.

I felt my brain begin to tick over. Sylvie felt as if she was alone, and she wouldn't let the women in, but if we showed her that she was welcome here, I mean if I showed her . . . I just had to figure out how.

'Poor Aleksy, it's just like Romeo and Juliet,' Matt said, and they all lapsed into silence.

It was clear no one knew what to do and it seemed that yet again it was going to be down to me.

I left them to see Tiger. George was still out and I assumed he would be with her. There was no sign of either of them, so I took one of my lives in my paws and jumped through the cat flap. Thankfully the kitchen was empty, and I made my way through to the living room where I stopped. Tiger's bed was in front of a fire, although it wasn't a real fire, and Tiger was alone in it. There was no sign of her humans, but Tiger was curled up. She looked up and saw me.

'Alfie,' she said, her voice quiet.

'Hey, is it safe to come in?'

'Yes, they've gone shopping for a bit, come on in.'

I made my way over to her bed, and sat down next to her.

'I thought George might be with you,' I said.

'No, isn't he home?'

I flicked my tail. 'No, and he's normally home by now.'

'Alfie, he seemed a bit angry when I saw him today. He was trying to hide it but he kept saying it was unfair that I wasn't going to be here soon. I tried to calm him down by telling him I'd always be watching him but I'm not sure he was buying it. Anyway, I think he might have needed a bit of time to himself.'

'I know and he's old enough, but Tiger, and I'm not telling you this to worry you, but he's been going out a lot more lately. At first I thought he was visiting Hana, which he does but not the whole time, so I'm not sure where he goes. I asked Rocky, Elvis and Nellie but they don't know either. He's not spending much time with them, it seems.'

'And asking George won't work, will it?'

'No, he gets defensive when I even ask him if he's hungry these days.' My lovely sweet kitten was becoming surly, mono-syllabic and he was actually behaving like a teenager, but of course cats don't normally do that. But, I accepted that, with the Tiger situation, normality had gone out of the window.

'Alfie, you'll have to follow him, just to check you know that he's safe.'

'I'm normally the one who would suggest such a thing.' I grinned. It was obvious. Why hadn't I thought of this? Although with everything going on, maybe it wasn't surprising.

'But just make sure that he doesn't see you. I'm not sure he'll take kindly to being followed.'

'And with all the mounting problems at the moment, having George angry with me is not one I want to add to the pile.'

'Please make sure you come back and tell me what you discover. If I can I'll come out, but if not I'll be right here. Even if my family is here – they are both quite sad at the moment, so they might even let you come in.'

'Right, Tiger, before I do anything more about the whole human situation I will make sure that I know George is OK and I'll find out where he's going.'

If George was acting like a teenager, I hoped he wasn't doing what I'd heard a lot of teenagers did, and getting into trouble. We had quite enough of that right now, thank you very much.

I casually established that George was going to see Tiger, and I lay in wait for him. Unfortunately it was cold, and I shivered in the bush in Tiger's front garden, where I had chosen to hide. I had followed many people before, but never George, and although I kept a close eye on him, I had to admit this did feel different. I felt as if I was betraying him in a way, although I knew, deep down, it was for his own good. I would let him have his freedom, just as long as I knew he was safe. I needed to ensure he was being careful and there was no danger.

I knew I should be thankful that he was going out during the day – if it had been night I would have had a whole heap of fears and worries. He could have been hanging out with unsavoury cats, fighting, hunting, getting up to all sorts of mischief. Though if he had shown any signs of that I would have got Dustbin on the case. I really had to stop worrying about things that hadn't happened, especially as I had my paws full with troubles that were very, very real.

It is characteristic of life, and I speak from my own experience, that when things start piling up the tendency is to fret more. It's a vicious circle: when things are good you enjoy them and try not to think of the bad times, but when things are bad you can only think of how they could get worse. So, as I waited for George, I tried to count my blessings. Firstly, the sun was shining. Yes it was cold and windy, but at least it wasn't raining. And I did have lovely families and friends. I might be losing Tiger but I was lucky to have had her in my life for as long as I had, and that was a gift. Although losing her wasn't a gift, it was the opposite of a gift, whatever that may be.

Just as I was running out of both blessings and optimism, George appeared. He didn't notice me as he set off down Edgar Road, towards where our cat friends met. I followed at a safe distance, hopping behind the odd lamppost to ensure I kept out of sight, but George didn't look back once. None of our friends were at the recreation spot but he walked straight past it anyway; that clearly wasn't where he was heading. As I carried on walking, I had a horrible feeling that I knew where he was going. As George stopped at the tatty house with the jungle garden and the horrible old man, my worst fears were confirmed.

I watched him from a safe distance as George played in the overgrown bushes which dominated the space. It really did look fun to play in; brambles and overgrown plants, a small, fat tree with overhanging branches and long grass. There were no flowers, no colour. But it was a garden you could definitely lose yourself in and I just hoped he was safe. I settled back to watch my boy.

After exploring the garden, he hopped up on the windowsill of the house and peered in. Next thing I knew, the old man from Halloween appeared and started banging a walking stick against the window in an angry fashion. George, however, sat on the windowsill and seemed nonplussed. Or nonpussed. I cowered behind a bush near the front wall, as close as I dared go. What if the man hurt George? He stood there shaking his fist and his walking stick. I saw him more clearly than I had in the dark that night. I could vaguely hear the words, 'Get lost', being shouted. George tapped his paw on the window one last time and hopped down, raising his tail in a salute. I quickly started running home.

All the way I tried to make sense of what I'd seen. George clearly knew the garden but the old man didn't want him there. The thing was that my George wasn't the best at reading signals, he'd thought Chanel liked him when she showed him nothing but disdain. But how could I discuss this with George without him knowing I was following him? I couldn't.

Another thing to add to my mounting problems; I would have to keep an eye on it. If this was where George was disappearing to most days I would need to make sure that he was safe. That walking stick looked like it could do some serious damage. The man looked as if he could do some damage too. And if the Goodwins were right and he was dangerous . . . I shuddered.

My other dilemma on the way back was whether to tell Tiger or not. On the one hand I didn't want her to worry, but on the other she'd asked me to treat her normally. Also, I had a vague idea that it might be better for her to tackle George about this, or at least to try to ask him about it. He was still talking to her, after all, whereas at the moment he seemed to be avoiding me as much as he could. Oh yes, he would still fill me in about Hana but it was as if talking to me was a duty rather than a desire. Our easy relationship, the one where we hung out, chased leaves, chewed the fat with other cats, talked through the day's events together in the evening, seemed to be over.

I just hoped it wasn't over forever.

I'd been at home for a while before George came in. I'd stopped at Tiger's but the cat flap was closed and there was no sign of her. I hoped she was resting. Every time I saw her she seemed weaker and the idea that, one day soon, I would go and see her and she wouldn't be there threatened to floor me.

I'd had a snack, a wash and a nap, only to be woken by the sound of the cat flap and the appearance of a very sad-looking George.

'Are you alright?' I asked, fussing despite saying I wouldn't.

'I'm a bit tired actually,' George said. 'I think I might have a nap. It's very cold out.'

159

He was chattier than normal, which I was happy about, but I also knew not to push it.

'OK, did you see Tiger mum?' I asked, casually.

'I did, earlier.' He turned to go, then he stopped. 'Dad, she's really not going to get better, is she?' His eyes were full of sadness and his whiskers seemed to droop. My heart broke and I wanted, so desperately wanted, to give him the answer he needed to hear, but of course I couldn't.

'No, son, I don't think she is,' I said, heavily. George, to my surprise, came up to me and nuzzled into me.

'What about you? Are you going to leave me as well?' he asked, his voice small.

'No, son, not for a very long time,' I replied and I crossed my paws and hoped, prayed, that that was true. No, actually I knew it was true. I wasn't going anywhere. I wanted to reassure him, but I didn't want to lie. 'You know, George, I would never leave you willingly, and nor would Tiger mum. She has no choice but I'm still here and, for as long as I am, I'll always be right by your side. I love you, son.' I nuzzled him and I felt his sadness through his fur.

As I watched George go to find his favourite chair to nap in, I felt my heart breaking for him all over again. I would be around for a very long time – don't ask me how I knew, but I did – and I would give George as much strength and courage as possible. That was what parents should do for their children, after all. That and try to keep him away from the scary old man at the end of the street, of course.

# Chapter Nineteen

# Chapter
# Nineteen

It was pouring with rain but I had promised myself that I would go to see Dustbin to check that all was well with Aleksy. Unfortunately I had heard nothing new; the situation, according to George, via Hana, via the door, was the same. George was being a supportive friend and their regular through-the-glass-door chats were helping her, he believed. I was trying to let George feel grown-up so I didn't intrude but I told him if he needed me, I would be happy to help. He was enjoying his friendship with Hana, although he was getting frustrated about not actually being able to see her properly or always hear what she had to say. That issue was already on my list, however. I felt that perhaps if I could get Hana and George face to face, it would help him through a tough time. I would have done anything to make George feel better about losing his Tiger mum, and though I knew that getting Hana out of the house wouldn't do it, not nearly, at least it would be something.

What I hated most about this situation was the feeling of helplessness. I was a cat who fixed things, who fixed hearts, who never gave up, but here there really was nothing I could do. If the vet couldn't fix Tiger, then I certainly couldn't, and I hated that feeling. My heart was going to break, as was George's, but I was powerless and that made me want to yowl in pain. All I could do was to be there for everyone, and that didn't seem to be enough, although it had to be.

'George,' I said, finding him tracing raindrops falling down the window with his paw.

'Yes, Dad?' he replied, but he didn't turn around.

'I know it's raining but I have to see Dustbin, Aleksy business. Do you fancy coming with?' There was a pause as George, head tilted, seemed to be mulling my offer over.

'No thanks, Dad,' he said eventually. 'It's quite far in the rain and I have to visit Tiger mum and also go and see Hana, so that'll keep me busy today.'

'Alright, son, I'll go on my own. If anyone needs me, let me know when I'm back later. I'm going to try to say hello to Tiger on the way, as well.'

George let out a big sigh. 'OK Dad, see you later.' He returned his attention to the raindrops, indicating our conversation was well and truly over.

Feeling like I wanted to say so much more, but unsure what, I waited a few moments before turning and heading out. Typical that I had to choose a day when the rain was beating down, although the grey sky matched my mood. But, never one to wallow, I went to Tiger's house. There was no sign of her and I butted the cat flap with my head, but it didn't move. Her family had locked her in again. Was this because she had to go to the vet? Or was it something even worse? My heart started beating fast as I made my way to the front of the house. I looked at the bottom window and there was Tiger, lying down. I jumped up onto the window-sill and she saw me. She looked frailer than ever but she managed to raise a paw and I did the same. Like George and Hana, we managed to exchange a few words, most of them lost in the wind. Her family was with her, in the living room,

I could see the lights on, the fire blazing red, and they were sitting on the sofa. I gazed at Tiger and mouthed, 'Goodbye', as I reluctantly left her to lay down her head again. I just hoped it wasn't going to be the last time I saw her. I hoped that every time, but I could feel her slipping away from me, and I knew that losing her was imminent.

My legs felt heavy with grief as I made my way to Franceska and Tomasz's house to find Dustbin. My limbs seemed to be filled with lead, my head ached, and I felt pain running through my whole body. I knew this feeling, I'd had it before; it was heart-break, pure and simple, the worst ailment to affect me. But I kept going. One paw in front of the other, me and my pain continued. I was almost glad of the distraction, but then I was sad I even needed a distraction.

'Dustbin.' I mustered all my cheer as I greeted him. He was having a snack; not a rodent, thank goodness, but some left-overs from the restaurant which looked very tasty. He did get pretty well-paid in his job. He had to see off all manner of nasty rodents but the food he was given was of the highest quality. I wouldn't have been able to do it though, not for all the sardines in the world.

'Alfie, what a lovely surprise.' He stopped eating. 'How are you, mate?'

I filled him in on the situation with Tiger, which he was very sympathetic about, then I shared my worries about George, and finally I asked about Aleksy.

'Oh boy, the drama just piles up, doesn't it?' Dustbin shook his tail. 'I feel for you, Alfie, I really do. And I wish there was something I could do. But if you think George is in any danger from this stick-wielding man, just say the word and I'll be after him.'

Dustbin was quite a keen fighter, not that I approved of violence, but Dustbin was a different type of cat to me. He didn't go looking for trouble, but he didn't shy away from dealing with it, which had helped me out quite a lot in the past. And for that I was grateful. He would never hurt anyone who didn't deserve it, I could vouch for that. He protected those he cared about, and I was grateful to be counted among those he did.

'I think George is OK, at least he hasn't got in with the wrong crowd. I'm worried about the old man, he seems very angry, but we can keep an eye on that. It's more the fact that he's shying away from me. We barely talk any more – well, we do about Aleksy, Connie and Hana, but not really about Tiger, or how he's feeling.'

'Give him time, Alfie, he's young still and doesn't know how to express himself yet. He will, and he'll come to you when he's ready. Just make sure he knows he can, which I know you do.'

'Thanks, Dustbin, you always say the right thing. What about Aleksy?' I gave Dustbin a quick affectionate nudge. He wasn't a touchy-feely type of cat but I like to think I had softened him up a bit over the years.

'He's a bit sad, the poor lad. He can't phone her so I don't get to overhear him any more, but he does mooch around quite a lot. His mum and him are talking more now though, which is a good thing, and he asked her for a job, so he can buy Connie a present to cheer her up. I'm not sure what kind of present though.'

Ah, Aleksy was a man after my own heart. He was going to do a grand gesture, a gift to show Connie that he cared. I had done the same in my time. Not that it was as simple for cats; not being able to buy anything meant that we had to be a little more creative. Digging up flowers and climbing trees, that sort of thing, but let's not go there. Anyway, Aleksy was showing what a considerate, caring youngster he was, which made me happy. And he and Franceska were on good terms again, which made me even happier.

'Did she give him a job?'

'She said he was too young to do anything official but he's helping with cleaning up and polishing cutlery at the restaurant and she's giving him extra pocket money, so yes it seems so. From listening to their conversations it seems that he still spends time with Connie at school. They are both sad about how her mother is but Connie says she won't budge. At least the mother/son relationship is good again, it's like he's stopped being a teenager.'

'Thank goodness. I miss the old chatty Aleksy and he and Franceska, who were always so close, need to be again. That at least makes me happy.'

'We need to count every single blessing at the moment, Alfie,' Dustbin pointed out.

'I agree, and if Aleksy is being sweet and it seems quite mature about this whole thing, trying to cheer Connie up rather than getting angry, well, I'm one happy cat.' I wasn't exactly happy. 'I just wish there was something I could do to get Sylvie to come round. Not only has she made the kids miserable but she's isolated herself now, so she can't be happy.'

'You'll come up with something. Oh look, it's that pesky rat. I thought I'd seen him off, excuse me a minute.' Dustbin turned, ran at breakneck speed and pounced on a rat. I turned my head away. It didn't look as if that rat would be bothering the restaurant again. It was the ugly side of being a cat and I could only be thankful that I didn't have to worry about it. There, I had found two blessings in one afternoon, which was better than none.

I saw Franceska come out of the restaurant, just as I was about to leave.

'Alfie, you came to see us,' she said, petting me. 'It's a long way, can I get you some sardines?'

'Meow,' I replied. She certainly could. And that was blessing number three.

# Chapter Twenty

# Chapter Twenty

December beckoned, with its demands for Christmas trees and advent calendars, and excitement was palpable among the young members of my family. The auditions for the nativity had taken place and everyone was waiting eagerly to learn of their parts. Even George forgot to be surly at all times. Although we were still shrouded in sadness – Tiger was getting worse, and the situation next door with Sylvie, Connie and Hana was no better – amidst all that, Christmas had officially started in Edgar Road.

Tiger was hanging on but we were seeing less and less of her. Not only was she hardly going out, but her family had started closing her cat flap more often, and so George and I were able to snatch only occasional moments with her, which were becoming rarer. If the cat flap was shut, she would try to make it to a window to see us, it had become our new thing, but it wasn't the same. Poor George had to talk to his new friend and his mum through a window, and I could tell he was getting frustrated with both. And he wasn't the only one. I had nothing. No plans, no schemes, and no idea how to fix any of the messes we were surrounded with. I was a cat without a plan and I was nursing a very bad heartache.

'Claire, how on earth are we going to get a tree that size home?' Jonathan said. Claire had been to the tree man down the road and had just announced that she'd reserved a tree which was over six-foot tall.

'Tomasz said he'd go with you in his van.' Claire indicated the conversation was closed. She was drawing up big plans for Christmas. She talked of something called 'hygge'.

'What on earth is that?' Jonathan had despair written all over his face.

'It's Danish and it's to do with cosy, simple pleasures, and I want to make our house feel like that this year.'

Jonathan just shook his head.

'I've got lots of candles and this is going to be a proper family Christmas,' she announced.

'Let's just hope we don't burn the house down,' Jonathan finished.

I left them, Claire talking through her plans for making the house Christmassy, and Jonathan still shaking his head, and went to find my boy.

George had reacted just as you would expect a child to react; he was angry, scared and he felt as if he was being abandoned. Parents are meant to protect their children and both Tiger and I had failed him in this. I remembered how I felt when my sister cat, Agnes, died when I was just a kitten. I'd been so lost without her and I didn't understand. My owner was beside herself and so I retreated into myself. I'd felt as if I had no one to turn to and then, when Margaret died a year later, I was utterly alone. But George wasn't alone; not that that would make him feel better right now. I was pretty sure that nothing would make him feel better right now. It broke my heart, which was already breaking over Tiger. I was worried there would be nothing left. But I had to pull myself together. For Tiger, and for George.

I set off down the road to find him. George was always home for tea, and with all the drama I realised I hadn't seen him for quite a while. He was loitering near the front of Tiger's house.

'Ah, there you are.'

'So?' George looked at me angrily.

'Well, it's just that I hadn't seen you for ages and it's teatime.'

'Whatever,' he said, sounding just like a teenager.

George looked at me with his beautiful big eyes, but I couldn't tell how he was feeling.

'It's about Tiger mum.'

'I don't want to talk about it.' He sat and flicked his tail angrily towards me.

'OK, then you can just listen. What has happened sucks.' I employed 'teenage' speak in the hope of getting through to him. 'For her, for me, and most of all for you. Saying goodbye is the hardest thing we have to do in our lives, and I know this as I've done it a number of times before. But, and this is where I need you to listen, if you don't say goodbye to Tiger mum, while you've got the chance, then you'll regret it, and I can't let you do that. I promise you that I love you, and I'll be here for you for a long time to come, but now I need you to talk to me about it.'

'But, I don't want to,' he said, his voice small, tinged with sadness. His tail was wrapped around his body as if he was trying to protect himself.

'I know, son, and if I could have it any other way I would, but I can't. You need to say goodbye and you need to say it now. Please don't leave it until it's too late. Don't regret it or be angry with us, because this isn't anyone's fault.'

George sat silently. I could tell he was mulling my words over, but I was determined. I would somehow drag him round there if I had to – although I had no idea how, he was quite a weight now. I crossed my paws that it wouldn't come to that.

'Should I go to find her right now?' he asked, his eyes full of fear.

'I'll be right with you,' I said, as we set off.

We made our way round to the back of the houses. It was eerily quiet, apart from the odd bird squawk or the faint sound of a car engine – it was like a ghost street. I could feel our uncertainty, shivering as we walked. We reached the back doorstep and looked at each other. I tipped my head slightly, and then I checked the cat flap. Thankfully it was open; I let myself have a huge sigh of relief. I gestured for George to go through first and then I followed, hot on his paws. I took a deep breath and prepared myself for the worst.

We both padded through to the living room, where Tiger was in her bed, in the same place I had left her last night. The fire warmed the room and I immediately felt my fur start to defrost. I nudged George slightly as he paused and we both made it to her bed at the same time.

'Tiger,' I whispered, hoping against hope that she was still with us. I almost didn't dare breathe.

'Mum,' George said, and I thought my heart would crack in two. After what seemed like an eternity she opened her eyes.

'My two favourites,' she said, her voice quiet and raspy.

'Mum, I'm sorry,' George cried. 'I just couldn't bear to say goodbye but Dad told me I would be sad if I did but even sadder if I didn't. I don't want you to go.'

'I don't want to go either, son,' she said. George hopped into the bed and snuggled into her.

They say cats don't shed tears but I swear my eyes were full of them.

'I will always love you, George,' she said. 'Remember that, and I'll always be part of you and you'll always be part of me.'

'And I will always love you too, Mum,' he replied.

'Be good for your dad, be true to yourself and you'll grow into a fine adult cat.'

'And wherever you are, you'll see me? You'll always watch over me?'

'I will, George, even though you won't be able to see me.'

'But I want to see you,' he cried. Tiger gave me an anxious glance.

'You know, George, your dad and my favourite thing to do was to watch the moon, and you know when we did we also saw lots of stars in the sky. If you ever want to see me then look into the night sky and I will be the brightest star. I won't be able to be with you but I'll always be there.'

'You'll be in our hearts forever,' I said, not for the first time, but I didn't know how else to say goodbye and I didn't trust myself to speak further.

'And you mine. Be the best you can be and, George, try to keep your dad out of trouble.' They both grinned and nuzzled.

'Oi,' I said, trying to sound jovial, but feeling as if the words were going to choke me.

'You two have each other, you need to be a team, a family, please remember that,' Tiger said. Before we could answer, I saw her body go rigid, then still. Her eyes closed. I looked at George, he looked at me. We both knew she had gone. It was almost as if we had seen her go and I was rooted to the spot. I watched my boy yowl into Tiger's fur and I knew that we would never see or hear her again. Not in the real world anyway. Tiger had breathed her last breath and now we had to find a way to carry on without her.

After a long while, I gave George a gentle nudge.

'We should go, son,' I said. 'Her family will be down soon.' I felt for them, how they would wake up today and find Tiger gone, that would be so hard for them, but I couldn't help. For once in my life I felt totally helpless.

'OK, Dad,' George replied, and reluctantly, wishing with our hearts that we didn't have to go, we both gave her one last nuzzle before leaving.

# Chapter
# Twenty-One

# Chapter
# Twenty-One

Tiger was gone but Christmas was coming. George and I were silent as we observed the house being decorated. We didn't talk about Tiger, neither of us were ready yet. I needed to see our friends, but for now I wanted to be silent in my grief. And from what I could see, George felt the same, so I was showing him I was there for him, whilst trying to hold myself together.

Our house looked beautiful with its big tree in the living room that Claire insisted on putting up on the first day of December. It took Jonathan, Matt and Tomasz to carry it in the house, which elicited a lot of words that neither children nor cats should have to listen to. And then they discovered it was too tall for the room, so Tomasz had to saw off the top. Although it wouldn't be Christmas if it all went smoothly! Claire was so happy about the tree that no amount of Jonathan's moaning could ruin it for her.

Despite the fact that we were miserable, we tried to enjoy the occasion the way we would most years. The children were so excited as they helped decorate it, as was fast becoming a Christmas tradition. It looked a little bottom heavy as a result but it also reflected our family. There were homemade decorations from both Summer and Toby, their favourite coloured baubles, which they were allowed to choose, and an abundance of tinsel. Toby even begged George not to try to jump into the tree this year. As George had done this every year since he'd been with us, we weren't confident.

Even though he said he would try his best, I had a sneaking suspicion he wouldn't be able to resist. Our living room had a sudden explosion of tinsel, lights and brightness, and it couldn't fail but to cheer us up. It was a burst of colour in our very black and white life.

Claire then did as she'd suggested she would and put out lots of candles. I wasn't sure about them – candles, cats and children weren't a good combination – but she said this was her nod to 'hygge'. She hadn't quite grasped what else it meant so to her it was just far too many candles and, as Jonathan said, 'turning our house into a fire hazard'.

Claire had also written most of her Christmas cards and she put one through the door at Sylvie's saying she hoped that they could have a drink over Christmas. Claire, like me, didn't like giving up, so she was trying to come up with ways to get Sylvie back into our Edgar Road fold. Jonathan told Claire to leave it but she rarely listened to him. I agreed, not just because we liked and cared about Sylvie, but also because both Aleksy and Connie were still being kept apart. I knew (via Hana and George) that Connie was still crying most nights, and Aleksy was miserable without his friend (via Dustbin).

Hana told George that Sylvie had found out that her ex-husband was having a baby with his new woman and that had set her off into deeper depression. He'd even suggested Connie going to spend Christmas with them but Sylvie couldn't bear to lose the only person she had left in her life. I understood. We were lucky with all the people we loved, despite losing Tiger, but she had no one. It was beyond sad.

I saw her in the street and tried to get her attention but she seemed to look through me as if I was invisible. I really was worried about her and her state of mind. It wasn't good, I could tell. I needed to do something, and through habit I went to see Tiger, momentarily forgetting that she was no longer there. I was alone to come up with a plan. I wanted to get Hana out of the house, but again, nothing. I thought if I got George in then that would be something, but they didn't even leave the top windows open any more, so I had no chance. There was literally no way in. George offered to see if he could fit through the letter box but even I knew that wouldn't work.

I was trying to make my list, in my head. Tiger, gone, but I wasn't ready to let go. Aleksy, missing his first love, and we all knew what that was like. Connie, isolated and angry with her mother. Sylvie, upset about her divorce but taking it out on the wrong people. Hana, a poor cat caught in the middle. And George, who was still disappearing regularly, still not quite talking to me the way he used to, and obviously hurting but refusing to let me comfort him. It was a lot.

Thank goodness for Christmas. The only speck of happiness on the horizon.

I sat with Claire as she made even more lists. She explained to me she was making a list of presents to get.

'Everyone likes getting gifts, Alfie, so I am going to make sure I put a lot of thought into it. It's how us humans show we love each other.'

*Ping*, I had a brainwave. Gifts, of course. That was the answer. I would win Sylvie over by getting her gifts. I went off for my afternoon nap and to try to make my own list of what I could get her.

★   ★   ★

'I am never speaking to him again,' I heard Toby shout as the front door opened and, along with a gust of icy wind, Claire, Toby and Summer burst in.

'Toby, calm down,' Claire pleaded. She chewed her bottom lip, worriedly. Summer was looking a bit startled, after all she wasn't the one being dramatic for once and she didn't seem to know how to handle that. Toby's face was red and angry. Oh no, what now, I thought. This was not good. Our Toby was such a star. He had come to us age five having been adopted, and not having had a great start in life. At first he'd had nightmares, which George had stopped, and then he'd had a fear of being sent away. But finally, he now seemed to feel, to believe, he was the important part of the family that he really was. It was both heart-breaking that he'd been through that but heart-warming that he had us now and we had him. We all loved him so much. Just as much as Summer.

'I will not calm down. It's not fair.' He sounded a bit like Summer as he stamped his foot. I guess he'd been taking lessons. I was glad for once that George was out; this scene would have definitely upset him. None of us liked it when Toby was unhappy, although I didn't recall seeing him this angry before.

'OK, but Tobe, you have to tell me, because you just sulked all the way home and neither you nor Henry would speak. So can one of you please let me know what's going on?' Claire ran her hands through her hair. Toby and Henry were best friends, inseparable, so I didn't like the sound of them falling out.

'I will not.' Toby crossed his arms and then looked a little unsure what to do.

'Oh Mummy, what happened is this,' Summer said. 'They

announced the Jesus play people in assembly today. I'm a star. Daddy says I'm a star anyway, so I think that's why they cast me.'

'I am guessing you mean nativity, and Summer, yes you are a star, but please can you tell me why this has made Tobe in such a bad mood.' Claire tried to hug him but he slipped out of range.

'He's Joseph, who is baby Jesus' daddy, but not his real one because Mary was a virgin.'

'Oh God, Summer, who told you the nativity story?' Claire asked, although it was a little off point.

'Daddy.'

Claire rolled her eyes. 'But Toby, that's the main part, along with Mary of course, that's amazing, you should be very proud. I'm very proud.'

I was very proud too, look how far Toby had come.

'Well I'm not, because I have to hold hands with Emma Roper. She's Mary and I don't like her. She's a girl.'

'I'm a girl,' Summer pointed out.

'You're my sister, that's different,' Toby said.

'True.' Summer nodded.

I saw Claire look between them, unsure where to go with this, and I have to say I wasn't sure either.

'OK, so you don't want to hold hands, but what has this got to do with Henry?' Claire asked.

'He's the donkey,' Toby said.

'Ah,' Claire said.

'I wanted to be the donkey. Everyone knows the donkey is the best part ever.' Toby burst into tears and ran up to his room.

183

'What on earth am I supposed to do about this?' Claire asked.

'Leave it to Daddy, he is so much better at all this than you,' Summer said sagely, and leaving Claire open-mouthed, and me a little bemused, she went to join Toby.

'He's really not,' Claire said.

'Meow,' I agreed; he really wasn't.

'I hope that she's only saying that because she's such a daddy's girl,' Claire added, stroking me.

'Meow,' I agreed. Claire and I would probably have to sort this one out, just as we sorted everything out.

The doorbell rang and Claire opened it to find Polly on the doorstep.

'I left Matt with the kids, but had to come and see you. Is Toby alright?' Polly asked, coming in and picking me up, taking me to the kitchen with her.

'I was about to go and see, but Sum's up there with him. He's really upset.' Claire's lips twitched, as did Polly's, and to my great surprise they both burst out laughing. What kind of parenting was this?

'Oh, I'm sorry Claire, but Henry was so pleased with himself. He kept saying how everyone wanted to be the donkey and he was chosen for his acting skills and the best thing was that everyone knew that donkeys didn't have to hold hands with girls.'

'Poor Toby is so distraught. I told him he'd got the main part but he wasn't having it. He said he doesn't like the girl who plays Mary, or he doesn't like any girls actually.'

'Poor girl, she'll get a complex. Anyway, Emma's a sweetie,

she was at Henry's last birthday party remember, and they all seemed to be friends then.'

'Oh, how things change in the minds of our babes. But what do we do? Summer thinks Jonathan is going to sort it all out.'

'Really? She's delusional when she comes to him.'

'Is Martha like that with Matt?'

'No, she knows he's hopeless at sorting things out, stemming from when he was out of work that time and I was at work most of the time. Things were chaotic.' Polly shuddered, as did I. It had been a bad time for all of them and Polly was right: the house was a mess, and everyone was struggling. It took Matt quite a while to learn how to cope with the children and the house. No one knew why he was so hopeless, although he's much better now.

'Anyway, I better put the kids' tea on, but what are we going to do?' Claire asked. 'Henry has always been such a good friend to Toby, and I couldn't bear it if they fell out.'

'Oh, kids fall out all the time, they'll be best friends in no time, and you know Henry can't hold a grudge, he doesn't have the attention span. A bit like his father. But anyway, what I will do is tell Henry to convince Toby that being Joseph is a really good thing. I'll bribe him somehow if I need to.'

'Oh thanks Pol, it would be amazing if we could sort this out. And I'll tell him that Joseph is an amazing part – oh, I'll say the sign of a good actor is pretending and if he can pretend to like the girl then that will show how amazing he is.'

'Perfect. Thank goodness for us. I'll bring Henry round before school tomorrow, and if you like I'll walk all the kids to school for you.'

'Oh, that would be fab. Now if only we could sort out Sylvie as easily.'

'I think that might take a bit more. But we'll come up with something.'

'Meow,' I shouted. They meant I would.

'Yes, Alfie, you'll help us as well,' Claire said, stroking me. Helping? Actually, it would all be down to me.

Toby sulked all through tea, despite Claire trying to convince him that he must be the best actor the school had ever seen. Summer thankfully agreed with everything her mum said, and I could see Toby wavering. He was listening, but he was also refusing to budge just yet. He did remind me of George.

That night I put the first phase of my plan into action. Giving gifts isn't easy for cats. We don't have money or go to shops, we certainly can't gift-wrap. But when I first moved to Edgar Road, I'd tried to win Jonathan over with my version of a present. He'd pretended he hated them but it must have worked because look at us now. So, confident in my plan and with a thought for how proud Tiger would be of me, I waited until everyone was asleep and went to find one of the street's nocturnal cats. I didn't spend much time with them, seeing as I was pretty much always asleep at night, but we were all friendly enough on our street. I found Lucky, a big black cat, and told him what I needed. I didn't have to wait long before he presented me with a juicy mouse, who unfortunately was no more. Despite my feelings of distaste, I took it to Sylvie's doorstep and left it by the front door. When she opened her door in the morning and saw the gift I'd left for her, she wouldn't be able to help but feel wanted on the street.

# Chapter
# Twenty-Two

Chapter
Twenty-Two

The following morning, as the house began to stir, George seemed to be in shock as he sat by his bowl in the kitchen, not wanting food, but not knowing what to do. Tiger's death had sunk in, but only a little. I tried to talk to him but he looked at me as if he couldn't hear a word I was saying. He just sat there and I stayed close by. I didn't know how to offer comfort any other way and I was desperately trying to suppress my own feelings for now.

We sat, side by side, as Claire ran downstairs, putting the kettle on, tipping food into a bowl for us, laying the breakfast table, before going to rouse the children. Jonathan emerged, fresh from the shower, poured coffee into two cups and took them back upstairs. Voices drifted down, children being chivvied, Jonathan looking for something, normal life going on all around us, when life felt anything but normal.

'I need to go,' George said, finally. His breakfast untouched, as was mine.

'Where?' I asked.

'I just need to be alone,' he said.

'Are you sure? Sometimes it's best not to be on your own.' I felt panicked, I didn't want him to leave, I wanted to stay with him to keep my eye on him. I needed him, but again, as a parent, I knew it wasn't about what I needed.

'I really am sure, Dad. Please, just let me,' he said sadly and I felt I had no choice but to let him go. As I watched him leave the house again, I was tempted to follow but then I realised that I needed some time as well. I had just said goodbye to my best friend, a cat I loved with all my heart, and I was never going to see her again.

I had to trust George would be alright for now, and I needed to trust that I would be too.

I was vaguely aware of the family going about their morning business. Claire made a mention of George, but Toby assured her that he had been in bed with him last night, so they didn't worry. I tried to eat a little but I felt the food would choke me. When something horrible happened it always struck me as odd, how normal life carried on around you.

Toby was still moaning about the nativity. Jonathan was trying to tell him how when he was a child he had always wanted to be Joseph, but that wasn't really working. I could see this situation was likely to go on a bit: Toby threatening to refuse to be in the play, Claire trying to cajole him, Summer saying it wouldn't be the same without him. I let it all wash over my fur. I couldn't really bring myself to get involved or be concerned at the moment. It was too painful, too hard.

A knock at the door interrupted as we were finishing breakfast and Jonathan opened the door. I stayed where I was as he came back with Polly, Henry and Martha all ready for school.

'Henry has something to say,' Polly announced before anyone spoke.

'Toby, I am sorry I said being Joseph was the worst thing ever and that Emma Roper would try to kiss you. I think it's cool actually and I am going to be the donkey, yes, but I will look out for you and if I think Emma Roper is going to try to kiss you then I'll try to stop her with my tail.' Henry stood back and looked quite pleased with himself. Jonathan stuffed his fist in his mouth as he did when trying not to laugh.

'Well, that's very kind of you, Henry, isn't it Toby?' Claire said.

'I still don't want to be Joseph though,' Toby said; he wasn't going to forgive so easily.

'I think it's great, one day I want to be Mary,' Martha offered.

'Why don't you children go and play for five minutes before we leave for school?' Polly suggested. They all went into the living room but as chatter started up, I realised that Toby was still not really talking. It seemed the nativity issue wasn't going to be resolved that easily.

'Right, I better go to work,' Jonathan said, standing up.

'Just a minute. We were on the way and we bumped into the Barkers, down the road. They were in such a state – turns out their cat, Tiger, has just passed away. She was very ill, they're so distraught, poor things, but I know she and Alfie were friends. And George too, I guess,' Polly said.

'They were, really good friends,' Jonathan said. They all looked at me, concern across all their faces. I started yowling and I lay down, finally able to fall apart.

'And they say cats don't have feelings,' Claire said, bending down and stroking me.

'Well they do, and none more than Alfie,' Polly added, as I just let myself go.

'That's awful,' Jonathan said. 'They're an odd couple, the Barkers, and although not particularly warm they did dote on that cat. Claire, we should drop round some flowers.'

'I agree, and I'll get a card,' Polly said.

As Claire picked me up and cuddled me to her, I showed my grief, and thought that at least my humans were lovely people, and they would show kindness to the Barkers, and I would pull myself together and take care of George. I would also have to go and see our friends later, because they would all be very upset, and I would have to learn to put one paw in front of the other and carry on. But for now, I would just take some time to wallow in my distress. As I felt the warmth of Claire's arms around me, I couldn't do anything else. Hearing them say it, my humans, made it abundantly real and I nestled into Claire's arms and let despair engulf me.

When everyone had gone out, and with still no sign of George, I cleaned myself and went out to see our friends, although it was the last thing I felt like doing. I understood George's desire to be alone, I shared it in a way, but it wasn't necessarily healthy and I needed to tell Tiger's friends what had happened and also find my kitten. It was too much for him to go through alone, even if he did think that was what he wanted. I mustered the tiny amount of reserve strength I had and set out.

I noticed that Connie was going out as I left but I didn't stop. I saw that Salmon's owners were at the Barkers' front door, and although they were terrible busybodies, I also knew they were friends and that they were hopefully going to be able to offer some small comfort to them in their hour of need. Again I didn't stop.

I carried on to the recreation ground, wondering if anyone would be there. It wasn't raining, but it was still bitingly cold, and a winter wind whipped around my legs as I walked. To say I arrived looking and feeling windswept was a bit of an understatement. I was relieved to see both Rocky and Nellie there when I arrived. No sign of Elvis, but they would be able to spread the word, and I was sure that Salmon probably knew already, so I wanted Tiger's friends to hear as soon as possible.

'Alfie,' Nellie said, with a sympathetic expression on her face. 'It's good to see you, I was wondering where you were. We heard about Tiger.'

'I take it you guys haven't seen George?' I said grimly.

'No,' Rocky said. 'Is the lad alright?'

'Oh guys, I'm worried about him.'

'Oh Alfie,' Nellie said, coming over to nuzzle me. 'It's all so sad. I'm going to miss her.' She hung her head.

'Me too, Alfie,' Rocky agreed. 'It's the saddest thing, losing someone you love.'

'And I know we all loved her, which makes all this so hard and not just for me. George said he needed time on his own but I really just need to know he's alright.'

I found fretting about George was overtaking my grief. I thought of two places he might be. One was Hana's house, but I discounted that on the grounds that he wanted to be alone. Then there was the house at the end of the street with the angry man. That made more sense. He could be hiding out in the garden, and no one would know he was there. Unless the old man saw him, of course – but if he wanted to be alone, hopefully he would have kept himself hidden.

'What do you want us to do, Alfie?' Rocky asked.

'Well, I wouldn't mind some help finding George,' I said.

I found it was a bit comforting being among friends but also people who loved Tiger too. As if they would prop me up and stop me from falling. I wanted the same for George.

'Let's go and find this jungle of his,' Nellie suggested. The three of us were about to set off when we saw Elvis coming towards us with George by his side. The sight of him was a huge relief. We all waited, glancing anxiously at each other.

'Hey,' Elvis said, solemnly, as they reached us. 'Sorry to hear about Tiger.' I noticed that George was looking at his paws.

'Are you alright?' I asked George. He swished his tail, sadly.

'I need to go, I have to eat something and then see Hana,' he said and without another word he left.

'I'm guessing George's not doing so well.' Elvis was a master at stating the obvious.

'It's very early days,' Rocky pointed out. 'I mean, it's barely just happened.'

'He saw the cat he thought of as his mum die,' Nellie pushed.

We all nodded. It was a lot for anyone, but especially for such a youngster. I knew, it had happened to me, but of course I hadn't had anyone else to turn to then. Not the way George had. But we needed to give him time, and some space. I was gladdened by the idea he was going to see Hana; I liked the fact that George had someone who wasn't connected to the rest of us, I think he needed that. A friend who was just his.

'I just had an idea,' Elvis said. We all raised our whiskers at him; he wasn't one for ideas. 'We should hold what the humans call a memorial or something like that, for Tiger.

They go to church which we can't do, obviously, but we can all gather here and say goodbye and talk about her. It might help the lad. It might help us all to say goodbye.'

'Elvis, you're a genius,' I said. Something, again, I'd never thought I would hear myself say. 'We'll invite all Tiger's friends, everyone who knew her, and make it a fitting goodbye.'

'It's a lovely thing to do, and sooner rather than later,' Nellie said. 'I'll help organise it.'

'And I'll get Dustbin to come too,' I said. 'Let's do it in a couple of days. Give us time to arrange things.'

'Hopefully it will help George,' Nellie echoed Elvis, and that seemed settled.

'How do you know about these memorials?' I asked Elvis.

'I watch a lot of TV,' he replied.

At home it was, for once, all about us cats. Toby and the nativity was a banned subject, as was Connie, Sylvie and Aleksy. Polly brought round some pilchards for George and I. And I have to say that even they failed to tempt me but I tried for Polly's sake. Matt even came to see us after work to give us both a hug. Claire and Jonathan fussed us, more than usual. George was quieter, he ate a bit but he still refused to talk to me other than the odd word. But I could tell he appreciated the care everyone was taking of him.

That night, I tucked him up with Toby, and I nuzzled him.

'I forgot to tell you, Hana said that someone left a dead mouse on Sylvie's doorstep. I of course said how kind, but Hana didn't understand – being a house cat she's never hunted and apparently Sylvie screamed and asked Connie if she knew anything about it.'

'Oh.' Not the reaction I was hoping for.

'I think she thinks it was because someone was cross with her. I tried to say we leave gifts like that as a sign of love but Hana didn't know how to tell Sylvie that.'

'George, it was me. I thought if we left her a gift she might feel wanted on the street.'

'But you don't hunt.'

'No, I got Lucky to do it for me. Never mind, I will have to try harder.'

I knew what I had to do. I had to leave her an even better gift. Oh, so much to do but I couldn't have Sylvie feeling sad about it, not now I'd started the plan. But I needed to talk to my son about something more important.

'I know you don't want to talk right now but I am always here for you, I need you to know that.'

'I do know, but I'm so sad,' George said. 'And I don't know how to act. I've never felt this bad before. Not even when I loved Chanel and I thought I'd drowned her.' His eyes were so full of pain. Although the less said about that incident the better.

'None of us do, George, but remember if you need me, or anyone, there are so many people who love you very much and we are all here for you. You don't have to go through this horrible, horrible time alone.'

'But I want my Tiger mum, and she's never going to be here again.'

I had no words, as I let my kitten wail into my neck and I silently wept right along with him.

# Chapter Twenty-Three

Chapter
Twenty-Three

It was the day of the memorial for Tiger. This was a day for her. There are not many areas where humans trump cats, but the memorial idea was one of them. I still didn't know much about it, but thankfully our television expert, Elvis, filled us in. Normally people wore black, sang songs and said a few words about the person they were saying goodbye to. We had adapted this to our lives and limitations, so we weren't going to wear black, obviously, but I had instructed everyone to look their best and we were going to each say something about Tiger, before we did a cats' chorus of goodbyes to her – our version of singing. I hoped it would help George with his grief; I didn't dare hope it would help me with mine.

But it gave me something to focus on, as we invited cats from our road, even Salmon who Tiger really wasn't fond of, but I knew that she would have liked having him there. Dustbin was coming as well; Tiger had become part of his life too, and he wanted to say goodbye. George had spoken to Hana about it and she'd told him about something in Japan where humans went to the temples – whatever they were – and left something as a prayer or an offering. George and I didn't quite grasp that but George was going to take his favourite toy mouse and leave it as something to keep Tiger safe which was very moving. Of course Hana couldn't come with us, which was sad but there was no way to get her out of the house, even if she had wanted to.

George was quite upset about that and I assured him that as soon as I could I would come up with a plan to get her out or him in. I could see how much he needed a friend and although he had us, she was really just his, and more his age. And also I remember Tiger telling me never to give up on my plans. I almost smiled as I could hear her telling me to never stop with my mad schemes – not that I thought they were mad, of course. And I wouldn't. Not that I could anyway. They were part of me.

But I thought that if I could find a way to get George and Hana together, it would help him. I wasn't matchmaking, don't get me wrong. I wasn't sure whether George liked her in that way, or she him, and goodness knows relationships among the young could be difficult, but I was determined that their friendship would be a priority for me. He needed her, I knew that. And of course, with everything going on in her house, she also needed him.

George and I had a thorough grooming before he took the toy mouse in his mouth and we set off for the recreation ground and Tiger's memorial. I could feel the sadness in the way we both walked, slowly, reluctantly almost, and I knew that wasn't going away any time soon. The grief we felt was inside us but also visible in the way we moved, and how we looked. There was no hiding from it. George dropped his toy a number of times but I didn't get irritated, I stayed calm. This wasn't easy for any of us, after all. When we eventually reached the recreation spot, I was moved to see that there was a good turn-out. As well as Nellie, Elvis, Rocky, Tinkerbell and Salmon, Dustbin was there, looking smarter than normal, and some of the other cats from Edgar Road we usually didn't see much as they were normally nocturnal. Tiger would have been pleased, I thought. I hoped she could see us all. I hoped she knew how many cats had turned out just for her.

Elvis, self-appointed expert on memorials, took the lead.

'We are gathered here today to remember a very special cat,' he said. Already I could barely hold it together. I glanced over at George who was staring very intently at the toy mouse. I stood as close to him as he would allow, but I wasn't sure it made any difference. 'Tiger was a feisty cat. She didn't go looking for trouble but she never shied away from a fight if she was protecting her friends and family. I remember the first time I met her, she was having an argument with Tom, and I tried to intervene but she told me that she could more than handle him, and she did. So much so that her and Tom ended up very good friends.' He paused and raised his whiskers.

I shivered. That was so Tiger. Tom had been a cantankerous cat who lived on our street and when I'd first moved here he really didn't like me. He wasn't that pleasant but Tiger sorted him out and they'd ended up very close. No one quite knew why and when I asked her she just shrugged it off and then he moved away with his owner. We had no idea where he was now, or even if he was still alive. Maybe they could both be in heaven arguing together now. I grinned at the thought.

'We all loved Tiger, we are all going to miss her, none more so than Alfie and young George, here. But it's only fitting that we remember the good things about Tiger, because there were so many of them, as we sadly say goodbye.'

201

Elvis was pretty good at this, I thought. He sounded as if he had done this before. He called each cat up in turn to speak about Tiger, recounting their favourite story, or memory. As I felt the love that everyone had for her, it warmed my heart. She would be so missed, but only those that were loved can be missed, I had to remember that. Soon, it was George's turn. I nuzzled him.

'Are you alright to do this?' I asked, full of concern.

'I need to do it for her,' he replied and my heart swelled with pride.

'Tiger mum was my mum,' George started. I swear there wasn't a dry whisker in the area. 'And she was a good mum. She loved me, she protected me. She let me climb trees when my dad didn't, and she took me on adventures. I think she was probably the best mum a cat could have, and I didn't want to say goodbye but my dad said we had to, and sometimes in life we had to do what we didn't want to do, so there was no choice, and I knew he was right. But I didn't want to lose my Tiger mum, and I just hope she knows how much I loved her, how important she was to me and how I will never stop missing her.'

'Oh George,' I said. 'That was beautiful.' He nodded, solemnly, and laid down the toy mouse for his mum. Nellie rubbed her eyes with her paws. No one had failed to be moved by George as they all told him how well he'd done.

And then all eyes were on me. I took a breath. I needed to do justice to Tiger, but also I had to do this for George and I guess for me too.

'So much has already been said about Tiger,' I began. 'And it's been so heart-warming to hear how much she was loved.

She was funny, feisty, yes, definitely, and loyal. Tiger was my first real friend on Edgar Road. I remember how I made her come for walks with me when she didn't want to – she was lazy and spoilt back then – but she soon found her adventurous side, and to be honest, soon became far more adventurous than me. She stood by me, even when she didn't always want to, she was the dearest, kindest cat ever, and to say I'll miss her will be a huge understatement. She was always there with a kind word, or a joke to cheer me, she would tell me off when I was behaving badly, or being annoying. She saved me on a number of occasions and, without her by my side, I feel as if I am half the cat I was before. But I know she will always be by my side, if not literally, and when I carry on with life, which at the moment feels impossible – but I know I will – I will remember her always. Tiger, no one wants to say goodbye to you but wherever you are be happy and know how very loved you are, and how loved you will always be.'

I stopped, exhausted, to find myself flanked by Dustbin on one side and George on the other. I let their warmth comfort me, as the other cats all began their cats' chorus in honour of Tiger. By the way, cats' chorus is probably not the best way to describe the horrible noise that came out of them, but it was well meant. We cats have never been known for melodic singing. But I hoped that it would bring a smile to Tiger's lips wherever she was and I looked up to the sky, raising my whiskers to the heavens and saying a silent goodbye. Yet again.

No one wanted to rush off, so we spent a pleasant afternoon in the cold, all huddled up to keep warm, lots of the older cats doing their best to cheer George up. Everyone was being kind to each other; even Salmon was upset and he never got emotional.

'Bad times, bad times, Alfie,' he repeated. I knew for him that was a lot. So as we shivered and nuzzled and basked in the glow of friendship that was around, I found some sort of peace. Sad, yes, but also it was good to see how much Tiger meant to everyone and to feel how much we all meant to each other. I knew that the coming days, months, years even, would be hard for us, George and I especially, but today, there was comfort of sorts and I took a mental picture so I could conjure it up whenever I needed to.

'George,' I said, gently. My fractured relationship with my son was still a little bit of a see-saw. One minute he was glad of my company, my love, the next he rejected it. I knew this was what I would have to bear for now, until he was ready to talk, or for our relationship to go back to how it was. No, that wasn't right, it would never fully go back to how it was, I knew that. It would always be different now, without Tiger, but I would wait until he was ready for us to move on to our next phase and hopefully that wouldn't take too long.

'Yes?' he replied.

'Would you like to go home? Warm up? Take a nap?' I knew I was fussing but then that was what parents did and I was now a single parent. That thought struck me so hard that it almost winded me. I was going to be doing this on my own from now on.

'No, I have to go,' he stated.

'Where?' I asked. 'Can I come with you?'

'Dad,' he sighed. 'I need to be alone, just give me some

space.' It wasn't a request and he said goodbye to the other cats and started walking in the opposite direction of our house. I knew he was probably going to his 'jungle' and the old man and I had to let him, but I also felt I needed to find out more about what he did there. I had only seen the one time when the man seemed angry, and I resolved that I would talk to him about it, later, I would get him to tell me exactly what he was up to there, after all that was what any responsible parent would do. Like it or not, I might be grieving, broken-hearted, exhausted, but first and foremost I was a parent and I needed to parent more than ever now.

However, my grief needed an outlet too, and so that night when everyone was asleep I went outside, and I yowled with all my might at the bottom of the garden, my cries being carried off in the wind.

I was about to go home, when I remembered Sylvie. I had organised another gift for her via Lucky again. After all, this plan was for Sylvie, for Connie and for Aleksy, as well as the friendship that I was trying to rescue and also in memory of Tiger.

The bird was waiting where I'd been told it would be – my new best friend was really proving helpful. As I picked it up and made my way to Sylvie's doorstep again, I nearly dropped it a couple of times, not least as I squeezed under the gate, but I made it. She would definitely know how much she was cared about now.

# Chapter Twenty-Four

Chapter
Twenty-Four

I was failing as a father and as a cat. My feelings of grief weighed heavily on me and I was finding it hard to muster any energy. I had always tried to put my feelings after those of others, but I couldn't do that as easily as normal right now. I was struggling with the day-to-day functions. Eating, with little appetite. Going out, knowing I would have to walk past Tiger's house, which was physically painful. Trying to talk to George who still had no real interest in talking to me.

The humans were being very considerate to us. They were sure that we were sad because of Tiger – we were – and so they were being extra nurturing. Toby and Henry were still at loggerheads – things had worsened when Henry had laughed at the play rehearsal when Emma Roper wouldn't let go of Toby's hand and Toby was angrier than ever about being Joseph – but I couldn't worry about that. Nor could I fret too much when Franceska came round to say how upset Aleksy still was, throwing himself into earning money so he could buy Connie a nice present, and how her mum was still unmovable. Apparently Connie had even asked her father to intervene, which he had, via Skype, but Sylvie said that he'd given up being a parent when he left them for another woman and it just made things worse. George was still visiting Hana, but he was so closed off that he didn't seem to want to talk to me about that either.

I did manage to ascertain that the bird gift hadn't gone

down very well. What was wrong with these humans? This time, according to Hana, Sylvie had accused Aleksy of doing it to punish her. Of course Aleksy never would but the idea that he was being blamed for my brilliant plan was devastating. I had to think like a human and not a cat. Despite being wrapped in grief, I needed to put this right, because so far my plan was making things worse.

I lay in my bed, in our empty house, and I talked to Tiger. I told her about the gifts and I could picture her there in my head. Her stripy fur, the way she would square up to any other cat, dog or anyone for those she loved. I knew that she would be sad about the way George and I were at the moment and I could hear her telling me that we needed each other more than ever, so to go and do something about it. It was startling how clear her voice was, how loud, how forceful. And I hadn't always done what Tiger told me to when she was alive, but I was going to now. Even if it was only a lone voice in my head. I needed to listen, I needed guidance. Sometimes when you felt at your worst, you had to pull through rather than give into it. Tiger was dead, that was the most horrible thing to recognise, but I wasn't, and I needed to keep living, but more important than that I had to show my kitten how to keep living.

With a slightly renewed sense of energy, I got up, stretched fully – I had been in bed longer than normal so felt very scrunched up – and cleaned myself up ready to leave the house. I walked past the living room where the Christmas tree lights were off, due to no one being home, and I thought about the festive period. It was a time for love, and goodwill to all men – and cats – so I needed to rally myself and my troops and make sure that I did Tiger proud by making this Christmas a good one. It wouldn't be the best, it couldn't be without her by my side, but it would be as good as it could be. And I was the cat to make sure of it.

Feeling amazingly confident and armed with my new purpose, I went to find George. He might not have wanted to talk to me but I would show him that he needed to. I made my way to the end of the street, it was drizzly, cold, and miserable but I kept going. I ignored the damp feeling in my fur, the ache in my legs, the pain in my heart, and I heard Tiger's voice egging me on every step of the way.

I got to the house and scanned the front garden for George. There was no immediate sign but then the garden really was an overgrown mess. I spotted George beneath a browning bush and I approached him. I wasn't going to pretend any more.

'What are you doing here?' he asked, raising his whiskers angrily at me.

'George, you know you are entitled to spend time on your own, and I'm not going to stop that, but I am your father, and I'm entitled to check that you're safe if I feel I need to.' I was stern.

'As you can see, I am.' He shuffled around so he had his back to me.

'George, I miss Tiger every second of the day, and I know you do too, but we've still got each other. We're lucky to have that so it's important you don't push me away.'

'But—' he started.

'No, no buts. I'm here for you, I love you and you have

211

to know that. You can be angry, you can be sad, you can be whatever you need to be, but you can't push away the people who love you, because that, George, isn't going to help at all.'

'I don't mean to push you away,' he said, his voice small.

'Then why do you?' I asked, kindly.

'Because I'm scared. I didn't know that you could get pain like this and what happens if I lose you too?' He looked at me, his words coated in sadness, his eyes spilling over with fear. My heart, which was already in pieces, shattered a bit more. 'I know you said you wouldn't go for a long time but then with Tiger mum, she didn't know, so that could happen to you.'

'I can't promise I'll always be here, George, I wish I could. But, we have been through this, you've got me for a very long time. I'm incredibly healthy, and I'm not going anywhere right now.' I was actually and on the whole took very good care of myself, I ate well, I exercised and I even ensured I drank plenty of water. 'And I'm younger than Tiger was. I'll take care of myself and do whatever I can to stick around for as long as I can, but you know what this whole death thing teaches us?'

'No,' he stated. I wasn't sure either, but I ploughed on regardless.

'It teaches us to make the most of living our lives. Make the most of our families, our friends, our fellow cats and our humans. If anything does happen to me – not that it will – you have Claire, Jonathan, Polly, Matt, Franceska, Tomasz and the kids, not to mention all the cats who were here for Tiger earlier. We are the lucky ones, George, and although

212

it might not feel like it right now, it might never feel like it, try to remember that. Live your life to the full, that is what Tiger would have wanted. And also don't push away those who love you. She would have told you that too.'

George stood up; he appeared to be thinking. I hoped, prayed I had got through to him.

'You're right, Dad, and I know it but the sad feeling is so strong.'

'I know, son.'

'But I will try and I'll talk to you more about how I feel. Is that a deal?'

'Yes, and not only will I listen but I will help you, that's what I'm here for.'

'Oh, come and meet my friend,' George said, animatedly, and I saw the glint of the kitten I used to know. He sprang up and ran up to the windowsill. I reluctantly followed him. He sat on the windowsill and I saw the old man sitting in a chair. It was dark in the house, and as soon as he spotted George, the man tried to pull himself out of the chair, which seemed to take an age; he didn't look in good shape. He finally hauled himself up and started waving his fist.

'Get lost,' he shouted. 'Get lost, I tell you.' His words flew through the window pane.

'George, he doesn't sound very friendly,' I pointed out.

'What do you mean?' George waved a paw at the man, who shook his fist again. 'We're waving, look.'

'He's telling you to get lost, and his face is all red,' I said carefully, glad that there was a window between us.

'Oh no, he thinks "Get Lost" is my name,' George said. 'He loves playing our game with me, we're very good friends.'

213

For a moment I was lost for words. I remembered back to how, when George got his first crush on the horrible Chanel, she would hiss at him and he took that as affection. Nothing I could say would persuade him otherwise. George did have a history of misinterpretation, and it looked as if this was a similar situation. I was still unsure how I would convince him that this man didn't like him, when the man suddenly came to the window and opened it wide, nearly knocking us both flying. I sprang back off the sill but George somehow managed to jump inside the house. I didn't realise it until too late.

'Get lost,' the man shouted.

I jumped back up on the windowsill. 'Oh my,' I exclaimed. What would happen to George now? I felt fear welling up inside me. This man could really hurt my boy, and I had to stop him.

'Oh, this is a new part of the game,' I heard George say as he dodged the old man. I was about to go in – no matter what, I needed to protect my boy – but then I stopped as the old man went a funny colour and then fell over. He was going to fall on George.

'Yowl,' I shouted and George managed to jump out of the way before the man reached the ground. 'Um, George, I don't think it's a game any more, he's lying on the floor.' I couldn't see much as it was so dark inside, but the man didn't appear to be moving and George sprang to his side.

'Do you think he's alright?' George looked at me, stricken. This was all we needed, having just lost Tiger, he couldn't lose his new friend. Even if the man didn't like him. I had to think and act quickly.

'I'll go and get one of the humans,' I said. 'They'll know what to do. Do you want to come with me?'

'No, I better stay here, I don't want him to be alone,' George replied.

I was in luck. Just as I was a few paw strides from the house, wondering who would be home, I saw Jonathan and Matt walking along the street. I ran in front of them.

'Hey Alfie, we're just going home from the pub, football,' Matt explained.

'YOWL,' I cried at the top of my lungs.

'Oh no, don't tell me this is another cat emergency,' Jonathan moaned. It wasn't my fault that there seemed to be quite a few lately. I jumped on his foot, which caused him to say a bad word.

'YOWL,' I screeched again. I then did my signal of running round in circles, before they both seemed to get it.

'Alfie, you do pick your moments, I'm really hungry,' Jonathan complained, but I was already hightailing it back to the man's house.

'Where the hell are we going?' They were finally following. I ran as fast as my legs would take me back to the open window. George hadn't moved, he was right by the man's side.

'Meow,' he greeted us with relief.

'What on earth,' Matt peered in the window, 'is that?'

'There's an old man on the ground, I think. With George,' Jonathan said. 'It's dark though.'

'I'm calling an ambulance. Thank goodness for these cats,' Matt said, pulling his phone out and dialling.

'I'll try to break in,' Jonathan said, shoving the front door

215

with his shoulder, which didn't move. 'Ow,' he said, rubbing it. I climbed in through the window, trying to show him how it was done. 'Oh, I guess I can go in that way,' Jonathan said. It was a bit of a tight squeeze but he made it.

'Great, why didn't we think of that?' Matt rolled his eyes as Jonathan came round and opened the front door for him. 'Ambulance is on its way.'

Jonathan's hands were shaking as he opened the door and they both ran in, with me on their heels. The house was freezing. Matt bent down.

'He's still alive,' he said, face flushed with relief. 'But he's so cold. Can you go and see if you can find a blanket?'

'Sure thing,' Jonathan said, rushing off. George nuzzled into him as close as he could.

'I'm going to try to keep him warm,' he whispered to me. I nodded. 'I can't let him die too.' My heart would have broken all over again but I wasn't sure there was enough left to break just at the moment.

'Get lost,' the man said, but so quietly that only we could hear him.

By the time the ambulance arrived, the man, whose name we didn't know, was wrapped in blankets, and his breathing was steadier. Looking a bit shaken up, Jonathan and Matt stood back to let the paramedics do their job. George and I did the same. Then the paramedics said if the man had been left in the cold for too much longer he might have got hypothermia. It seemed we had saved him and it was all really thanks to George.

Jonathan established what hospital they would be taking the man to and he told them that he and Matt would go there to try to sort things out as they didn't know anything about him or his family. There were a few photos on the wall of a woman and a boy, and then of the same boy as a young man. Matt searched and found a wallet in the man's coat pocket, which was hanging by the front door. It had a bus pass in it, for a Harold Jenkins. But there was no other information to hand.

'Hopefully when he comes round we'll be able to find out who his family is,' Jonathan said. 'God, I wish Claire was here, she'd know what to do.'

'Meow,' I said. They could figure this out, surely.

'Shall we see if we can find some pyjamas to take for him? Maybe a book or something, that's what Polly would suggest.' Thank goodness, I thought, at least they were being a bit practical.

'Good thinking.' Matt and Jonathan went upstairs and we followed them. The house was a bit of a mess, and none of the lights seemed to work, although they found one that did in the man's bedroom.

'Bulbs need changing,' Matt said. 'God, being old and alone is depressing.'

They found some clean pyjamas in a drawer and a pair of reading glasses by the bed. They took them and a few bits from the bathroom, which looked as if it was in need of a clean.

'He obviously can't really cope on his own,' Jonathan said. 'I hope he's got family. I think I need to start training Summer and Toby up to take care of me when I'm old.'

'I hear you,' Matt said. 'And good work, Alfie and George, he'll probably be alright thanks to you,' he finished, as he ushered us all out of the house, locking the door behind him.

I looked at George as Matt and Jonathan set off to get to the hospital.

'You did so well,' I said.

'I hope he's going to be OK?' George looked at me, his eyes full of fear.

'It sounds as if he will be and it's all thanks to you.' I nuzzled him and then I took my son home.

# Chapter
# Twenty-Five

Chapter
Twenty-Five

'These guys really earned their pilchards today,' Jonathan said, jubilantly, as my families all sat round the dinner table. Although we'd had little to celebrate lately, I was slightly buoyed by the fact that today had turned out so well, as was George.

'Tell us exactly what happened,' Franceska pushed. I licked my lips. So, yes I had been off my food since losing Tiger, but the fresh, plump pilchards were mouthwatering, particularly after the busy day we'd had. I'm only a cat, after all.

'So, we were on our way back from watching football . . .' As Jonathan launched into the story, George and I launched into our dinner. George was happier now that Harold was safely in hospital, and was going to be alright. Jonathan and Matt had gone to see him, taking him his things, and had found he was stable. He had something called a blood sugar problem which caused him to faint, but I didn't understand much about that, not being a doctor. The point was that it wasn't serious. But what was serious was the fact he wasn't taking care of himself, or according to the hospital, not capable of taking care of himself.

It turned out that Harold had a virus and had been struggling to go out. So although he'd had some food delivered, he hadn't seen anyone, not even a doctor, because he 'didn't believe in them'. Which was a bit rich when he ended up in hospital surrounded by them. He hadn't been able to pay for his heating, because for that he needed to go to the post office, so that was why the house was cold. He was too proud to ask anyone for help, so he'd been suffering alone and it could have ended very badly for him.

'But surely he has family?' Claire asked.

'Thankfully, he has a son, Marcus, who he'd fallen out with. Not sure exactly what happened but something to do with him getting divorced – Marcus not Harold – and Harold doesn't believe in divorce,' Matt explained.

I wondered what Harold did believe in – not doctors, not divorce, nor cats, it seemed.

Matt continued. 'He lost his wife, Marcus' mum, to cancer a few years ago, and he's a proud and stubborn man. So Marcus and he haven't spoken for over a year. We persuaded him to give us his number though,' he said. 'I said if the hospital didn't think he had anyone to help him they'd never let him out. That did the trick.'

Jonathan smiled. 'Yeah, and I called Marcus and he seemed pretty nice. He was upset that he had let things go this far with his dad though, and he rushed to the hospital. I gave him our number because he said he was going to sort the house out, and so I said we'd help. I mean, the state of the place.'

'Where's the son from then?' Tomasz asked.

'He lives nearby, which is the worst thing, about ten minutes away from here, but he has been through a divorce and various job issues, so he's been a bit preoccupied. But he seems decent,' Matt said.

'Yeah, it sounds as if he's had a hard time, as well as his dad, but Harold is quite a difficult character by all accounts. So although it's sad they fell out, it's not irrevocable. It's like

George and Alfie brought them back together.' Jonathan grinned. 'With our help of course, eh Matt?'

'I'm so proud of you, you are such a softy underneath it all,' Claire said, giving her husband's hair a tousle.

'Get off,' Jonathan said, but he was pink and smiling, under his not-so-tough exterior.

'The thing is that Harold told us that George had been visiting him for a while and he kept telling him to get lost but he wouldn't, which of course sounds just like both our cats,' Matt explained.

'And now, because George and Alfie saved him, he said he would welcome him anytime. Poor old chap, miserable because he can't cope with not coping, if you know what I mean,' Jonathan added.

'Pol, I said you'd help Marcus get the house sorted, if you don't mind? It's just a dump at the moment, dirty, threadbare carpet, furniture falling apart, and Marcus said he would pay for anything, he feels so guilty. And I also said we'd help do the garden,' Matt explained.

'Which is so annoying because it's December and freezing,' Jonathan pointed out. Not to mention that he didn't even do any work in his own garden. Claire normally did it.

'We'll all rally, that's what this community is all about,' Claire said. 'I can give his son the number of a cleaner, so the house can be spotless, and we have some old furniture you might be able to use, Polly.'

'When he comes home from hospital we should throw him a welcome-home dinner,' Franceska suggested. 'I will bring food from the restaurant and then he knows he has friends around here.'

'That is such a lovely idea,' Polly said. 'And of course I'll get the house sorted. God, getting old isn't much fun, is it?'

'Polly, we're no way near there yet,' Tomasz pointed out, and they all laughed.

As I licked my lips after polishing off the pilchards I smiled at my humans. I had taught them all well. And my kitten, well, I couldn't be prouder of him either and I knew Tiger would have been too.

George and I left the adults planning how they were going to help with Harold and Marcus, and went to check on the children. It wasn't a happy sight. Summer and Martha were both unnaturally quiet, Toby and Henry weren't talking and Tommy and Aleksy were trying to bring about some kind of truce. In my experience, once one thing got sorted, another problem reared its ugly head. And suddenly there was no shortage of them round here.

'Right, so have I got this straight?' Aleksy asked. 'Toby is not talking to Henry because Henry is a donkey and Toby is Joseph?'

Both boys nodded and Tommy and Aleksy exchanged a smile. I couldn't believe the change in Aleksy since the last time I saw him. He was happier, he was engaging with the younger children and the adults, and more importantly with me. He was like a different person and I hoped that it was because things with Connie were settling down, or he was being grown-up about it. Whichever, it was great, and one less thing for me to worry about.

'Toby, Joseph is the main part. I was Joseph once and I loved it,' Aleksy said. Toby glared at him, suspiciously.

'But you did drop the baby Jesus,' Tommy pointed out.

'Yes, but I picked him up quickly,' Aleksy replied. Both boys laughed.

'Hey, I've got an idea,' Tommy said suddenly. 'I will make sure that you are remembered for being Joseph and you, Henry, as the donkey, will be able to help too. But before I share this idea, you two have to be friends again.'

Henry and Toby glanced at each other uncertainly.

'What's the plan?' Henry asked.

'No, no friendship, then no plan.' Tommy whispered into Aleksy's ear, and he laughed.

'We will get into so much trouble, but what a brilliant idea,' Aleksy said.

'OK, let's be friends again,' Toby said, unable to resist, and he and Henry shook hands. Tommy gathered us all close in and he whispered the plan. He even let Summer and Martha in on it, but everyone, including me and George, were sworn to secrecy. I didn't know what to think, as I listened. The kids thought it was great, I wasn't so sure. I knew some of my plans were a bit crazy, but this really took the biscuit. Or the baby Jesus. Aleksy was right, we would get into trouble. Big trouble.

'Are you sure?' Toby asked. He wasn't very good at not doing what he was told, he was such a good boy.

'I am, I think it's brilliant,' Tommy said, immodestly.

'I think it's amazing too,' Martha said.

'Meow,' George agreed. Well, he would.

'And, you know, it will remind us that we're not just friends, but family, and therefore we do it for each other,' Aleksy said, which made me want to weep. OK, that did it, so I was in too.

'Meow,' I agreed.

As they discussed the finer details, I hoped that it wouldn't go wrong as many of my plans had in the past, but then I decided that we all needed cheering up and this might just do it. It might do the opposite, but I wasn't going to think about that. It had reunited and bonded all the children. George was hopping with excitement and I knew this would take his mind off Tiger a bit, which could only be a good thing. So, I high-fived Tommy with my paw, to reiterate that I was all in.

'You did such a great job today,' I said to George as we took our last bit of air in the garden before bed. We were both exhausted, it had been such a long day.

'I didn't know he was that bad, but I'm glad I could help him,' George said. 'And doubly glad he might call me George now instead of "Get Lost".' There was no convincing George that the man didn't like him.

'Well, I am incredibly proud of you,' I said. I thought that if I reminded George every day how great he was, it might make things a bit easier for him, navigating his grief.

'Thanks Dad. I'm just happy he has his son now, and it made me realise how bad it was when I tried to pull away from you. I'm sorry.'

I was so choked up. 'Don't be sorry, but let's not do that again, I missed you, I missed our relationship, doing things together. How's Hana, have you seen her?'

'Not much, but it's funny, she said that her owner, Sylvie, is still upset about the mouse and the bird. Apparently she keeps going on about it.'

'Right, we better put this right – I mean, I better put this right. I know, women like getting flowers.' I had tried to woo Snowball with flowers once. It hadn't gone to plan but she had appreciated the gesture.

'They do. Claire loves it when Jonathan gives her flowers.'

'So, let's go and get some flowers and leave them on her doorstep. Then she will know that they're gifts and nothing bad.'

'Great idea, Dad, I'll help you dig some up. Polly's are nicest. But, there is something I'd like you to do.'

'What's that, son?'

'Figure out a way for me to get to see Hana, properly, I mean. I've been wrapped up in my sad feelings but she is sad too. She loved being an indoor cat in Japan, she had lots of people around her, but now she's alone a lot and her house is very unhappy, so she needs a friend like me.'

'I'll do whatever I can,' I said, meaning it. 'Everyone needs a friend like you, George.'

# Chapter
# Twenty-Six

Claire came into the house, having dropped all the children off at school and immediately called Franceska on the phone.

'Hi,' Claire said. 'I just bumped into Sylvie. I'm seriously worried, she said that someone is out to get her.'

There was a pause.

'Because she's had a dead mouse, bird and now dead flowers left on her doorstep. I tried to reassure her that no one would do such a thing but she's not convinced.'

Another pause.

'Yes, I'm sorry, Frankie, but she thinks it might be Aleksy.'

Pause.

'I told her he wouldn't do anything like that, but it is a bit weird, isn't it?'

Pause.

'Yes, but of course it's not Aleksy, and I told her, don't worry, but I thought you might need a heads-up. Oh, and Polly was telling me today that someone had taken some of her flowers from the garden. How weird is that?'

It was beginning to sink in that my plan may have been a bit foolish. I hadn't taken into account that Sylvie was a mere human and not as highly sophisticated as us cats. Yet again I had expected too much and I wondered if Tiger would be laughing at me in heaven or wherever she was – of course she would. No more ill-thought-out gifts, I would need a new plan.

On the plus side, we were about to have a breakthrough with the Hana situation. I gleaned from Claire and Polly's conversation about the dead things that Sylvie was still refusing to have anything much to do with us, but she was working longer hours, and had told Claire that a lady called Susan had just started coming to the house to clean it – apparently so Claire didn't think she was a burglar. I think that Sylvie was showing that she did want to communicate after all but she still didn't know how, that was my take.

I immediately formed a plan, and explained it to George. All we needed to do was to find out when this Susan came, and then get George into the house with her. It would bank on her not throwing him out but, after all, no one could resist George. OK, well perhaps Harold could, but we had a feeling this Susan loved cats and so wouldn't be immune to his charms. Hopefully anyway.

So, George and I cased the house, waiting for her. We knew Susan came after Connie had left for school and Sylvie for work. It became part of our daily routine. We would breakfast, then clean ourselves, and when everyone from our house left for school we would go and camp out next door. We'd wait in the front garden, sheltering from the cold under a fat bush, and if there was no sign by lunchtime we would know she wasn't going to turn up, so I'd head home and George would go and visit with Hana through the glass. The routine helped me; although I was still pining for Tiger, I appreciated being kept busy. As did George. It was helping us to rebuild our relationship too, spending time together. We chatted as we waited, and I felt closer to George, once again.

We struck lucky on the third day, when a lady unlatched the gate and made her way up the front path. She was wearing jeans, had her hair tied back and looked very friendly, I thought. As we watched her approach the front door, I gestured for George to go.

'Go in with her, quick,' I said as the lady stood on the doorstep, fumbling around in her pocket for a key. He started to move towards her and then stopped.

'Dad, you forgot to tell me how to get out again?'

'Make sure you leave when she does, son,' I said. Bless him, I thought, he still had a lot to learn. I crossed my paws that this would all work out as I watched George slip in between Susan's legs as she began to walk through the door.

'Who do we have here?' she said, bending down.

'Meow,' George said. I saw Hana come to the door, and I saw her eyes widen as she saw George there. They greeted each other with a nuzzle and then Susan shut the door. He was in.

I felt warm; George and Hana were together for now and I hoped they had a nice time together. I also hoped he came back with a lot more information. Actually, more than anything, I hoped he remembered to leave with Susan.

Feeling satisfied, I stared at the closed front door for a few minutes before I headed back. I imagined that, as Susan got on with her work, George and Hana would have a tour of the house, as I had that time I'd got stuck inside, and they would play together, chat, really enjoying their time together. I raised my whiskers at another job well done.

Back at our house, I found Claire, Polly and a man I hadn't

met before sitting round the kitchen table with a notepad and pen in front of them. I was curious as I jumped up onto Claire's lap.

'Marcus, this is Alfie, one of our cats who alerted us to your father.' Ah, so this was Marcus. He was nothing like I'd expected. I'd expected a slightly younger version of the angry, red-faced man, but he was tall, slim and about the same age as Matt and Jonathan at a guess. He had curly dark hair, glasses, and he looked very kind. Nothing like his father.

'I still can't believe your cats saved my father, it's crazy,' he said, with a small laugh.

'I know, it takes a bit to get your head around how Alfie and George are,' Polly explained. 'It's taken us years to get used to it, but Alfie is a remarkable cat and we like to think he's training George up to be the same.' She stroked me and gave me one of my favourite head scratches. Just what I needed.

Marcus leant over and petted me. I immediately liked him, he had very soft, warm hands.

'How do I thank them?' he asked. 'I'm guessing, no matter how clever they are, they won't read a thank you note.' The women both laughed and I added good sense of humour to his list of attributes.

'Buy them some fish, that always works,' Claire said, still tittering. 'Or any kind of delicious treats.'

'Meow!' It really would.

'Right, I can do that. So, let's look at the list. I can't believe how nice you've all been.'

'Hey, don't mention it. I wish I'd known that he was there before, we could have helped,' Claire said. A darker look passed over Marcus' face.

'I feel so damn guilty, but it was a really bad time. My wife cheated on me, my dad didn't approve of me divorcing her, then I sold my company, because I wanted to have a fresh start, and that took quite a lot of work. I still work for them, but as a consultant . . . Anyway, there was a lot going on in my life, and I let my stupid pride get in the way. Dad and I are both too proud for our own good actually, it's one of our biggest faults, but I should have kept an eye on him, I should have made sure he was alright. I'd have never forgiven myself if anything happened to him.'

'Hey, it all worked out. You've had a wake-up call and now you are going to make sure your relationship is repaired,' Polly pointed out. My women were so kind.

'So you're single?' Claire asked and I swished my tail; Claire and I did like to matchmake but perhaps this wasn't quite the time.

'Yes?' he replied, sounding worried.

'Ignore her, Claire is the matchmaker of the group, but Claire, we don't know anyone we could try to set Marcus up with, do we?' Polly stated, firmly.

'Well, no, apart from Sylvie.'

'Who's not even talking to us, remember,' Polly said.

'Who's Sylvie?' Marcus looked confused and I couldn't blame him. Although it wasn't a bad idea. If Sylvie hadn't been totally insane, of course.

'No one to worry about right now, but what we do need to sort out is the house. How long before your dad is out of hospital?'

'They said about another week. But in that time I need to get it cleaned up and sort out some furniture. I'd like to

235

redecorate but I don't see that we have time, not to mention that garden and getting the front of the house painted.' He looked worried.

'That's why we're here. Polly and I are going to put together a roster. We've cleaned the house, so that's a start,' Claire said. 'Although it won't all be finished, we can get a lot done in a week.'

'Thank you so much.'

'So, painting first off. I've roped a couple of guys in to help us, and the carpets can be laid, all you need to do is choose the colours. Then there's furniture – we can get some of it sorted now but some might need to be ordered so we will make do with what we've got for now. The garden will be tidied up a bit before your dad comes home, but again, that might take longer, and the outside painting will be last.'

'As I said, I'm willing to pay, and also for your time,' Marcus said.

'Marcus, we are doing this out of friendship, that's what we do. But let's go to the DIY store now to get supplies, and you can bring your credit card for that,' Polly said.

'I'll pick up the kids and give them tea,' Claire offered. 'That way you guys have longer to get everything you need.'

'What would I have done without you, cats and husbands included?' Marcus said, shaking his head as if he couldn't believe it.

'Well, luckily you don't have to worry about that, you're part of our Edgar Road family now. And I know you're going to stay with your dad for a bit, but it'll be good to know that we're just down the road when you're not there.' Claire smiled.

236

'That means a lot. I'm a bit thin on the friendship ground, what with the divorce and everything.' He looked sad but then he smiled; I could tell he no longer felt alone.

I raised my whiskers, all this friendly chat and caring was making me very tired. For the first time in days, I drifted off into sleep, feeling almost peaceful.

Someone licked my head, interrupting my dreams. I opened my eyes slowly to see George standing over me. I'd almost forgotten to worry about him, actually I had. The sleep that I'd had was desperately needed, I couldn't remember the last time I'd had rest like that.

'Dad,' he said, as I extended my paws and started to stretch.

'You got out OK?' Thank goodness. That wasn't my best parenting – going to sleep and forgetting about my child – but thankfully it had been fine, he was fine.

'Oh yes. It was so good, and I got out easily. I told Hana that we would stay close to Susan, but not so she could hear our chat, but so we knew when she was leaving. It was so nice to see her properly and have a conversation which we could actually hear. The house is very nice. Not much stuff around but Hana said they lived in a smaller space in Japan and did something called "minimalism".' His voice was so animated, I hadn't heard him so full of enthusiasm since before Tiger told him she was ill. 'The best thing is that Susan is coming back in two days, she comes in twice a week now. Apparently Sylvie isn't very good at cleaning and also she worries about Hana being left alone, so she comes in, for two hours twice a week! Which means that I can see Hana all that time.' He sounded happier than I had heard him in ages.

'So how was it?' I asked. I didn't want to burst his bubble but I was curious.

'Well, as I said, the house was lovely, and Susan is sweet. Hana has raw fish for food nearly all the time! And she eats rice, and I got to try some.'

'Rice, really? And did you like that?' I'd never tried rice.

'It was OK. I prefer my food to be honest but it was good to try it. But Hana is lonely though, we were right.'

'Go on.' We were getting to the interesting part, I could tell.

'Well, she loved her life in Japan. She didn't spend much time alone, there were always people around. Sylvie, her ex-husband, Connie, and the house was normally full of their friends too. But now she's alone so much and when Sylvie and Connie are home they don't really talk to each other and they shout if they do.'

'We guessed that was the case, didn't we?' I tilted my head sympathetically.

'Yes, but things have taken a turn that you and I didn't even think of,' he said.

'What, George?' I had a bad feeling in my fur.

'Remember you said how Aleksy was working to buy Connie a present?'

'Yes.' I willed him to hurry up, but he wasn't one for rushing a story.

'He lied to his mum a bit, because he bought her a phone yesterday, and she hid it under her pillow and they do that talking thing where you don't talk but write.'

'George, are you talking about texting?' I had a very bad feeling.

'Yes, they do texting, which means that of course Hana doesn't know what they are saying because she can't read. She thinks they do still talk but only when Connie shuts the door and Hana is outside. Of course her mum doesn't know.'

'George, I have a bad feeling about this. Was there anything else?'

'Sylvie cries a lot, she's very lonely, she isn't coping so well. It's not a happy house at the moment, but it is very nice and clean. Susan is a very good cleaner.'

# Chapter
# Twenty-Seven

# Chapter
## Twenty-Seven

'Perhaps I should go and see Dustbin, just in case, see if he knows anything.' I said later, starting to fret yet again after having had time to digest all the information George had given me.

'OK, but I'm tired, so I think I better wait here for Summer and Toby. It's been another busy day,' George yawned.

'And you know if Dustbin did know anything urgent, he would come and find us, so he probably doesn't.' The idea of walking all that way right now wasn't appealing to me either.

George and I made our way downstairs, me trying to decide what to do. We had reached the kitchen when the cat flap bashed loudly. We both ran as quickly as we could and slid through, to find Dustbin standing on the other side.

'Talk of the devil,' I said. 'I was just trying to decide if I had to come and see you, because George found out that Aleksy got Connie a phone,' I gushed.

'Ah, you know about that, yes he did. And I came to you as soon as I could, but I was very busy. The rodents seem to be more determined in winter.'

'At least you're here now. There'll be big trouble if anyone finds out about the phone,' I said, raising my whiskers worriedly. Aleksy and Connie were playing with fire. I understood how frustrating love could be, especially when you were young, but still.

'Yeah, it's worse than that,' Dustbin said.

243

'What?' My fur stood on end.

'I heard him speaking to her last night in the yard. They are planning on running away.'

I wondered if Tiger could see me and what she would be thinking if she could. Slightly out of ideas, we held our crisis council at the recreation ground. Thankfully, as Dustbin, George and I approached, Nellie, Elvis and Rocky were all there. It was a good time, before tea and before it got dark, and I was grateful for my friends. We needed to come up with a plan; it needed to be quick and I needed their input.

'According to what Dustbin heard, we think they might be planning on running away tonight, late, when it's dark and everyone is asleep,' I finished, having filled them in the whole situation.

'Oh dear,' Nellie said, licking her paws in concern. 'I don't like the sound of this.'

'The poor kids just want to be together,' Elvis said. 'I saw something like that on TV once, and I have to say I don't blame them. Parents have a lot to answer for.'

George flicked his eyes towards me worriedly.

'Not you Alfie, of course.' Of course not. I'd tried to help George get together with Hana, not keep them apart – although that was just friendship. And yes, I had tried to warn him off Chanel, but that was because she didn't like him. No, in the case of Aleksy and Connie, I was fully supportive. But not of them running away. Running away never solved anything. Not to mention that London at night was full of danger.

'Well,' Rocky said. 'I think there's only one thing for it.'

'What is that?' I asked, impatiently. If there was a solution, I wanted it. What with how full my head was at the moment, I was finding it hard to think.

'Stop them,' Rocky said.

'Great, I think we know that,' I said, a little snappily. 'But how?'

'Don't snap, Alfie, we're only trying to help,' Nellie bristled.

'Sorry, sorry, it's a bit tough right now.'

'But hey, Rocky's right, we just need to stop them, literally.' Dustbin's eyes lit up as he seemed to be thinking. And then I got it.

'Sorry Rocky, you are right. We need to lie in wait for Aleksy, and make so much of a commotion that he'll think we're going to wake his family up, or we actually do wake his family up, and he'll have no choice but to abandon running away.' My brain was back in proper operation now.

'Oh, good idea, Dad, but what about Connie?' George sensibly asked.

'Go and tell Hana, if you can. I know it'll be through the window but fill her in and see if she will try to stop Connie. It'd be easier if we could get in there to help but it'll have to be down to her, I'm afraid. Once again, thanks guys, you are the best friends a cat could have. And I hope that Aleksy and Connie appreciate us.'

'They probably won't, not if you stop them running away,' George pointed out, sensibly.

'Not right now but my job, our job, is to keep them safe,' I explained.

'And it's not safe out there, not for teenagers or most cats,'

Dustbin explained. 'Honestly, if they did run away, I shudder to think how they'll manage. I mean, Aleksy hasn't exactly got survival skills.'

'I'll go to Dustbin tonight, and help him stop Aleksy. If he sees me there he'll know that somehow we've foiled his plan and it might make him think again.'

I was a little cross now I thought about it. Aleksy was normally the sensible one but running away, late at night, was not clever and it was far from sensible. It was also not going to happen. As the others discussed the plan, I listened but I couldn't help but think about the other day, when Tommy had come up with his plan for the nativity and Aleksy had said he'd help, as if nothing was amiss. And his good mood must have been down to this crazy running-away idea. I wasn't happy with him at all.

I would not let this family fall apart. I would not let Aleksy and Connie run away. Yes, their situation was unfair, and yes, they should have been allowed to have their relationship, within the limits of their age, but this was not the way to go about getting Sylvie to change her mind. I worried that if she got wind of it then she'd lock Connie up at boarding school, far far away, whether she could afford to or not.

I calmed down as George and I headed home, and I felt confident in our plan. George had asked to come with us but I pointed out that Toby would worry if he wasn't there. Although our plan didn't involve any of my usual dangers, things could always go wrong, so knowing George was safely tucked up at home would be one less thing for me to worry about. The ideal outcome would be that we stopped Aleksy without his parents finding out and the same with Connie.

Then they would realise how foolish they were being and rethink their behaviour. George and I parted ways and he went to Hana's house and I went back to ours.

Marcus was at our house again. He had paint smeared on one of his glasses lenses, and he and Jonathan were both drinking beer and laughing. They seemed to get on well and I thought he would be a welcome addition to Edgar Road – although I had said the same about Sylvie not long ago.

I didn't have much time to listen to their conversation though I picked up a bit. Harold was recovering well, but wasn't coming home until the doctors were confident that he had the right medication. But that was all I managed to glean as I ate, had a quick wash and, after putting George to bed – he felt he had successfully communicated what he needed to to Hana – headed out to meet Dustbin. I was beyond tired, and my exhaustion was added to by the thought of the long night ahead. I wasn't sure what time the kids would think about trying to escape, but I knew it would probably be fairly late if they were waiting for the adults to go to sleep. Just the idea of it made my fur feel weary.

Dustbin was hard at work when I arrived, evenings being his busiest time. It was pitch black, as the nights were now, and the street was lit only by a handful of stars and eyes of the cheeky rodents that Dustbin was charged with getting rid of.

'Why don't you get some rest while I finish up here?' he suggested, kindly, when I told him how tired I was. I didn't need asking twice, I curled up by the back door to Franceska's house and I took my forty, or so, winks.

I was woken by Dustbin nudging me and although I was

startled I shot up to see Aleksy opening the back door to their house. He was wearing dark jeans and a black hoody, and had a backpack with him. It didn't look as if he had much stuff in it, I thought, as he was carrying it with ease. Dustbin and I blinked at each other and we turned to face Aleksy.

He jumped at the sight of me. 'Alfie, what are you doing here?'

'MEW,' I said at the top of my voice. That was our cue. Dustbin and I yowled and meowed at the tops of our voices.

'Shush, please shush,' Aleksy said. We didn't. He picked me up but I wouldn't stop and I wiggled until I had to, reluctantly, give him a tiny scratch, which made him let go and drop me onto the floor. It wasn't one of my best experiences. Dustbin, give him his due, thankfully kept going – turns out he had quite a pair of lungs on him. We saw a light go on inside the flat above the restaurant, and I saw Aleksy notice it too. I imagined them looking out of the window at us. Thankfully neither Tomasz or Franceska seemed to have heard us though.

'Can you both please just be quiet, you'll wake Mum and Dad.' I could hear the desperation in his voice but I wasn't going to be silenced.

'Yowl,' I shouted over and over.

'Alright,' he said, suddenly sitting down on the doorstep and pulling out his phone. We both stopped shouting and waited. 'Hi, it's me.'

I couldn't hear what Connie was saying.

'Hana tried to trip you up?' There was a pause. 'She woke your mum up?' Another pause. 'What did your mum say?' Silence. 'Oh, you shut yourself in the bathroom, quick thinking. But Alfie is here and he and Dustbin made such a noise when they saw me that my parents will wake up soon, and the flat next door is already looking out of the window. They haven't seen me yet, I don't think.' Pause. 'No, I agree, we can't risk it tonight.' He sounded crestfallen but it was for his own good. 'I'll text you and let's talk at school tomorrow and come up with a new plan.'

That wasn't exactly what I wanted to hear but at least he and Connie were safe and had aborted their running away for now.

'Alfie, why are you here?' Aleksy asked, after he hung up. 'Did you know I was going to try to be with Connie?' He narrowed his eyes. 'No, that's silly. Of course you didn't know, you just came to see your friend, Dustbin.' He nodded. If it was easier for him to believe that, then who was I to argue?

'Alfie, I'll walk you home,' Dustbin said, after we watched Aleksy go inside. I was glad I hadn't woken Tomasz and Franceska, but also a little surprised. The fact that they had slept through me and Dustbin at our nosiest was slightly worrying. If that didn't wake them then what on earth would?

'You don't think he'll try to come out again?' I asked. I was longing for home, for my bed, but I didn't want to lose Aleksy.

'No, we'll wait a few minutes just in case. But that doesn't mean that's the end of this.'

'We'll keep our ears to the ground,' I said, but I didn't mean literally.

'Sure, but we're both tired, it's been a long day. Let's sleep on it and see what tomorrow brings.'

'Oh goodness, I need a rest. In a few days we have the nativity play to look forward to. Maybe that will give us some light relief.' I filled Dustbin in on Tommy's plan as he walked me back to Edgar Road and even Dustbin thought it would be a riot. That was what worried me: it might cause a riot. I wasn't sure how much more this cat was up to at the moment.

# Chapter
# Twenty-Eight

# Chapter
## Twenty-Eight

I knew the nativity was a big deal, but today it was all anyone talked of over breakfast. Summer was so excited, she kept saying she was literally the star of the show. Toby mumbled how there were loads of other stars but he was too miserable about having to hold Emma Roper's hand to make a huge fuss. They didn't mention Tommy's plan and I was impressed with the fact that Summer hadn't spilled the beans, she just kept saying it was going to be the best nativity ever. The performance was after school, which was why all my families could go, and of course that included Tommy and Aleksy.

It had been a few days since we'd foiled Aleksy's running-away plan, and according to Dustbin he and Connie seemed to have been a bit put off the idea; Aleksy hadn't mentioned running away when he'd listened to his snatched conversations. That gave us some time, thank goodness, and we could focus now on the nativity and then Christmas. Although George and I were on good terms, I knew the first Christmas without Tiger would be incredibly hard for him, for both of us, and I was mindful of that. I was also feeling the stress of the past couple of weeks. So much had happened: Tiger, Harold, George and I, Hana and getting George into Hana's house, and of course the attempted runaways. It was a lot for any cat to cope with, and the strain was definitely being felt. Yes, I was coping, yes I was grieving, and yes I was exhausted with the emotion of it all.

I didn't feel like myself at the moment. There was something missing, and everything felt as if it was such a huge effort. I wanted to enjoy Christmas and all that entailed but I was also dreading it, knowing it was the first one without Tiger. I missed her, and that was exhausting too. I didn't like to complain but all I wanted to do was to yowl in pain. But of course I couldn't do that.

Thankfully we had Tommy's caper to distract us. I was still unsure about the finer details of how they were going to pull it off, but for once I didn't have to worry about that. It wasn't my plan, I was just an innocent part of it. That made a refreshing change to be honest. It was almost like having a day off, and that was how I was going to look at it. After the drama of the last few days and the ache that I carried constantly from missing Tiger, no one needed a day off more than me.

Thankfully, it really was a day off for me, as I needed more than anything to catch up on some rest. Claire was helping at Harold's house; everyone else, including Marcus, was working, so she was supervising the new carpets. George was visiting Hana. Aleksy and Connie were both at school and I would be seeing Aleksy later, so I didn't have to worry about him for now.

I spent the day catching up on my sleep, before making a quick visit to our friends. I also checked on the Barkers, a habit I'd got into. Since Tiger had passed away they never left the cat flap open, of course, so I couldn't go in, but I just felt that it was my duty to go by and see their house. If I saw them I would try to be friendly, and they did pet me kindly; I could tell they felt Tiger's loss keenly. We all did.

Grief hung over Edgar Road, despite the approach of Christmas. The Barkers hadn't even bothered to get a tree from what I could see through their front window, which meant they must have been in a bad way. I felt so bad for them; I understood how they felt, after all.

I added them to the list. I didn't know how I could cheer them up when I couldn't really cheer myself up, but I was concerned. I knew Tiger would have wanted me to try and I owed it to her, so I would do all I could. But time was ticking on, and problems were piling up, and I was shrouded in grief, so it was all so hard. When I got home, I took another nap.

The light outside was beginning to fade as I heard the door open and Aleksy and Tommy appeared. Luckily, George and I were in the living room and were ready, having had something to eat and groomed ourselves thoroughly.

Aleksy picked me up and told me I would have to hide in his jacket. Tommy did the same with George.

'Quick,' Tommy said. 'Before Mum notices I stole the key.'

'You didn't steal it, you borrowed it,' Aleksy replied, far less dramatically.

'I know, but the grown-ups might not see it that way. Anyway, we better go, I told Mum we'd meet her at the school so we could get good seats.'

'We need to get the best seats to watch what you've got planned,' Aleksy said, and I agreed. I noticed he stopped at the gate to Connie's house and looked longingly up at the window. He didn't mention anything about the other night to either me or Tommy.

'Come on, honestly her mum will come round, I heard Claire say that,' Tommy said, patting his brother on the shoulder and nearly dropping George in the process. 'Oops, sorry George, I must be more careful.'

'Meow,' I yelled from the warmth of Aleksy's jacket. Yes you must.

It was a pleasant journey after that. I could just about poke my head out and check out the scenery, which was always different from this vantage point. Instead of seeing – and dodging – feet, we could see the people more clearly. And the cars – there were so many cars revving along the road. Although it was warm inside Aleksy's jacket, the top of my head felt cold. I willed Aleksy and Tommy to be careful when crossing but they were very sensible, thankfully. I noted a couple of dogs being taken on their walks and women pushing prams, the way our ladies used to when our children were younger. Goodness, when I first met Tommy all those years ago he was still just about in a pushchair. And look at him now. Time passes, that's what it does, and although we have to carry our hurts and our grief with us, it showed me, yet again, how we all have to keep moving forward.

It was funny, on this walk I was watching life, and it was passing us, bumping us, moving around us, and that was what life did. It made me realise, from my home in Aleksy's jacket, how absorbed we get into our own little worlds and I found some kind of comfort in seeing a bigger world. I wondered what Tiger would have thought if she'd known what we were about to do. I imagined her chuckling and telling us how mad we were but also being impatient for us to get back and relay the story to her. She would have told me to make sure George was alright but, other than that, she'd have liked this one. I would tell her later, in my head, and in my heart, because that was where she lived now.

I tried to rein in my emotions as we reached the school. Tommy told us both to keep down as they zipped their jackets up. Surely it was obvious we were there, bumps poking out of coats? It was pitch black so I couldn't see anything, but my hearing was very good. Aleksy greeted the adults, Tommy was quiet. Claire had got them all seats near the front and so they rushed in. Aleksy sat down with me on the end, hoping no one would notice me, and Tommy said he needed the toilet. Luckily he had been to this school himself, not so long ago, so he knew where everything was. I was still locked in the jacket so I couldn't tell you what was happening but by the sound of scuffles on the floor and chairs scraping impatiently the hall was filling up. People greeted each other, chattering excitedly. Parents were all desperate to see their little ones appear on stage. I just hoped that we weren't going to ruin it for them. Although I thought that, mad as Tommy's plan was, it was also quite funny and harmless. And it had brought Toby and Henry back together, so I was still very proud of the boy.

Tommy reappeared and took his seat next to Aleksy with his dad on the other side. I was pleased that all the family was here, but then, as Tomasz said, it wouldn't be Christmas without going to a nativity, and now his boys didn't have them any more, he was glad they could still come. Not long ago I had thought that Sylvie and Connie would be joining us but, of course, that hadn't worked out. I knew that not everyone could be friends, but I still didn't understand why not. The loneliness coming from next door was bothering me but, as the lights were turned down and the headmistress appeared on stage, I put that to one side. We had a play to watch.

I was allowed a peek out of the jacket to watch. I didn't dare look around too much, lest I was noticed. But after the headmistress welcomed everyone – I like to think she included me – she introduced the play and then I noticed people taking out their phones. Tommy did the same; they were either taking photos or filming.

The music struck and the singing began. Toby looked so cute in a robe and what looked like a tea towel on his head, but I noticed the donkey couldn't stop laughing as Toby kept trying to pull his hand away from his Mary. I saw Summer twirling on the stage as a star and she really did pretty much command the centre of the stage, which I wasn't sure she was supposed to. Then Martha came on as an angel and, actually, she really was a little angel. The angels sang a song and then the oldest one spoke to a scowling Toby and his Mary.

At one point a teacher appeared to move everyone, as it had got a little confusing. I was pretty sure I knew the story of the nativity well; I think Summer was supposed to move with the other stars to the back of the stage after singing to the shepherds, but she seemed to want to stay right at the front. I imagined Claire had her head in her hands at this point. A shouty boy told Toby there was 'no room at the inn'. I have to say Toby looked quite relieved but I'm not sure he was meant to. Then they were directed to the stable and I braced myself.

There was another song, and then the shepherds gathered, and the wise men, and they were all supposed to give gifts to the baby Jesus. Tommy stuffed his fist into his mouth, and held his phone up high, while Aleksy giggled into my fur. Toby and Henry exchanged a glance and then, just as the first wise man approached the manger, he shouted:

'It's a cat. The baby Jesus is a cat.' I could hear Jonathan's groan from my seat. Then George, who I assume must have fallen asleep, jumped up from the manger where they had wrapped him in a tea towel.

'Mewmewmewmew,' he said.

The audience erupted in laughter, the room echoing with it as Toby grabbed hold of George and cuddled him to his chest. I peered out and looked at my family. Claire *did* have her head in her hands, Jonathan and Matt had tears running down their cheeks from laughter, Aleksy was giggling into my head, Franceska, Polly and Tomasz's shoulders were shaking as they tried and failed not to find it funny. A teacher ran on stage but didn't know what to do when she got there, and Henry, the donkey, laughed so much he had to lie down.

'It's George, the baby Jesus,' Summer shouted, as she spun around. Only Mary/Emma Roper didn't look happy. She was still trying to hold Toby's hand even though he was now clutching a cat.

Finally, Jonathan, having been shouted at by Claire, approached the stage, looking a bit embarrassed, and got Toby to give him George. The applause was deafening and if George hadn't been clamped so tightly to Jonathan's chest I know he would have taken a proud bow.

'High-five,' Aleksy said to Tommy, and as we all high-fived, I felt as if it had given us some much-needed fun.

The children were all squashed onto our sofa, the parents lined up in front of them. George, unsure where to go, finally perched on the arm of the sofa and I, of course, stood with the parents, although I was pretty sure this time I was in trouble too.

'Tommy, it was your idea?' Franceska asked, with her arms folded.

At the play, the audience hadn't stopped laughing until they reluctantly filed out of the hall, collecting their children as they went. The headmistress had a face like thunder, as she told my adults that the nativity, which they had all worked hard for, had been ruined. Although parents did come and stick up for us, saying it was the best nativity they'd ever seen, I'm not sure it helped, the woman was so angry. Claire was embarrassed as they got a ticking-off, and it didn't help when the headmistress told Toby that he wouldn't be trusted with the role of Joseph again, and he replied, 'Thank goodness.' The adults made the children apologise. Tommy stood up and took responsibility, but the headmistress pointed out that Toby and Henry knew George was in the manger all along and if they weren't 'in on it' they should have told an adult. The upshot was that everyone was in a bit of trouble, and although actually it was worth it, they had to at least pretend to be cross. Although thinking about it, I think Claire really *was* cross; sometimes she forgot her sense of humour.

'It was all my idea,' Tommy said, again. Give him his due, he always owned up. Like the time it was his idea to take

George to church in our holiday home in Devon – I haven't forgotten how they left me behind – and George saw Chanel, the cat he had a crush on, and it didn't end well. Or when it was his idea to take us both crabbing with them, on a boat no less, and George got bitten on his nose by a crab. That *did* turn out well, as we all got ice cream, but you get the gist.

'That's a surprise,' Franceska said with her best cross voice, but I could tell she wasn't actually that angry. Apart from Claire, I could see them all struggling to keep straight faces.

'But the rest of you all went along with it,' Claire pointed out. The children, including George, looked a little guilty beneath their smiles.

'But apart from me, George was the best thing about the play,' Summer pointed out. Star by name, star by nature.

'Where does she get it from?' Claire hissed.

'Don't look at me.' Jonathan shrugged.

'Let's get back on topic,' Polly interrupted.

'It was quite funny,' Matt added. 'No, it was incredibly funny. "The baby Jesus is a cat" classic line.'

'Yes, it might well have been, but Mrs White, the headmistress, didn't find it funny, she's angry and for some reason she blames us. Honestly, Claire, we'll be made to bake cakes for every occasion as penance,' Polly said.

'You can't bake,' Matt pointed out. He was right, she couldn't. She bought all the cakes, then put them in tins and took them to school, we all knew that.

'Not the point,' Claire replied. 'Right, why did you do it, Tommy?'

'Well, Toby was so upset about being Joseph and he and Henry weren't really being like friends and I wanted to make them happy again, so I came up with the plan to get them together.' Ah, he was a boy after my own heart. 'And Aleksy was so sad about Connie and the fact her mum won't let them spend time together, and I thought it would cheer him up. I roped them all in, honestly, and Alfie, well I didn't want Alfie to miss seeing George as the baby Jesus.'

'Of course you didn't.' Jonathan grinned and shook his head. 'Look guys, Tommy meant well and no harm done. I mean, everyone thought it was funny. Apart from Mary but then she had just given birth to a cat.'

'Jonathan,' Claire snapped. 'They have to apologise to Mrs White.'

'We can do that,' Tommy said. 'I'm happy to write her a letter, not that she deserves it,' he mumbled.

'Toby?'

'OK, I'll say sorry. It was worth it, wasn't it, Henry?'

'Sure was, Tobe.'

I agreed. It really was worth it.

'What about me?' Martha asked. 'Do I have to say sorry?'

'Well you should,' Polly said. 'You knew all about it so that makes you guilty too.'

'OK.' Martha shrugged in the good-natured way she always did.

'But not me?' Summer said.

'Why not you?' Jonathan asked.

'I'm a star, I'm allowed to do what I want,' she said.

'No, you are not.' Claire rolled her eyes. 'You apologise too, young lady.' Summer scrunched her nose up.

'And guess what?' Aleksy said. It was the first time he had spoken and his voice was animated as he looked at his phone.

'What?' Tomasz asked.

'George is trending. The video is on the internet already and "cat as baby jesus" already has thousands of views. George, you're famous,' he said, punching the air with joy. 'Tommy, the video you put on YouTube is being watched and shared. We might get rich!'

'Good thinking, boys. We could make some money out of this.' Jonathan rubbed his hands together.

'Jonathan, don't make this worse,' Claire warned.

'Oh come on guys, look how happy it's made the internet.' Matt grinned.

George looked nonplussed as he licked his paws.

Everyone was relaxed again. The kids were playing by the Christmas tree. The adults all had drinks and snacks and Claire had lit her hundred candles. To be honest, I didn't expect this to last long – they took ages to light and to blow out so she didn't bother too much. Her interest in 'hygge', whatever that was, was definitely waning. But it looked and felt Christmassy, as the tinsel glinted, the tree lights sparkled and the candle flames danced. I thought of Tiger, of course, and how much she would have loved to be around for Christmas, how much we would have loved having her around. That was the weird thing about grief, it appeared at the strangest times. I was happy, with my families, but then I thought of her and I was sad again. But happy, and sad. It was most confusing.

'Oh no, George is on fire,' Tomasz screamed.

'Yowl,' George said. He had caught his tail on one of the candles and it was now on fire. My poor boy. I ran around in circles looking for something to put the fire out with, as did the adults.

Thankfully Aleksy and Tommy were quicker than all of us. Aleksy grabbed George, holding him away, and Tommy threw a glass of water over his tail, then grabbed one of Claire's 'hygge' blankets – there were quite a few – and wrapped it around him.

'Oh my goodness, is he alright?' Claire asked, tearfully. I felt my heart pounding.

'Meow,' George said. I knew that meant he was in pain but he was alright.

'I think so,' Aleksy said.

'Tommy, Aleksy, great job,' Jonathan said. 'But we need to get George to the vet, there's a clinic I can take him to,' he said.

Not the vet, I thought, but this time I agreed with them.

'I'll drive, I haven't been drinking,' Tomasz said.

'Oh, that was so scary,' Polly said.

'I think I'll get rid of the candles,' Claire finished.

# Chapter
# Twenty-Nine

# Chapter Twenty-Nine

It was very exciting, Harold was coming home. Well, it was to everyone else, because I, quite frankly, was having a down day. There would be all these distractions that I was used to, being the kind of doorstep cat I was, but then I would remember how much I missed Tiger and my heart would collapse all over again. I tried to keep my tail upright but, sometimes, it just didn't want to do it and all I felt capable of was curling up in my bed and yowling. George was my salvation in the darker days, him and my families of course, but mainly him.

Since becoming the star of the school nativity play, and actually getting to spend time with Hana, he was doing pretty well. Of course the tail incident was still fresh in our minds, but apart from it being painful and singed, George was fine. The vet had given him an injection which took some of the pain away and my resilient boy had bounced back. Toby said all of the school now wanted to come to our house to meet George, and Summer suggested selling tickets – Jonathan was proud at this, Claire not so much so. And George took being famous in his stride but I could tell he quite liked it. He still talked to me about missing Tiger mum, and how hard he found it to walk past her house. I knew that one. Some days I would find myself in her back garden, staring at the closed cat flap as if she would slide through it, but of course she never would. Sometimes seeing her house, knowing she wasn't there, floored me, so I understand how he felt. One day, I literally froze as I approached the house and couldn't bring myself to walk past it. It was beyond hard.

After the apology at school, the children had returned to normal for the last week of term. Well, as normal as they ever were at Christmas. Summer declared that she was going to be a famous actress when she was older and Toby said he wouldn't want to be an actor, because there were too many girls involved, so he was going to do something like be a spaceman, where you didn't have to hold anyone's hands. Henry and Toby were firm friends again and Martha, with her customary laid-back manner, was just lovely Martha.

So many people had viewed the video that George had even been mentioned in a newspaper, and now he felt that he was the most famous member of the family, which of course he was. But no one dared tell Summer that.

Amidst all the chaos, Christmas was drawing closer and closer. More and more of the advent calendar doors were open, festive food was being bought, presents wrapped, cards displayed. The weather was also getting colder, frost greeted us most mornings and everyone talked of snow. Despite the ache that now sat with me daily for Tiger, I couldn't help but enjoy everyone's festive spirit. I knew they felt as if it was the most wonderful time of the year and I tried to bask in their happiness even if I wasn't going to ever say this was my favourite Christmas.

It couldn't be, not without Tiger here. The thing was that, last year, when we went away to our holiday cottage in Devon for Christmas, I hadn't seen her but I'd known she was there. And when we had returned home, we'd all been so excited to share our stories. She'd told me that she got extra turkey, some toys and a very fetching new red collar for Christmas. In return, I'd told her that we'd spent time with our friend Gilbert in Devon and, although the beach was freezing, we had braved it, and I'd managed to keep George out of the water this time. It was moments like these, sharing moments, that kept friendship and love alive, I believed, and so I was still sharing with her; every evening I had a chat to her before going to sleep. It was just very one-sided.

'I can't wait to see my friend Harold again,' George said, hopping with excitement, as we sat on the windowsill looking out at the quiet street. Marcus was collecting Harold this afternoon, and Polly and Franceska were at his house now, getting it ready for his welcome-home party. We were both invited and I just hoped Harold wouldn't tell us to get lost or wave his stick at us now. Apparently he wouldn't, he'd told Jonathan that we were both welcome in his house after all. George was so looking forward to it; he'd taken ages getting himself looking his best, as had I. I was one cat who always took care over his appearance – even when I was heart-broken, I had learnt not to let myself go.

Claire returned with Toby and Summer and shortly afterwards the doorbell announced the arrival of Franceska, Tommy and Aleksy.

'Meow?' I asked as I greeted them. Where was Tomasz?

'Tomasz is going to meet us at Harold's later, he had to sort something out at work,' Franceska explained as she petted me. But I think she was talking to Claire.

'Come in for a bit, have a coffee. Boys, can I get you anything?' Claire asked, as coats were shaken out and hung up.

'No, we're good, thanks,' Tommy answered, shooting worried glances at Aleksy who was back to not talking. Franceska shook her head and followed Claire into the kitchen.

'Where are you going?' Franceska asked as Aleksy headed out to the back garden, carrying me for some unfathomable reason.

'Alfie wants to go out, I thought I'd go with him,' he replied, looking at his feet. I had no idea what sort of pawn I was now, but I didn't want to go out, I wanted no such thing. I had just got myself all smart and the wind and the cold would probably ruin all my hard work. But I didn't say anything. I knew, better than any cat, when one of my humans needed me and Aleksy clearly did. No one argued as he opened the back door and we went into the garden.

It all became clear. Aleksy started walking around the garden, trying to find a vantage point where he could see into Connie's house. I stood there, freezing and quite astounded, as he even tried to climb the fence. Was he mad? Yes, he was but then I remembered what young love could do to you.

'Yowl!' That wasn't a good idea. I had done the same thing when I was trying to woo Snowball, of course, but it seemed humans were slightly happier for cats to get into their gardens than other humans.

'It's no good.' Aleksy looked so downcast. I sighed. It was always down to me. I led him to the bottom of the small garden, where a table and chairs sat. They were covered for the winter but if he stood on a chair, he might see something. 'Alfie, you're a genius,' he said, as he took one of the chairs over to the fence and climbed on it. 'Bingo,' he shouted as he saw Connie appear in one of the upstairs windows. He started waving wildly at her.

I have to say, as I climbed on top of the fence to watch, her face seemed to beam as she waved back. He took his phone out of his pocket and pointed at it. I looked around. I saw how Claire and Franceska were pretending not to watch us from the kitchen as a number of annoying birds flew overhead. But I knew that for Aleksy and Connie they were the only two people in the world right now, I could see it on their faces. I saw Hana appear on the windowsill and I tried to wave my paw but I nearly lost my balance so I stopped. I could see she was raising her whiskers though. I couldn't help but think how sweet this was, and also how unfair. I had to find a way to get these two kids together.

Fourteen years old, responsible enough, hard workers, they weren't the worst teenagers by a long shot. They should have been allowed to be together with adult supervision at the very least. I felt angry with Sylvie.

Speak of the devil.

'Yowl!' I tried to warn Aleksy as Sylvie appeared in the window behind Connie, and not only did she see us, but she also saw that her daughter had a phone. I tried to get Aleksy's attention by tapping him, but I wobbled and fell on him. The shock of seeing Sylvie, coupled with me landing on him, meant he lost his balance and fell off the chair.

'Ahhh,' he shouted as we landed on the grass. Luckily for me, I was on top of him. But his face was stricken as he scrambled up, dropping me into a patch of mud as he did so.

'Meow,' I complained. But he didn't seem to hear me as

271

he ran round to the front of the house. I got up, certainly not looking my best now, and ran after him.

Connie was outside the front of her house, sobbing, when we got there. The rain had started in earnest, so we were all getting soaked.

'I'm sorry,' he said.

'It's not your fault,' she replied. I ran around in a circle, what on earth could I do? Sylvie appeared, then Claire and Franceska came out of our house. I could hear Claire shouting at Tommy to look after the kids and we all stood around. No one seemed sure what to do next, as we shivered in the rain.

'Your son gave my daughter a phone, although I forbade it,' Sylvie shouted. A vein seemed to be throbbing on her head, and although her face was red with anger, it was also puffy as if she had been crying. She needed someone to support her, I knew that, and if she'd had such a person maybe she would have been handling this whole situation better. But there was no one for her: her ex-husband didn't want to know and she had pushed everyone else away.

'Aleksy, that wasn't good,' Franceska said carefully. 'I promise you I didn't know, but Sylvie, can't we work things out? The kids want to spend time together, and they are both good kids.'

'Good kids don't lie and get phones when they've been forbidden.'

'I agree, Sylvie, and I will punish Aleksy but they just want to see each other. Perhaps if they were chaperoned?' Franceska suggested.

'What is this, the 1920s?' Claire said, unhelpfully. She blushed and shut up but I agreed with her.

'No, that won't work. I mean, who will do it? You work, I work, and well, just no. I told Connie she can date when she is sixteen,' Sylvie replied.

'But that's two years away!' Aleksy was horrified, and I noticed that he was still holding Connie's hand. My heart went out to him. Love was hard enough without it being forbidden.

'Can't we figure this out somehow?' Claire said. 'Sylvie, look at them, the lengths they've gone to to try to be together. Aleksy doesn't lie but he has done now, and that's only because you won't let him see Connie.'

'Oh, you mean leaving dead mice, birds and flowers on my doorstep.'

'Eh?' they all said. I wasn't sure how to own up to that, but then, as Sylvie continued, I decided not to.

'It scared me, like someone was warning me off,' she stormed. 'Why would you do that?'

'I didn't do that.' Aleksy scratched his head. 'I would never do anything to upset you.'

'Well, actually you have. The lengths you both have gone to are not acceptable, and I want this to stop now.'

If only you knew the lengths they were going to go to, and still might, I thought. Perhaps Dustbin and I should have let them run away. I mean, I have kind of championed running-away plans in my time . . . Well, actually only one, which ended up with George getting catnapped. And also Snowball had run away once when her family were all having a terrible time – that had been nothing to do with me, but she nearly died. Luckily Dustbin rescued her on my behest. But no, it was far too dangerous. And it would probably just make Sylvie lock Connie up. Oh, why was this one so hard to crack? I wished I had Tiger to talk through my thoughts with, she had always been my sounding board. She was also often my voice of reason, not that I always listened to her. And I wondered what she would say about the 'gifts' plan. Though I had a feeling she'd just laugh about that.

'Claire, Franceska, I have said it before, I think Connie is too young for a boyfriend, and it's as simple as that. She lived a very sheltered life in Japan and quite frankly I am looking to move her to an all-girls' school now. Her father thinks she should go back to Japan.' She looked and sounded threatening.

'But I love my new school, I've made friends, you can't send me away.' Connie burst into loud, angry tears.

'I think we need to sort this situation out, somehow, please,' Franceska pleaded, putting her arm around Aleksy. 'The children are so unhappy, surely we can work something out.'

I thought Sylvie might crack. Her daughter sobbing, my families being sensible, Aleksy so sad . . . But just as I thought she would, she shook her head.

'No, not at the moment. And take your phone back. When I say my daughter shouldn't have a phone, I don't expect to be defied. You say they're good kids but look, they went behind our backs. I can't stop you seeing each other in school for now.' She crossed her arms as if she would do soon. 'But I'm seriously looking at alternatives, so that is that. And you.' She pointed at Connie. 'Are grounded until further notice.'

'I'm never allowed out anyway,' Connie shouted and ran back in the house, slamming the door. With a final glare at Aleksy, Sylvie followed.

'Aleksy, that wasn't good of you,' Franceska said.

'But—'

'No, you never used to lie to us, but now look.' Even Franceska was angry now.

'Mum, please.'

'No, Aleksy, I support you as much as I can, but not when you lie to me and to Sylvie. It makes her seem less mad and more right, and for now I have to agree with her.'

It had put a bit of a dampener on the day, but George's excitement infected me. He was really looking forward to seeing Harold again, and after all he'd been through lately I certainly wasn't going to rain on his parade. Ha, the irony as the rain had ruined my neat looks and I had to dry myself off and then lick myself smooth again. Claire gave me a rub with a towel to help with the worst of it, then she went to change, and lent Franceska some clothes. Aleksy, covered in mud, had to get into a bath – thank goodness I didn't have to – before Claire sponged the worst of his trousers and then dried his clothes off on the radiator. It was quite a mission and we were worried we would be late for Harold's party with all that was going on.

Aleksy was upset, though everyone gave him a wide berth.

'Mum, can I go home rather than come to the party?' he asked, as he sat in his pants and socks. 'I really don't feel like it.'

'You come to the party,' Franceska stated, indicating the case was closed.

We set off, picking up Matt, Polly and the kids on the way. Toby was insisting on carrying George, but I had to walk,

275

and thankfully the rain had stopped as quickly as it started. I listened to my humans chatter as we went towards Harold's house. George and I had visited a few times while Harold was in hospital, seeing the progress being made. Having been around Seabreeze Cottage while they did lots of building work, I was quite the expert in home renovations, I liked to think.

'Oh no, my garden,' George said as Toby set him down in front of the house.

'Sorry, son, but they were always going to tidy it up for Harold,' I pointed out. It was no longer a jungle, but a very neat front garden. Grass trimmed, bushes cut back, and although the house wasn't quite painted yet, the front door had been smartened up, and I could see it was going to look very nice soon. Even if poor George no longer had his jungle.

Polly opened the door and let us in and the warmth hit me first, followed by the light. No more gloomy interior, that was for sure, and all the lights worked. Walls had been painted a bright white, the living room furniture had been replaced by a nice sofa and one of Claire and Jonathan's old armchairs. A coffee table sat neatly over new carpet and a bigger television hung on the wall. I ran to see the rest of the house. It was such a transformation. Still quite simple, but more homely. The kitchen hadn't changed but had been cleaned up, the hallway carpet had been replaced, there was a small dining table at one end of the sitting room, over-looking the small, but tidy, back garden. I thought Harold would be very pleased, even if George was not.

They had even insisted on getting Harold a small Christmas tree, which sat in the corner of the living room. It was adorned with lights and baubles, and I saw George eyeing it up.

'George, you cannot attack the tree before Harold even sees it,' I said.

'There is no fun in this house any more,' he complained as he slunk away. I flicked my tail. Kids!

Claire and Polly supervised Matt and Jonathan hanging a 'Welcome Home' banner across one wall. Franceska got Tommy to help her with the food in the kitchen, which as usual looked delicious, and Toby, Henry, Summer and Martha played happily in the living room with George. It was heart-warming after what we had just witnessed with Sylvie. If only she and Connie would be part of this, I knew it would help them, but it seemed there was no way to win Sylvie around. She didn't even seem to notice me, let alone allow me to charm her, and I had no ideas left. But I knew we would have to do something, we couldn't go on like this. Not my poor Aleksy. But clearly dead things as presents were off the menu.

We were all lined up in the living room when Marcus texted Matt to say he was just outside. Tomasz had just arrived, with even more food, and as we all stood there Harold came in, with his stick in one hand and his son holding the other arm.

'Welcome home,' everyone cheered at once and as Harold's eyes took in the scene they filled with tears. Oh no, we'd made another person cry today.

'I can't believe it,' he said. My eyes widened; he sounded moved rather than angry. 'I don't know how to thank you for all of this. I'm such a cantankerous old man, I don't deserve it, but I'm so happy to be home and what a lovely home it is. I don't know how to thank you. And you . . .'

I almost ran in front of George as Harold slowly bent down. Was he going to hurt him? Instead though he gave him a pet. Wow, who was this man?

'Thank you, clever cat, for saving my life, I'll never tell you to "get lost" again.' George purred and nuzzled into him, and I wondered where my thanks were. After all, I had gone and got the humans. I should have been used to being ignored by now, but you know, some appreciation would have been nice.

As they all crowded round Harold to show him the work they'd done to the house and then sat him down with food and a cup of tea, George, his new best friend, sat proudly next to him. I softened a bit. OK, so I was underappreciated at times but I had my George, so it was alright. And George needed any cheering up he could get.

'And I have told Dad that I'm moving in here for a while,' Marcus announced.

'You don't have to, son, and I'm sorry again about the whole divorce thing,' Harold said. Being in hospital had really changed him.

'No, we've put that firmly in the past where it belongs. Dad, I should never have let our row get out of hand. We're family, so I'm staying at least until after Christmas and then we'll see. I've arranged some home help for when I'm working, so you'll be looked after as you should.'

'And we're going to pop in and see you as well,' Jonathan said. He was quite fond of the old man; apparently they shared the same taste in football teams.

'Oh, and I was thinking, we're having a big Christmas this year, at our house,' Claire said. 'So why don't you both join us?'

I felt like squealing; this was the sort of situation I loved, bringing more people into our family circle.

'That's so kind,' Marcus said. 'And if you're sure we won't be in the way, then we'd love to. I'm not much of a cook.'

'He isn't,' Harold laughed. 'He can burn water.' Everyone laughed although I didn't quite understand what that meant. It was a shame I couldn't get Sylvie there, after all she and Marcus, well they were both divorced, both nice-looking, a similar age . . . Although one of them was insane. But then no one, not even me, was perfect.

'You might have to bring a couple of chairs,' Polly laughed.

'Deal.'

'Daddy, George is in the Christmas tree,' Summer shouted and everyone moved at breakneck speed to find George sitting in the middle of the tree, a tangle of lights.

When he'd been untangled and sat back on the floor I went up to him.

'What did I say?' I chastised.

'You said, don't attack the tree before Harold sees it. Well he's seen it now.'

I couldn't argue with that.

# Chapter
# Thirty

Chapter
Thirty

How we got to Christmas Eve, I don't know, but it was now upon us. December tended to do that. With the excitement of the decorations, the nativity, Aleksy and then Harold, it had been one of the busiest Decembers for my humans, and especially for me. It was flying by, and giving me very little time to enjoy the festivities or to grieve, both of which I wanted, and needed, to do. However, I was trying very hard to put everything aside to enjoy today.

Christmas Eve was a very special day with all my families. Even Tomasz took the day off from the restaurants. And he closed them all on Christmas Day and Boxing Day, he said it was important for him and his staff to have family time. The only problem was that my families weren't together on Christmas Eve, so I had to travel if I wanted to see everyone. Claire and Jonathan were busy with last-minute preparations for the big day. Claire was preparing any food that she could ready in advance and Jonathan had to try to keep two very hyperactive children and one hyperactive kitten entertained and calm, which was no easy feat. I did try to help him but it was impossible. He gave up and took them out to the park to try to run off some of their excitement, and he called for Matt, who came with Henry and Martha. Polly was doing some last-minute shopping, which she always did. She was always a last-minute person, whereas Claire was super organised. I just hoped she remembered to buy enough cream for pudding because I was especially looking forward to that.

I was determined to put any sadness about Tiger away for the day; if George could do it then so could I. I still missed her and I knew she would be the one cat I wanted to visit today but couldn't. Nonetheless, Christmas was a time for fun, and I was going to do my very best.

It had been a bittersweet time since Harold's welcome-home party. He and Marcus were firmly part of our family now. They sort of fitted in as if they had always been there, actually. Marcus was funny, kind, and had been very hurt by his ex-wife, which would have made him perfect for Sylvie, if she hadn't been quite so unhinged. Though I had to stop thinking that, as I had quite enough to cope with without trying to matchmake. But I couldn't help it, I was still hoping for a way to get my next-door neighbours back into the fold, but so far my one-sided conversations with Tiger hadn't yielded any inspiration.

My other friends hadn't exactly been full of helpful advice; even Elvis hadn't seen a TV show about it. It was as if, without Tiger, we were devoid of plans, and I hoped that my career of helping people hadn't died with her. The gap she left in our friendship group, our family, our relationships was vast and obvious to us all. She had been like the glue that held us all together in a way and, without her, we had to try that bit harder, but all the while knowing something, or rather someone was missing.

George was now coping so much better than I ever imagined he would. He missed her, he talked about his 'Tiger mum' a lot, in a way which made me want to weep, but he also kept himself busy. He visited Harold, those two were thick as thieves, and I let him have space for that friendship, as I did with Hana. He told me how he would sit next to Harold on his new sofa, watching a TV show about 'very old things' and eating biscuits dunked in tea, which was now George's new favourite food. I have to admit I couldn't resist going to spy on them a little. I managed to watch them sometimes, keeping out of sight on the front window, and they did look very sweet together – not something I ever thought I would say about angry Harold. But he wasn't angry any more, he was happy, and as I knew from my years of experience, happiness changes people for the better, which was why I was such an advocate.

George had also been spending time with Hana in their house, though sadly that had stopped this week, as Susan, the cleaner, had gone away on holiday until after Christmas. He was trying to persuade Hana to come outside but she wouldn't, or rather she couldn't. But, George, a chip off the old block, wasn't giving up, and said that he was going to redouble his efforts in the new year and was hopeful that by summer she might have experienced the great outdoors. I was happy for him to have a project. She was lovely, Hana, but he said she was homesick, and also of course she was living with two miserable people. Although Hana didn't complain, it was all so sad for her, and now George couldn't even go in and cheer her up and they'd had to go back to having their through-the-window conversations.

'You see, Dad,' George explained to me, very maturely, I may add. 'I miss Tiger mum, but I know she would be pleased because I am spending time with a lonely person and cat, and then they aren't quite as lonely when I'm there.'

I thought I would burst with pride for my lovely, kind, caring kitten. Tiger and I had both taught him well.

Christmas Eve passed in a whirl of activity with all the families that George and I decided to visit. We always spent Christmas Eve together and liked to think we were a bit like Santa cats as we delivered good cheer to everyone we cared about. Although we didn't dress up. Claire had tried to dress me up once and let's just say it didn't end well for any of us.

We started with Harold. Marcus and he were laughing in the living room as we sat on the windowsill until they let us in. Their Christmas tree was wonky and even George didn't seem keen on trying to jump onto it any more, which was a bit of a relief for me. They were both preparing sprouts, which they were going to bring to us for lunch tomorrow, and some other vegetables which were all very sensible, and not terribly tempting for us cats. But Marcus said he also had bought some nice wine, chocolates for the adults and a big jar of sweets for the children, which I knew would be gratefully received. He looked at George and I, and then winked at his dad.

'We've got a present for the lovely cats too,' he said. My ears pricked at this and I hoped it was some kind of fish. Although I think George was hoping for dunked biscuits.

'We better had, these cats deserve a medal,' Harold said, affectionately, and I basked in the fact I'd been acknowledged for once. But I would much rather have had pilchards than a medal. I wasn't even sure what a medal was.

We left them a little while later full of good cheer and went to visit Polly and Matt. Matt was trying to get the children to sit still and watch a film, but they weren't really in the mood. They were both so excited, babbling about what Santa would bring them, and even Martha, who was normally quite chilled out, was bouncing around.

'Alfie and George,' Henry beamed, as we entered the living room.

'Oh good, we can play,' Martha said and Matt just shook his head in defeat. Their living room was decorated beautifully but then as Polly was an interior designer we all expected nothing less. Their tree was so tasteful, and she got away with it by giving the children their own tree to decorate, which was in the corner of the living room and was a bit of a mess. Polly told Claire it was alright because you couldn't really see it, but George loved it because he could jump on it, which totally ruined it, but made the children laugh. I despaired along with Matt, but Polly said he could do anything to that tree as long as he didn't touch hers. For once, George actually took notice of this and didn't dare go near her tree. No one did, not even Matt.

Matt and Polly were the best at decorating, they had lights outside the house and reindeer scattered around the small front garden. Claire had begged Jonathan for something similar but he'd refused, saying that he'd probably fall off the ladder, or it would take him all of December to do, as our house was bigger, so it was left undecorated outside. It was the only battle that Jonathan won really, and as Claire wasn't going to do it herself she said the kids could just admire Polly and Matt's.

Polly came downstairs, looking a little flustered, which wasn't like her.

'I've run out of Sellotape,' she said. 'And I've still got loads of wrapping to do.' You see, she was so disorganised.

'The shops will be closed now,' Matt said. Even he looked alarmed. 'Are all the kids—'

'No,' Polly said quickly. 'I need more.'

'Meow,' I said. Claire will always have spare, I tried to tell her. Claire had drawers full of it, we never ran out.

'Oh Alfie, thank goodness, I'll just nip to Claire's to borrow some. Are you sure you're OK with the kids?' Polly asked.

'Not really, but then they've eaten a mountain of choco- late coins, so what did I expect?' I'd never seen a man look so defeated. 'Actually, shall I go get the Sellotape?' he asked, smiling at the idea of escape.

'No, I think I'd better go,' Polly said. 'After all, we've still got loads to do before the carol concert and you'll probably have a drink with Jonathan . . .' She was right, he would, and I could see from the disappointment on his face that that was what he had been hoping for.

I cheered up at the mention of the concert. There was always a Christmas Eve carol concert for the children at the local church, and although George and I didn't get to go, it meant that Franceska and family would visit us either before the concert or after, so I would get to see them briefly. I'd have liked to have seen Dustbin but we really didn't have time. Christmas Eve was a busy day for us all, as I've said.

After we left Matt and the children trying to sort out the small Christmas tree that George had all but squashed, we went to see our friends. They were all waiting to wish us a

Merry Christmas and we chatted about what we were looking forward to most about the following day.

'Food,' I said, which was true. 'And all the humans I love being together of course.'

'I like the wrapping paper,' George said. He hadn't grown out of playing with that yet either.

'Oh, I do love the fact that we have visitors all day and they make such a fuss of me,' Nellie said.

'I like the fact I get to sleep a lot, because my lot go out for quite a while and there's nothing like a good Christmas Day nap.' I wasn't sure I agreed with Rocky but as long as he was happy.

'I like the Queen's Speech,' Elvis declared. 'She does it every year on TV, and when she comes on we all go quiet and listen very intently. It wouldn't be Christmas without it.'

No one knew quite what to say about that. I had never even heard of it. But anyway, we passed a pleasant few minutes before I felt something wet landing on my fur.

'Oh no, it's raining,' I said.

'No, Dad, it's not raining, it's snowing!' George said. 'Look.' We all looked up at the sky and snow was actually falling. We all stuck our tongues out to catch it, and it definitely made us all feel even more Christmassy.

'Do you think Tiger sent the snow?' Nellie asked as a fat snowdrop landed on her head.

'Probably, she hated snow,' I laughed.

Walking home, George kept trying to catch the snow with his tongue, and because he wasn't looking where he was going he walked into a lamppost.

'Ow,' he said.

'Look where you're going, silly,' I replied, but actually catching snow was quite fun, I had to concede. We both stopped naturally when we got to Tiger's house. There were lights inside and I wondered how the Barkers were coping without Tiger. There was still no tree, I could see through the window, and only a small amount of decorations, but I hoped they were OK. I would have liked to have seen them really, but since Tiger had died they never opened the cat flap, and as it was so cold I doubted they would venture out.

'Do you think Tiger mum is happy where she is?' George asked, suddenly.

'I do, son,' I replied. 'She can't be over-the-moon happy because she's not with you, but I think she's not in pain and that must be a good thing.'

'I know, I miss her but I'm glad she's not in pain, any more. Dad?'

'Yes, George?' I could barely speak.

'Loving is about letting go, isn't it?'

'Yes, George,' I managed, my throat choked up. It really was.

When we got home, thankfully the warmth hit us as soon as we got through the cat flap. Everyone was in a state about the snow.

'What if it settles?' Claire panicked. 'People won't be able to get out and then it could be a problem.'

'Everyone can walk here and if we need to help, like with Harold, I can go and give Marcus a hand. So don't worry, it'll be fine, darling. In fact, more than fine, it's going to be the best Christmas,' Jonathan reassured. 'We're together, we've got our gorgeous two children, our amazing cats and our best friends coming, what more could we want?'

'I know, I'm sorry. I wish that Sylvie and Connie would come though, I feel so sorry for them, and I know they'll have a miserable Christmas. Especially Connie.'

'You might need a Christmas miracle for that one. I'm not sure even Santa can sort that out.'

I wished I could give them that miracle but I was all out of ideas. Part of me still wondered if Dustbin and I had been right to stop the kids from running away but I knew, deep down, it had been our only option. It was too dangerous out there for them. I was going to have to keep thinking, or – like Claire – hope for a miracle.

By the time Tomasz, Franceska and the boys arrived before the carol concert, I was exhausted from trying to think. However, Aleksy took me aside immediately. Well, he picked me up. I narrowed my eyes at him. What was he up to now? I hoped we weren't going to try to look for Connie again. But instead of heading outside, he took me upstairs.

'Look, Alfie, I know you were only visiting Dustbin the night I was running away, but it was probably good that you were there,' he said when we were out of earshot in Toby's bedroom.

'Yowl.' I wasn't, I was trying to stop you.

'I thought it was a good idea, when you and Dustbin made the commotion and stopped me going, I really had to think about things and Connie did too. We realised running away was a terrible idea. We have very little money, I spent most of mine on her phone, and what job would I get at my age?'

'Meow.' I raised my eyes to the heavens, it was madness.

'And it's dangerous out there, I know that, but you see Connie was so sad and I just wanted to make things better. But somehow I made them worse because now she doesn't even have the phone any more and her mum hates me.'

'Yowl.' She does.

'Anyway, I have a plan and I think you might approve of this one.'

I put my paws over my ears. I had a bad feeling.

'No, honestly, there's no risk to either of us. You see, tonight I am going to come to Connie's and she is going to meet me and then we are going to hide, so that come morning when everyone gets up they'll see we're missing and they'll worry but then we appear and say we were pushed so far to make a point that we want to be together and then they have to let us.'

'YOWL!' Could I voice my disapproval any more? Doing this on Christmas morning! It was a terrible idea. The worst.

'Right, of course how did we concoct this with no phone? Well, that's the clever part. Connie's best friend, Sophie Hawker, is also my friend and we live on the same street. She went to visit Connie and she gave her a note from me. Her mum didn't even suspect a thing. Clever, huh?'

He looked so pleased with himself, I really felt like scratching some sense into him, but I wasn't going to use violence, it didn't solve anything. And I couldn't do that to my Aleksy. Not unless I really had to.

'And then Connie gave Sophie a note for me agreeing to the plan!' His eyes sparkled.

'Mewmewmewmew.' This was quite possibly the worst plan I'd ever heard. What Aleksy was suggesting was ruining everyone's Christmas morning by going missing. I knew how I'd felt when George went missing, it had been the worst time ever. Aleksy was going to put his parents, Tommy and Sylvie through that? Even for an hour it was too much and it would ruin Christmas. Totally ruin it.

'I knew you'd approve. And we won't ruin Christmas as we'll only be gone for a bit.'

'Yowl?' How could I stop this one, I thought, as my poor overworked brain started whirring.

'The best bit is that we're going to hide in your shed, so we'll only be in your garden. And I'll set my alarm so we don't leave it too late to tell everyone we're fine. Hopefully before they call the police.' His eyes clouded over slightly at that mention.

Oh no. I put my paws over my eyes. Of course, they'd call the police straight away. This was not good. Not good at all, I had to put a stop to this madness, but how?

# Chapter Thirty-One

Chapter
Thirty-One

This Christmas Eve was not going according to plan at all any more. I should have been relaxing in the warm with my boy while the families all went to the carol concert, but no, no I had to go and clear up yet another mess that my humans were making. I knew Aleksy was young so I really tried to give him some kind of concession, but this was possibly the worst plan I'd heard, and trust me, I had heard and even been the mastermind of quite a few. None that involved ruining Christmas, though.

And now I was going to have to save it.

I toyed with the idea of not telling George, but after all I had told him he needed to be open with me, so I felt I should do the same with him. I filled him in, but I downplayed it a bit; even so, he was shocked. He had been to visit Hana to wish her a Happy Christmas Eve through the glass door and she obviously had no idea what the kids were up to. I said the best thing would be for him to stay home to make sure all was alright here, while I went to see Dustbin. By giving him a very important job I managed to persuade him to wait at home. I was a little annoyed, as I was looking forward to a relaxing festive evening with my family, but of course life didn't always give us what we wanted, did it?

My legs were so weary as I made my way there, but I had no option. The snow was falling more heavily – I had to be careful, as it was slippery under paw in certain parts. I felt as if my fur was freezing to my body, as worry flowed through me. We had to sort this out, and I had only one idea. Dustbin was in the yard having a rest by the bins. Obviously the rodents had scrammed.

'Alfie, what a surprise.' He stood up and stretched out. Poor Dustbin seemed tired as well.

'I know. It's Christmas Eve and it's snowing, and I've had a really full day, but Aleksy came to my house and he confided in me that he and Connie are going to run away tonight.'

'Oh no, that's terrible.'

'Yes, but the best or worst bit – I can't figure out which – is that they are only planning on hiding in our garden shed for a while. They think if they scare the parents just for a short time, they will see sense, or Sylvie will, and let them see each other.' I was almost tripping over my words.

'This sounds like one of your plans,' he pointed out. Not terribly helpfully, I might add.

'Well, yes, normally I would, perhaps, agree but I wouldn't do anything at Christmas. Christmas is, well, Christmas, no one should mess with Christmas.' I was getting quite worked up now. 'Imagine Franceska, Tomasz and Tommy waking up on Christmas morning to find Aleksy missing, it'll be awful, and the same for Sylvie, only worse as she's all alone. And then they'll call Claire and Jonathan, which will ruin Christmas morning for the little ones, and the same with Matt and Polly as everyone aborts normal Christmas festivities to find the idiots!' The more I thought about it the worse it sounded.

'Oh dear, what a mess.' Dustbin could sometimes be a bit too calm, although as I was so worked up, that might not have been such a bad thing. 'So, we'll stop him like we did last time,' he suggested, licking his paw.

'No, we can't because Connie is going to meet him in the garden shed.' I was so agitated. I suddenly wanted to knock the heads of a number of my humans together. Sylvie, for being so ridiculous about keeping these two apart, them for this silly plot, and well the mood I was in, I could probably find a reason for all of them. Happiness was so precious, so fleeting, why couldn't they see that?

'Um, I see.' Dustbin licked his other paw and glared angrily at a mouse who was trying to approach. The mouse took one look at him and scurried away. 'I almost feel bad not letting them in in this weather, but you know, a job's a job.' He raised his tail.

'Dustbin, back to the matter at hand,' I snapped.

'Oh yes, so what do you think we should do?' he asked. He looked at me with sympathy in his eyes and I knew I was being unfair, snapping at him, so I tried to calm down.

'Well, I was thinking there is only one thing to do, and that is for me to somehow get Jonathan and Claire to discover them tonight, so the morning isn't ruined.'

'Good thinking. So what can I do to help?'

Now I could see us being able to foil this plan, I was beginning to feel calmer.

'It's a big ask but I wondered if you could follow Aleksy, you know, make sure he's OK. He shouldn't be wandering the streets at night, even if it's only to our house.'

'Right, that's good, yes that'll work. And then when I get to your place I'll bang on the cat flap to let you know they are in the shed, so you can alert the humans straight away.'

'Perfect. You really are such a good friend, Dustbin.' I felt emotional, probably because I was so tired, angry, missing

Tiger, and the idea that Christmas might be ruined, it was all getting on top of me.

'No, you are. And you take care of these families so well. Right, so I'll let you know when they are there. You will have to really make a fuss to get Jonathan and Claire out though.'

'Oh, don't worry, I seem to have had a lot of experience doing that lately.' I really had. And although they sometimes could be a bit slow on the uptake, they seemed to get what I was telling them in the end. After all, that was how I had saved Harold. I just hoped I could stay awake long enough, I was so cat-tired (Yes, I know the expression is dog-tired but I would never compare myself to a dog.)

'Right you are. We'll sort this out and, you never know, the shock of them actually running away, albeit to a garden shed, might even make her mother see sense. I hope so, Aleksy is such a good lad.'

I nodded, I did understand. Love wasn't always easy; I had learnt that the hard way.

My house was once again a hive of activity when I returned home, brushing the snow off my fur and warming my bones by the radiator.

'Oh there you are, Alfie. I was wondering where you'd been. I can't believe you went out in this weather,' Claire said.

'Meow.' It wasn't my choice.

'Never mind, it's so Christmassy, isn't it? The first white Christmas in goodness knows how many years. The kids were so excited at the concert and getting them into bed was a mission. Thankfully they know that Santa only visits sleeping children, so they seem to have gone off now. And

George is tucked up with Toby, in case you were wondering.'

I was, but I'd assumed that was where he'd be. When I was dry and warm I was going to go and say goodnight to him.

'And Jonathan and I have quite a lot to do before we're ready for tomorrow. But I'm so excited. The snow, the big lunch with all our friends. It's going to be wonderful,' she gushed, she was so full of Christmas cheer. I hoped it was contagious.

As I thought about Aleksy and Connie, I wondered what would happen when they were discovered. Either all the parents would be so angry the teenagers would be grounded forever, or they would see how much the two of them meant to each other and Sylvie would relent and maybe we'd all spend a wonderful Christmas together. I knew which one I wanted it to be. I also knew which one I thought it would be.

After kissing my boy goodnight, I went to wait by the cat flap. That way, I knew if I went to sleep I would hear Dustbin when he arrived. I wondered what Tiger would have said to me if she was here, but I thought I knew. She would have said that Aleksy's crazy plan was too much like one of mine, and that perhaps my humans were more influenced by me than we'd realised. I would be to blame for all of this, but then she would have approved of the way I was putting it right, I'm sure. I did feel responsible but then I cared too much about everyone's happiness. I was learning that there was only so much this cat could do, however, and although I would never give up trying, sometimes I couldn't find ways to solve everything. I still hadn't figured out how to bring Sylvie and Connie back into the fold, and I hadn't found a way of getting

Hana out of the house – although of course I had discovered a way to get George in. Harold and his son had been reunited thanks to George and I, but that had been mainly George. Although I had achieved a fair bit, thinking about it. Just not everything, and I wasn't a cat who liked loose ends.

Claire and Jonathan approached.

'Honey, can't we go to bed yet?' Jonathan yawned.

'Not until all our gifts are under the tree, and let's have a last glass of champagne, so we can toast our Christmas Eve together. And it was perfect, wasn't it? I can't believe that Harold even sang at the carol concert, he really enjoyed himself.'

'Yeah, and Marcus is a top bloke. I like him.'

'If only Sylvie would meet him, he'd take her mind off all the awfulness in her life,' Claire said.

'Meow,' I agreed.

'Oh Alfie, I thought you were asleep. Why are you lying by the cat flap?' Jonathan asked. 'Santa comes down the chimney, not through the cat flap,' he laughed. I swished my tail. Very funny.

'Very funny, Jon, now come and have a drink, honestly, it will help you finish the wrapping.'

'We'll be up all night at this rate,' he complained.

'I want it to be perfect for Summer and Toby when they wake up at the crack of dawn,' Claire said. I thought Jonathan might voice another of his objections but instead he put his arm around Claire and kissed the top of her head.

'And so do I, darling, so let's get going and be tucked up in bed in time for the real Santa to come.'

I let Jonathan scratch my ears and I hoped that Dustbin would arrive first.

# Chapter Thirty-Two

Chapter
Thirty-Two

I must have fallen asleep, but I heard the cat flap bang and jumped up in an instant. I put my head through and saw Dustbin's eyes staring back at me. In a second I was out in the freezing cold next to him.

'They're here?'

'Yup, they went through with the crazy plan. Aleksy shivered all the way here, it's so cold, and the shed is probably freezing. It's lucky we're not leaving them until morning, they'd probably get hypothermia,' Dustbin replied. 'Anyway, I checked they were inside before I came to get you, didn't want them seeing me this time.'

Although the snow had stopped, there was a thin carpet of it in the garden. I could see their footprints, and also Dustbin's paw prints.

'Right, I guess it's showtime,' I said. Dustbin nodded.

'Good luck, Alfie, I'll wait just round here out of sight in case you need me.'

I went back inside. Claire and Jonathan were in their pyjamas, just about to switch the lights off in the living room and go to bed. Oh boy, I thought, as the tiredness weighed heavily on me, I had to get this right.

'MEWMEWMEWMEWMEW,' I screeched at the top of my lungs. Then I ran in circles.

'Oh, not this again,' Jonathan said. 'What now? For goodness sake, Alfie, it's midnight, on Christmas Eve, which means it's technically Christmas morning and I for one want my bed.'

'Alfie, shush, you'll wake the children, now go to bed,' Claire said. Oh dear, they were obviously so tired they weren't getting it.

'YOWLYOWLYOWL.' I tried to stand on Claire's foot but she pulled it away and I fell on my tail. I got up and ran some more circles. Normally Claire was the quicker of the two but it was very late.

'I really think he's trying to tell us something.' Jonathan scratched his head. Thank goodness. I headed to the back door, mewing all the way.

'He wants us to go outside?' Claire said, uncertainly.

'What, in this weather? Alfie, you've got to be joking.'

'MEOW.' I really wasn't. I headed through the cat flap, crossing my paws that they would follow. After a few seconds I saw the door open and two sets of eyes peered out at me.

'You go, Jon,' Claire said.

'But I've got my slippers on.'

'So have I,' Claire replied. I wished at least one of them would just hurry up and come.

'OK, let me just put my shoes on.' Jonathan went off and came back, his feet stuffed into some trainers. 'Come on then,' he said, glancing back at Claire as he stepped outside. 'This had better be good.'

Oh it would be, I thought, as I started to lead him to the shed. He ran his hands through his hair and turned back to Claire.

'I think he wants me to go to the shed,' he said.

'What if there's someone in there? They might be dangerous,' Claire replied. She went to the kitchen and came back with a saucepan. Forgetting she had her slippers on, she ran to Jonathan and handed it to him.

'What's that for?'

'In case you need to hit them,' Claire said.

'You honestly think Alfie is telling us that there's someone dangerous in our shed?' He sounded a little bit panicked.

'No idea but to be on the safe side,' Claire said sensibly.

'It's probably a cat. You know, a stray cat that we'll end up having to give a home to, or maybe it's Santa.' Jonathan laughed and I swished him with my tail again, this was no time for jokes.

'YOWL.' Would you just open the door already? Claire gave Jonathan a little push and, saucepan in hand, he tentatively opened the door. A scream from inside filled the air, as Jonathan flung the door wide open.

'Oh my goodness,' Claire said as the three of us stared at Aleksy and Connie, huddled together in the shed, wrapped in dusty old painting blankets.

'What the hell?' Jonathan shouted. He was still holding the saucepan up.

'Oh dear,' Aleksy said. Yet another understatement. Jonathan shook his head, and looked at Claire.

'Right, I'll go and call Franceska,' Claire said. 'And then I'm going to get your mum, Connie.' She sounded angry. 'Blimey you two, it's freezing, are you both mad?' Without waiting for an answer she ran back to the house. I was tempted to go with her but I wanted to see how this was going to play out.

'What were you thinking, Aleksy? You idiot.' Jonathan didn't mince his words. He finally let his arm with the saucepan drop.

'We just want to be allowed to see each other,' Aleksy said, his voice wobbly. He was still my sensitive boy and he seemed younger than ever as he held onto Connie's hand.

'Yeah, mate, but running away on Christmas Eve, it's madness. What if your mum, dad and Tommy woke up and found you weren't there? And you, Connie, your mum is alone, she'd be absolutely terrified. Honestly, I could bang your heads together. It was irresponsible and stupid and you could have ruined Christmas. Right, come inside before I get frostbite.'

If I could have spoken, I would have said exactly the same, I thought proudly.

As both Connie and Aleksy slunk into the house after Jonathan, I went to see Dustbin.

'Great job tonight,' I said. 'Thank you so much.'

'You did well, Alfie. Try to get some sleep though, big day tomorrow.'

'Everyone is coming here, why don't you pop over?' I said. I didn't like the idea of Dustbin being alone on Christmas Day, although I knew he wouldn't mind. He liked being alone.

'Nah, big rodent day, they think they deserve to get more food at Christmas, so can't risk taking any time off,' he said. I grinned and raised my whiskers.

'You work too hard.'

'You and me both.' He wasn't wrong. 'See you, Alfie.'

'Happy Christmas, Dustbin,' I said.

'And to you. I know it's going to be hard for you, missing Tiger, but keep the courage, Alfie, and I'll see you soon.'

I watched as he seemed to disappear into the night.

★     ★     ★

Aleksy and Connie were sitting on the sofa looking very guilty. Jonathan was pacing up and down, delivering a lecture about how irresponsible they were. He seemed to be enjoying it, and actually was doing a pretty good job. I gave Aleksy my best disapproving look.

'How come you came to the shed?' Aleksy asked.

'Alfie made us.' They all turned to look at me. I examined my paw closely; honestly, sometimes humans weren't the smartest.

'But how did he know?' Connie asked.

'I told him,' Aleksy said. They all glanced over at me again. My paw was suddenly very interesting. 'I had to confide in someone but I didn't think that he understood it.' He turned to Connie in confusion.

'He's a cat,' she said.

'Yes, we do know that,' Jonathan snapped. 'He probably just heard a noise from the shed and thought I should investigate it.' Their suspicious glances were increasing.

'But he's a cat,' Connie said again. 'He can't have known we were there.'

'He's more than a cat,' Aleksy said and I felt proud. At least he noticed. 'But maybe he did just hear something, but that other time—' Aleksy quickly clamped his hand over his mouth.

'What other time?' Jonathan narrowed his eyes. We all stayed quiet. 'Anyway, back to the matter at hand,' he said. 'I know you think your mum's being unreasonable and unfair,' he went on. 'But Connie, she's had a bit of a hard time. I lived in Singapore and I lost my job, and had to come back here. I know it wasn't a divorce, actually it was worse than that.'

'Meow.' OK, maybe not that good of a job.

'Oh right, maybe not worse, but anyway it was a huge adjustment and I had a very hard time processing what happened to me. I probably was depressed and not very nice to anyone, actually including Alfie.'

'Meow.' He certainly wasn't very nice. He kept throwing me out of the house in actual fact.

'I definitely was depressed. Anyway, when people are depressed they sometimes act in a way which might not seem rational.' Like throwing charming cats out of your house, I thought. 'Connie, you are the casualty of this, I can see that, but you know you and your mum need each other and you're a team. I know it's a lot for you to have gone through too, and you are the kid, but she needs your support. Don't get me wrong, I'm on your side here.'

Really? It didn't sound like it.

'But you know, you have school and your new friends, and your mum, well I think she's a bit lost at the moment. So as much as it's not your responsibility, you need to try to understand, honestly it will make life better for both of you. And then she might come round to Aleksy, you know.'

I take it back, it wasn't that bad after all.

'Jonathan, we are sorry,' Aleksy said. 'I just didn't know what to do, and it seemed a good idea.'

'It was a terrible idea. Aleksy, tell everyone you are sorry and that you will never do anything so irresponsible again. Making people worry isn't the way to solve anything.'

I purred my agreement, I had thought it a good idea once but not any more.

Claire, wearing a coat and some boots over her nightwear, came in, her arm around a crying Sylvie.

'Your father is on his way too, Aleksy,' Claire said. 'Your mum couldn't leave Tommy on his own so she'll save her shouting for when you get home. She really wasn't happy with you.'

'I'm sorry, Mum.' Connie burst into tears and flung herself at Sylvie.

'Oh Connie, to think you had to run away. What have I done?' They were both sobbing, arms around each other, as Tomasz arrived.

'So, Aleksy, you want to tell me what happened?' Tomasz said. He looked as if he had been woken up, thrown on the first clothes he could find, his hair was dishevelled and he didn't even have that much of it.

'We were stupid. But you know we just wanted to be able to see each other. We weren't going to do anything bad, but we wanted you to know how serious we were and the only thing I could think of was running away, but the first time we tried—'

'You mean you tried before?' Claire screeched.

'Oh.' Aleksy clearly regretted mentioning it again; when would he learn? 'Yes, we did, but then I got downstairs and Alfie and Dustbin started making such a noise that I thought they would wake you up – so we had to abort it and then we realised that London was dangerous and so we weren't going to run away because that was silly.'

'I'm not sure I've heard anything like this before,' Tomasz said. He looked a little lost.

'So then we thought we'd just pretend. And yes, we realise now it was very bad to make you wake up on Christmas morning with us gone, but we were desperate.' He had tears in his eyes, which I knew he would push back. Aleksy felt he was too grown-up to cry. In truth, no one was ever too grown-up to cry.

'And you were going to sleep in the shed all night?' Tomasz continued. Sylvie was listening, but she was also still hugging Connie.

'Well, actually I don't think we would have in the end, because it was very cold.'

'Worst runaways ever,' Jonathan said, and Claire swiped him as that wasn't very helpful. 'Honestly, it was just like the nativity scene,' he continued, rubbing his arm. 'Mary and Joseph wrapped in old blankets in a shed.'

'It wasn't quite like that, Jon.' Claire rolled her eyes.

'I am sorry,' Sylvie said. 'To all of you and to Aleksy and Connie. If I'd known how miserable I was making you, but then . . . I'm struggling, Con, darling. I miss having your father help me with parenting and I feel a bit lost in London, like I don't know anyone, and well I shouldn't stop you from having a life. I still think you're too young for a boyfriend but if you're willing to abide by rules then I guess we can figure it out. I don't want you to feel that you want to get away from me, I love you.'

'I will, I'll do anything,' Connie said, her eyes full of hope.

'Me too,' Aleksy said. 'Even if we aren't alone ever, we don't care.' He sounded so excited.

'But you will be punished,' Tomasz said, unsurely.

Jonathan patted him on the back. 'Hey, how about we let

it go for now? It was stupid but I think they've learnt their lesson and it is technically Christmas Day.' I went to rub Jonathan's leg; he was right. 'We'll put him on washing-up duty or something tomorrow,' he laughed.

'And I know Frankie will just be relieved to have her boy home,' Claire added.

'OK. So maybe no punishment, I don't know what to do in this situation but we better get home and let Claire and Jonathan go to sleep.'

'Yes the kids will be up early and we've got a big lunch to prepare. Sylvie, Connie, please will you join us?'

'Oh, no, we couldn't. Sorry, but we just couldn't.' Sylvie said, almost pushing Connie out of the house.

'Please?' Aleksy asked.

'No, we have plans, I'm sorry,' she added and they were gone.

'That was strange. Just as I thought she was being reasonable?' Jonathan said.

'I think perhaps she's too embarrassed to see everyone at once,' Claire said. I agreed with her. 'You know she's sort of fallen out with all of us, and she probably thinks she needs to build bridges but Christmas Day, us all en masse, it might be a bit much.'

I thought that Claire was spot on. The thing was that a broken heart was a terrible thing, and Sylvie definitely had one of those. As did I. However, I seemed to be coping better, more rationally, than she did, which was darn lucky for my family.

'You see, I'm no good at this stuff, I never even thought of that.' Poor Tomasz looked perplexed. 'Right, young man, come on, let's get you home.'

Aleksy was smiling, he was allowed to see Connie. Tomasz, Claire and Jonathan seemed pleased with the outcome, and I was too. It was a Christmas miracle after all and it seemed I had saved our Christmas.

# Chapter
# Thirty-Three

The excitement of Christmas Day was something I would never tire of, despite being incredibly worn out. But we had rallied, when woken by the kids at 'silly o'clock', as Jonathan called it. George was excited by the prospect of his wrapping paper and so was encouraging the children to rip open their presents, hopping around them as they did so. As he blew a stray piece off his head, I looked on affectionately. Happy Christmas.

Everyone was fizzing around, a bit like the drink that Claire and Jonathan had. Although it was champagne, it had orange juice in it which made it suitable for breakfast apparently, although not for children or cats it seemed.

The presents were soon opened. Toby was so happy he was beside himself, and Jonathan who had to help him with some very complicated Lego, was beside himself but not with happiness as he struggled. He kept scratching his head and looking pleadingly at Claire. Summer had added even more dolls to her collection and apparently Santa was the cleverest person in the world, as he had got everything right. George was in wrapping-paper heaven although we did have to untangle him at one point when he got himself stuck with Sellotape, but everyone was cheerful. Including me. Because seeing everyone I loved having such a nice time warmed my heart. I knew how lucky we all were: we were warm, fed, loved and it made me sad for anyone who wasn't as lucky as us. But I couldn't dwell on that today, I had a kitten to unwrap from the tinsel he'd liberated from the windowsill.

I hoped Tiger could see us, she would have enjoyed this scene, and although I missed her with every piece of fur on my body, I couldn't help but smile as I heard her voice wishing us, 'Happy Christmas.' It was a happy Christmas, but a sad one too. But then life was all about balances and contrasts in feelings after all.

'Right, I've showered and now I better start cooking,' Claire said. She was wearing a bright red jumper with a Christmas tree on it. Jonathan was supposed to wear a matching one but he claimed to have lost it. I knew that it was hidden as I heard him say it was 'ridiculous' and that he wouldn't 'be seen dead wearing it'. Which was a phrase I didn't understand. But anyway, Claire looked quite Christmassy as she tied on an apron. I was not only excited for lunch but also the knowledge that my other families would be here soon.

'Do you want a hand?' Jonathan asked, looking pleadingly at her as he studied the Lego instructions. Jonathan didn't like cooking but it was clearly easier than putting a Lego spaceship together.

'No, you carry on with Toby.' Claire grinned.

'Yay!' Toby said, and then stared very intently at Jonathan, who was still scratching his head.

'Mummy, can you help me with my car?' Summer asked. She'd been given a pink car which spun around when operated with a remote control. She wasn't the best driver, though, my tail had already been run over and George had had a few close calls.

'Darling, I have to start cooking. Toby, can you help her for a moment?'

Toby looked thoughtful, as if weighing up the Lego or his sister.

'OK, but only for a minute,' he said, as suddenly and without warning the Christmas tree lights went off.

'Oh no, they must have fused,' Jonathan said, jumping up and trying the living room lights. But they didn't come on either. 'Strange, I wonder if it's tripped?' he said, going to the hallway where the fuse box was. 'No, it's not tripped,' he said, sounding confused just as the phone rang.

'Oh my goodness. The power in the whole of Edgar Road is out,' Claire screamed, as she lowered the phone from her ear.

'What do you mean?' Jonathan asked.

'No power. None at all. How am I supposed to cook Christmas lunch?' She looked at the handset, which she was still holding. 'Sorry, Pol, I'm just in shock, I'll call you back,' she said, hanging up.

'What are we going to do?' Jonathan said. We all stood in the semi-darkness in horror. What was Christmas without food? For me, that was the best bit. I was so looking forward to my Christmas dinner. George looked horrified, Toby concerned and Summer played with her dolls as if nothing was wrong.

As panic continued all around me, I tried to calm myself and think. I had saved Christmas once already this year and now I needed to do it again. And I was still sleep-deprived from a long, long day yesterday, an early morning today and not even any turkey to show for it. No, we couldn't have that. As they say, a cat's work is never done.

★　　★　　★

I listened as Summer suggested they eat sandwiches for lunch and Toby chocolate coins – although he had already put a fair few of those away, as far as I could tell. He even offered to share round his selection box. Which was all well and good, but what about us cats? We didn't eat chocolate and as for sandwiches, unless they had pilchards in them, or some other kind of fish, I simply wasn't interested. No, I wanted my traditional Christmas lunch and by the look of horror on Jonathan's face, so did he. And what about all the people who were having lunch with us? What about the rest of the street? This was a disaster.

The phone rang again and Claire snatched it up. After a few moments she replaced the receiver.

'That was Marcus. Apparently there's a fault and it's down as an emergency but they don't expect it to be fixed until tonight at the earliest,' she explained.

'Oh no, Christmas is ruined,' Jonathan moaned.

'Shush, of course it's not. We just need to think,' Claire said sensibly but she had panic in her eyes too.

Of course, as soon as it went quiet, it came to me. They said the fault was with Edgar Road, so Tomasz and Franceska's road might be fine and their restaurant was closed today, so we could all decamp to their place with our food, cook and eat it there. Brilliant and simple. Now, how to convey that? I looked at them, licked my lips. I mewed and then ran to the front door.

'Now what?' Jonathan said as he glared at me. OK, so that wasn't clear. I took George aside and told him my idea.

'Such a good idea,' my boy said. 'But how are we going to tell them?' I thought and thought.

On the table by the front door were leaflets for take-aways that Claire and Jonathan sometimes had; would that give them a clue? I jumped on the console table and knocked them to the floor.

'What the hell is he doing?' Jonathan asked.

'Yowl,' I said. This wasn't easy. Then I saw it. Aleksy had left his backpack here in his rush to get home last night, and Claire had put it by the front door. This had to work, I thought as George and I climbed on it, mewing loudly.

Claire and Jonathan looked at each other.

'I'll call Tomasz,' Jonathan said. Finally. 'Oh of course, the restaurant is closed today and they probably haven't lost power!' He sounded jubilant, as if it was his idea.

I was feeling a little smug, as George nuzzled me.

'I miss Tiger mum, but I am lucky to have the cleverest dad in the world,' he said and I couldn't be any happier at that moment, or sadder, because I really missed Tiger mum as well.

It was all organised. Well, in a very disorganised way. While Franceska stayed to organise the restaurant, Tomasz drove over with the boys to pick up the food that needed cooking to take back. Jonathan and Matt went along the street inviting any of the neighbours who were stuck to come and join us. I went with them and was delighted when Tiger's family agreed to come. They were fretting about being without power, and on top of missing Tiger, I was glad they would be with us.

Marcus and Harold were on board, although Marcus was going to drive his dad there, as it was too far for him to walk, and he offered to take anyone else who needed a lift. I wondered if that meant me? The busybody Goodwins also agreed to come and Jonathan didn't even complain about that, in the interest of it being the day of goodwill to all men – and cats. And in that vein, I invited Salmon who said he would love to come with us, as it was the only way to guarantee any Christmas dinner. There was no sign of my other friends, though, and I could only hope that they would be alright.

'This reminds me of the Blitz spirit,' Vic Goodwin said, as he and his wife, in matching Christmas jumpers, started to gather their food to contribute.

'I'm far too young to remember that,' Jonathan replied.

'Well, so am I,' Vic said, and we were all uncertain how he knew if that was the case. But Vic did say something useful, he said they should all get torches to take with them in case we all had to come back to houses still without light, so they rounded up all they had to ensure that every family who needed one had one.

Luckily many of the families had either gone away or had somewhere else to go, but there were a fair few of us as we organised getting everyone to the restaurant. Jonathan and Matt led the way and Polly, Claire and the children got ready to bring up the rear, along with me and George.

'I wish Hana was coming,' George said, and I realised there was still something left to do. No one had gone to see Sylvie, probably because she had told them that they already had plans, but I didn't believe her.

I stood on the doorstep and meowed loudly.

'Oh goodness, look, Claire, we didn't think about Sylvie,' Polly said. Everyone stood at the front gate, but George sat beside me at the front door.

'Last night she was really adamant that she had plans but we thought she might be too embarrassed to face us all.' Claire had told Matt and Polly what had happened with Aleksy last night, so they were up to speed with the situation.

'But she probably hasn't, has she?' Polly said, as she opened the gate. 'Look, it's Christmas and if Connie and Sylvie are on their own, we need to persuade them to come with us. No one should spend Christmas in the dark, for goodness sake.'

'Of course,' Claire said, uncertainly, as they unlatched the gate and came to join me at the door. Henry reached up and rang the doorbell as we all huddled like a group of carol singers on the doorstep. After a while we heard footsteps and the door opened. Connie, looking very sweet in a jumper with a reindeer on it, stood before us. She looked a little relieved to see us.

'Hi, is your mum in? Oh, and Happy Christmas,' Polly said before pushing past her into the house. We all followed. Sylvie was in the kitchen, where George ran up to Hana and they nuzzled like the old friends they were.

Claire seemed a little taken aback. 'How are they friends? She never goes out?' she said. No one answered.

'Hello, and Happy Christmas,' Sylvie said but she was a little red-faced.

'Look, I know you said you had plans but it doesn't look like it, and you can't spend Christmas with no power. We and a few of the neighbours are taking our food and drink to Tomasz and Franceska's restaurant where we are going to have a lovely, if slightly unconventional Christmas lunch together,' Polly said.

'That sounds like fun,' Connie said, hopefully.

'We can't, I just can't.' Sylvie burst into tears.

'Connie, take the children to see your tree in the living room,' Polly commanded, and Connie, although looking shocked, did as she was told.

'Right, now what's this about?' Polly said.

'Apart from the fact that my daughter ran away last night because I'm a terrible mum, I've been horrible to all of you who have done nothing but be nice to me, my ex-husband is spending Christmas with his pregnant girlfriend, who he has moved into my house in Japan, what else could there be?' she sobbed.

Put like that, it didn't sound good.

'Listen, your ex, I can't do anything about. But you and your daughter seem to have built bridges by the looks of it,' Polly said. Sylvie nodded. 'And you are not a terrible mum, you were trying hard to protect your daughter, we all under-stand that, but she doesn't need protecting from Aleksy, by the way, he's about as harmful as a houseplant.'

'Well, I'm not sure I'd compare him to a houseplant,' Claire said.

'First thing that came into my mind. You know I mean a flower . . . he's as dangerous as a delicate flower.' I really had no idea where they were going with this. 'Anyway, that's beside the point.' Even Polly looked as if she'd forgotten what the point was.

'No, the point is that we are all fine, we understand, you've had a terrible time and it really hasn't been easy. We all still want your friendship and want you to have ours, and today of all days we can't let you two be alone, in the dark,' Claire said, and we were back on track. 'So, come with us today and you can start building those bridges.'

'But Franceska must hate me. I was so horrible to her, and her son,' Sylvie said. Her eyes were full of tears. 'It'd be so insensitive of me to swan into her restaurant, when I've no right.'

'Oh, Frankie couldn't hate you. All you have to do is apologise and it'll be forgotten. I mean, she's about as good at holding grudges as . . .' Polly narrowed her eyes as if she was thinking.

'A houseplant?' Claire suggested. They all laughed. 'Honestly, Sylvie, she'll be so happy you've come and you know whose Christmas you will really make?'

'Connie and Aleksy's,' Polly finished as if there was any doubt. And mine, and George's, I silently added.

'OK, give me five minutes to clean myself up and put some make-up on.' Sylvie smiled. 'I really am so sorry for behaving so badly and I really do hope you can forgive me.'

'Already done,' Polly said as she went to give Connie the good news.

'I am so glad that everyone's happy again,' Hana said. 'And George says it's down to you, Alfie.'

'Not entirely,' I started modestly.

'It really is down to us,' George countered, immodestly. 'But now, your family are coming with us, and you will be here on your own. In the dark.' He raised his whiskers, hopefully.

'Hana, come with us,' I said.

'But I've never been out and it's been snowing and I didn't know what snow was until Connie told me last night.'

'Yes, your paws will be cold and it might be a bit slippery but only like a polished floor,' I pointed out. 'Listen, Hana, you have to come with us, you need to start going outside. Honestly, you'll like it, trust me.' I hoped I was right.

'But I'm scared,' Hana said.

'But I'll be right by your side and nothing will happen to you,' George said.

'Come on, your family need to know that you are still a family and that includes you,' I stated, nudging her with my nose towards the front door. 'Not to mention the food we're about to eat, no self-respecting cat would pass up this opportunity,' I pointed out.

'Hana?' Sylvie asked as they came to the front door to see Hana sitting by it.

'She should come with us.' Claire looked worriedly at the three of us and I nudged Hana again. She couldn't have been any closer to the door.

'But she doesn't go out,' Sylvie said.

'Meow,' Hana said. It seemed she was learning.

'Maybe she wants to come with us,' Connie said.

'She definitely does. I can tell, I know a lot about cats,' Toby said.

'Me too, and yes she absolutely does,' Summer, not to be outdone, added.

'Right, well you'll have to carry her then, Con, darling, I don't want her to get cold paws,' Sylvie said, uncertainly, as Connie scooped her up. It wasn't quite what I had in mind but, as I blinked at George and he blinked back, it would have to do for now.

★　★　★

'I am so full I don't think I can move,' I said later, as we all rested after our meal.

'Me either, Dad,' George said.

'Being outside is quite nice,' Hana said, although she was currently inside.

'Right, well I better get back to work,' Dustbin said. 'Those pesky rodents will have taken advantage of my absence.'

'Can I help you?' Salmon, who was on his best behaviour, asked.

'Nah, no offence but you don't look like the sort of cat who gets his paws dirty,' Dustbin replied, but without malice. Salmon wasn't, he could probably talk the rodents to death, but that was it. Like cat, like owner, in that respect.

Although in fairness the Goodwins had been on pretty good form. Seeing them play charades was a sight to behold. Although not as good as Harold, who guessed every single one incorrectly and then accused the person acting the charade of being wrong. All the adults were laughing so much they were nearly crying.

It had turned out to be a wonderful Christmas Day. The food was delicious – and there was plenty of it as everyone had pooled their resources. The children had a table set up on their own and were behaving beautifully. The younger ones had brought some of their new toys with them. The older ones were supervising, well Tommy was but Aleksy and Connie were staring at each other with dopey expressions on their faces. Tommy despaired, but no amount of teasing would stop them. I even noticed they were holding hands under the table whenever they could. Ah, young love.

As I'd weaved in between everyone's legs I felt a warmth

327

in the atmosphere that I relished. The adults were all behaving pretty well. Sylvie had apologised to Franceska, and cried a bit, and Franceska, who was just too lovely, had hugged her and told her that they should forget it. She told her she would never let Aleksy take advantage of Connie or hurt her, and Sylvie had said she did believe her, but that after her husband had hurt her she was so scared of her daughter going through anything like that. It all made sense in a way, because of course heart-break wasn't rational. I knew that better than most. Sylvie was back to being the woman we'd first met when she moved here and somehow Claire had manoeuvred it so she and Marcus were sitting next to each other at lunch. I had hope they might fall in love, but I didn't think either of them looked as if they'd be jumping into anything anytime soon. Harold was on good form, though he and Vic Goodwin had a slight disagreement about the reason for the rise in crime, which Jonathan had to diffuse. But other than that, everyone was getting on well.

I'd felt choked when the Barkers raised a toast to Tiger, and I nuzzled close to George who shook, when they talked about how much they missed her. We both went over to them and rubbed their legs to let them know we felt the same, which they seemed to appreciate. However, I was alarmed when they said they were going to the shelter in the new year to adopt a cat, but an older cat, as the house didn't feel right without one.

Replace Tiger? How could they?

'We're never going to be able to replace Tiger,' Mrs Barker said. Phew. 'We had her from a kitten and as we never had children she was our child. We miss her so much but we have a good, warm and kind home and I know Tiger would want us to help a cat who needed a home.'

They were right, she would. She would have been proud of them, and I would just have to get used to seeing another cat come out of that cat flap. And, as hard as it would be, I would welcome them with open paws. Again, it's what Tiger would have wanted.

It was getting late when Marcus, who hadn't had a drink, drove his dad and the Barkers back to Edgar Road. The clearing-up had been shared by everyone – although Franceska had tried to get them to leave it, the Goodwins insisted and they loved bossing everyone about and giving them jobs to do. I went out to the yard to say goodbye to Dustbin who was busy working.

'It's been a grand Christmas,' he said.

'It has. I wish Tiger was here but, apart from that, it's worked out wonderfully,' I replied, with a sad grin. 'And of course I am still tired from the incident last night.' I was pleased and a little surprised that no one had talked about that today, but that was Christmas for you, it wasn't a time to speak of anything bad.

'She'd be proud of all you've done,' he said, and I really hoped she would.

'Mewwwww!' We turned to see Hana tentatively putting her paws outside, with George encouraging her. The snow was slushy now and not deep but she still found it cold. Well, of course it was cold.

'You did it,' George cheered. 'You've officially stepped outside now!'

'Well, so I have. What a Christmas,' Hana said. 'But is it always this cold?'

'No, one day soon it will be warmer and I will insist you try coming out more often,' George said. 'So we can hang out.'

'I'd really like that.' She waved her tail before jumping back inside.

'Incoming,' Dustbin shouted and dived to catch a mouse behind one of the bins.

'Happy Christmas, Tiger, wherever you may be,' I whispered, staring up at the brightest star in the sky, and then I turned to go home.

# Chapter
# Thirty-Four

Christmas is the most wonderful time of the year. It's also the hardest for a lot of people. Among the trees, the happiness, the presents, the food and the excitement, it's a good time to remember that it's not all plain sailing for a lot of people – and cats. That was my Christmas message this year, and I told George that. As we said a silent prayer for Tiger, as we rubbed our full bellies, as we yowled together at how much we missed her, as we watched our children enjoy their gifts, it was a very mixed kind of Christmas for us this year. And we were the lucky ones. I drummed that into George until he told me he got it and please would I 'just stop lecturing me'. Teenage George was back at times. Although perhaps I had laboured the point a bit.

It was all over for another year. As Jonathan said, it took months to prepare for Christmas and then it was all over in a flash. But although that was true, Claire pointed out that for that flash it was worth it. And this year certainly had been. Everyone pulling together like that, friendships forged, upsets mended, and even the busybody Goodwins involved, that was what life should be about. I was saving that lecture for the new year though.

The power came back on when we got home on Christmas night, and as the children almost fell asleep the minute we walked through the door, along with George, we tucked them all up and then Claire, Jonathan and I sat in the living room, enjoying the peace and the twinkle of the Christmas tree lights. I fell asleep at some point on the sofa and woke there in the early hours before I wearily made it up to my bed. It had been a bittersweet Christmas, but then life was going to be bittersweet for a long time to come, I knew.

It was now New Year's Eve and we were having a party at our house to say goodbye to another year and hello to the new one. Claire had been planning this party for months and even Jonathan was keen. All the children were having a sleepover with us, and Polly and Matt and Franceska and Tomasz would be there. Connie was coming with Sylvie, Harold was going to walk down from his house with Marcus, and even the Barkers had said they would pop in for a sherry early on, though they wouldn't stay up until midnight. The Goodwins were coming, but they said they had to keep watch because it was a known fact that lots of crime was committed on New Year's Eve. Jonathan offered them a pair of binoculars and said they could station themselves by our curtains. They were happy to agree to this, but were bringing their own binoculars; they didn't trust Jonathan's would be good enough. In actual fact he was joking, he didn't own any, but luckily they never discovered that. Jonathan had invited a couple of people from his work who didn't have plans and Claire had asked some of the women from her book group and their partners. It was going to be quite a gathering. And a party was possibly just what I needed, to say goodbye to what had been a good but also a terrible year and welcome a new one, which I hoped would be better.

George appeared fully groomed and looking smart.

'Hey son,' I said, giving him a nuzzle.

'Hi Dad, I've just been at Hana's.' There was no stopping

those two, although as far as I could tell they were just friends. Now Sylvie and Connie were back as part of our family, George was in and out of the house more frequently when he saw one of them, and they didn't mind. Connie had even suggested to her mum that they have a cat flap fitted into the side door, so that George could visit and keep Hana company. We were so excited about this prospect. And I thought that it would be lovely for both of us, especially George, to have another home to add to our collection. You could never have too many, after all. However, they were still not sure that Hana should go out, and neither was she, but George was working on it. It was his New Year's resolution.

'How was she?'

'Yeah, good. She's not coming tonight – she said she's had so much excitement that she needs a quiet night in. I think I understand. Hana is a very quiet cat, who's used to being calm. I think us Londoners are a bit of a revelation to her.'

'Of course,' I replied, seriously. It was possibly true, Hana was used to a calmer life than we were. I couldn't remember what a quiet life was, to be frank.

'It's been a hard year, well the end has, hasn't it?' he said.

'Yes, son, and you have been coping so well. I don't know how you've done it but I am very proud of you.' I meant every word.

'I think it's just that thing, really, knowing how Tiger mum would like me to live my life. I hear her talking to me all the time and I also know . . .'

'What, son?'

'I know she would want you to be happy. At the moment you're not but you need to be. She would want you to make

335

the most of every minute and not wallow. And you say that you carry those you love around with you in your heart and she's in mine.'

'Mine too.' I felt so emotional. My kitten was so wise.

'Well then, we will both be alright. But, Dad?'

'Yes, son?'

'I don't want you to get another cat girlfriend, if you don't mind. I think it's best you stay single and just be my dad.'

'OK son, that's a deal.' I was sure I didn't want another girlfriend either. I'd been lucky enough to love twice in my life and that was quite enough.

'Good, because I don't want a new mum.'

'You won't ever have a new mum, you'll always have Tiger mum, even if I did get a girlfriend, but I won't. I'm too busy looking after you lot.' I raised my whiskers.

Wasn't that the truth?

The party was in full swing. Music blared out and it was lucky the neighbours were here so they couldn't complain about the noise. I wandered around, taking it all in, enjoying myself the way I had promised George I would.

The Goodwins were stationed behind the curtains, with their top-of-the-range binoculars and alcohol-free drink. Nothing was happening but they had their eyes trained just in case. The Barkers were sipping sherry on the sofa, and chatting to Harold who had a beer and was waving his stick around, enthusiastically, as he spoke. He was happy and not angry at all any more. Polly and Matt were dancing with some of Claire's friends – badly, I might add. Tomasz and Jonathan were chatting to Marcus; there was lots of laughing and back-slapping going on. Sylvie had insisted on helping

336

Claire in the kitchen and they were filling plates with food and also topping up drinks, and Franceska was of course in the thick of that. They were laughing and joking as they did so, and everyone seemed at ease with each other once again.

I went to check on the children upstairs. Tommy was supervising games night with the younger ones, who were all too excited to go to sleep. Toby and Henry were playing Hungry Hippos, Martha and Summer were playing with some cards, but apparently neither of them knew the rules, which made Tommy exasperated but he kept sneaking his iPad out, in between barking instructions and breaking up squabbles. They were all happy though, as they snuck up some food, and some fizzy pop which Claire never normally let them have. They'd have sugar rushes for hours, I was sure. And George was with them, being fussed, getting in the way, being cute. Aleksy and Connie, who were supposed to be helping to supervise, were on the landing, holding hands and chatting. When Tommy asked them to help him they kept saying, 'In a minute.'

'Alfie, I am never having a girlfriend,' Tommy said to me as he broke up a minor altercation when Summer was found to have stuffed some of the cards down her dress. 'If it turns me into a soppy guy like my brother, I'd rather not.'

'Meow.' You'll change your mind when it's time, I thought. Although I couldn't imagine Tommy ever being soppy.

I split the evening between upstairs and downstairs, before Franceska went to get Aleksy, Tommy and Connie for the midnight countdown. Thankfully the younger children had worn themselves out by then. Toby, George and Henry were fast asleep in one room and Martha and Summer were in bunk beds in Summer's room. I went with the adults.

'Right everyone, it's countdown time,' Jonathan shouted. 'Ten, nine, eight, seven.' Everyone joined in. 'Six, five, four, three, two, one. HAPPY NEW YEAR!' the room shouted with loud cheers. People in couples kissed. Marcus hugged his father, then Sylvie hugged Harold, and Marcus grabbed Sylvie in a big hug and kissed her cheek. She blushed and I noticed. As, I saw, did Claire.

Connie and Aleksy snuck off and I looked around and saw they were sharing their first kiss – I assumed it was their first – under the mistletoe in the hallway. So much for them being chaperoned at all times. But, I was pleased, it made me feel warm for them, for everyone.

Old friends hugged, and new ones, and then they started singing this unfathomable song called 'Auld Lang Syne', which I didn't understand, although I did catch a bit about old acquaintances and I think it meant don't forget them or something. Surely they could have made it clearer though, as people sang it every year and no one really understood the words as far as I could tell. In fact, most people didn't seem to even know them.

Satisfied that everyone was happy, having fun, and no one needed my help, I went outside to get some air.

The cold air wrapped itself around me. The snow had settled into a thin blanket and the air was cold and crisp. The sky was clear as I looked at the moon, something Tiger and I used to do together. We loved watching the moon and it was one of her favourites tonight, round and clear. I wondered if wherever she was she could see it. I felt his presence before I saw him, as George appeared.

'What are you doing up?' I asked, as I nuzzled him.

'I heard Tommy say it was New Year now, and so I wanted to come and wish you a Happy New Year.'

'Thanks, son, and Happy New Year to you too.'

'Promise me, you'll be happy, Dad.'

'I promise.' Just then a star appeared to wink at us. It was the brightest star I'd ever seen.

'Wow, there's Tiger mum, just like she said,' George said.

'She's with us. Happy New Year, Tiger,' I said into the wind.

'Dad, make your resolutions now,' George said.

'What do you know about resolutions?' I asked.

'Claire is going to drink less, Jonathan moan less, and Summer be more amazing than she is. Oh, and Toby is going to keep away from girls.'

'OK, here goes. Firstly, I will take excellent care of you. You are growing up to be such a fine young cat. And my second is that I will never stop missing Tiger, or loving her. My third resolution is that I will never stop with my plans to bring people together or keep them together. People and cats of course. Finally, I resolve to live every day to the full. How about you, George?'

'I think I might just try not to set myself on fire again.'

We laughed and I told him what a good resolution that would be. I watched him hop back into the house before I followed him. As I left my footprints in the snow, I felt happiness and sadness, love and loneliness, the contradictions of life. And in the opening minutes of a new year, I gave a thought to all of those I loved, past, present and future.

One ordinary neighbourhood.
One extraordinary cat.

Read the *Sunday Times* bestseller and find out how it all started. The tale of one little grey cat and his journey to become a Doorstep Cat.

They were a family in crisis.
He was a friend for life.

**Read the follow-up to the smash-hit bestseller,**
*Alfie the Doorstep Cat.*

# One little kitten.
# A whole lot of trouble.

**The *Sunday Times* bestseller returns –
and this time he has a sidekick!**

# It's time for Alfie's first ever holiday!

Alfie and George are back for more
adventures – this time taking them a long
way from home . . .

Ring 24/4/19